A SINGLE SUMMER
WITH LORD B.

By the same author

A DANDY IN ASPIC

MEMOIRS OF
A VENUS LACKEY

A SINGLE SUMMER WITH LORD B.

BY DEREK MARLOWE

NEW YORK · THE VIKING PRESS

Copyright © 1969 by Derek Marlowe
All rights reserved

Published in 1970 by The Viking Press, Inc.
625 Madison Avenue, New York, N.Y. 10022

SBN 670-64709-8

Library of Congress catalog card number: 72-83235

Printed in U.S.A.

Originally published in England
under the title *A Single Summer with L.B.*

CONTENTS

1 Exiles — 9
2 Billets-Doux — 32
3 Alienations — 45
4 Reminiscences and Recollections — 59
5 Alarums and Excursions — 75
6 Victims — 92
7 Laudanum and Vampyres — 114
8 Abelards — 135
9 Venus to Polidori — 157
10 Lament — 168
11 Old Mother Stale — 188
12 Revelations and Anniversaries — 202
13 Flicflac — 212
14 Dismissals and Arrivals — 233
15 Exeunt Omnes — 246

ACKNOWLEDGMENTS

Acknowledgments must be made for the help and enthusiasm of the following: Michael Wells, Ken Russell, Christopher Logue, Sukie Marlowe and Michael Hastings, as well as the generous resources of the London Library.

AUTHOR'S NOTE

Apart from John Polidori's letters to Florence, which are the author's creation, all quotations and much of the dialogue are taken solely from the letters and journals of the personages involved, or extracted from contemporary sources.

I am very pleased with Lord Byron. I am with him on the footing of an equal—everything alike.

John Polidori, letter to his sister Frances, May 2nd, 1816.

A SINGLE SUMMER
WITH LORD B.

[1]

EXILES

THE land now began to sink into the sea. Slowly at first as the packet-boat hesitated, and then more quickly, evenly, without effort (a momentary obliteration by a sail, nothing more), and then it disappeared altogether below the waves and was gone. Only the sky remained, surprisingly clear, and then that too vanished all too willingly, and the boat plunged into the deepest trough yet, its bow disappearing, and the sound of horses was heard from the decks below. Then a half-dozen unrelated things, each seen in turn with detached interest, like a series of mediocre engravings placed before one, merely to pass the time. A loose piece of rigging frozen upside-down in mid-air, the face of a man appearing suddenly from the galley, his tongue abstractedly licking some grease from a finger; a belaying pin rolling across the deck, north to south, to come to rest temporarily against a mast.

Other things, perhaps. No more dramatic than those, but to be recorded. A sailor leaning against a rail and lighting a pipe, despite it all, and glancing at a small boy, hat tied to button, gloves to sleeve, intently plank-walking the deck. A hover of sea-gulls above, and below them, Claire staring into the water, her face white, her hair black, curly, shifting only perceptibly in the wind. Then she too drops from sight as the boat rises, levels out, and the coast is seen once more on the starboard side and a little nearer.

At the stern of the boat, a young man slowly realizes that he is cold. He hasn't moved since the voyage began, but has sat hunched up in a worn greatcoat (grey, ankle-length, a size too large) on the open deck, staring fixedly at the oncoming light from the east, obscured at first by the darkness and the rain, but clearer now, whiter and already casting shadows. The other passengers had boarded the boat, hands clutching children or small bundles, had hesitated in small shy groups, craving sleep but remaining doggedly and a little wistfully to stare up at the dark cliffs as the packet eased slowly away from the harbour and headed out to sea. Within half an hour, cheated by the cold and the dark, they had hurried below to find a bed or some food or merely to join in the prayers. Only the young man had remained, sitting on a wooden bench, his back to the shore, one hand resting on a leather box, the other carefully around the waist of a young girl of eighteen, her light brown hair and the lower part of her face hidden behind muffler and bonnet, leaving only her eyes, almost elliptical in shape, but hedge-brown in colour and temporarily closed.

At a casual glance, she could be taken for the youth's younger sister, for they both share the same high forehead, the same colouring (though his eyes are blue, almost mazarine), and the same thin delicacy in cheek and bones. A pallid skin, commonly called consumptive, but the adjective is a description rather than a diagnosis. There, however, the resemblance ends. If one could lower the woollen scarf and see the girl's mouth, it would be with disappointment. Not full and sensuous (and perhaps a little too sulky) like the young man's, but thin, tight, almost spinsterish. The mouth of a friend's great-aunt, even at the best of times. At worst, that narrow upper lip and those deadly even teeth could well belong to a fragile and rather precious lizard.

Strange that the man should be the prettiest of the three — for there is a child too, a boy of five months, now fortunately asleep in the girl's arms. The father's eyes, but the mother's mouth and grandfather's name. Same hair too, inevitably, as its parents' (auburn to fair, thin, wispy, worrying in a man), though the father at twenty-three wears his hair long, uncombed, descending loosely to the shoulders. If desired, one can stare longer still and observe the scuffed, worn shoes, the frayed trousers, the absence of rings on any of the hands, for the young man, though awake, seems to have cut himself off from everything around him and remains as immobile as his companions, as if they were all posing for a rather unfashionable but pedantic village painter. A family group for the mantel. To the other passengers who are now reappearing on deck, the trio must look from a distance like three adolescent and rather poor émigrés, too impoverished to rent a berth below. In a sense, they are right, except that the young man is the heir to a baronetcy, the young girl (Mary by name, and thus enhancing ironically the pious tone of the pose) is his mistress and their poverty is a cause rather than an inhibition. The young man is also a poet, which ought to account for many things, but which, in truth, accounts for none. Bells are now rung, and the passengers turn away and gaze towards the horizon now that they can see it, and discover with relief that land, at last, lies close ahead.

It appears to be a flat land, a black midriff between light grey and dark, and like any other from a distance. But the young man remembers it from the previous visit as being blissfully mediocre, and if not quite the dullest stretch of earth in the world, certainly the most irritating. Little wonder that in its history it has bred so many sensational battles—good flat land, strong turf, fair odds—but not a single great man. It is a land to enter without fuss, cross quickly, preferably at night with heavy curtains drawn round snoozing passengers, and then forget. A muffled and tedious bridge to the sun and the mountains along straight roads, dark fields and scattered poppies, and lying now perhaps three miles from the packet, its main port highlighted only by the embers of a bonfire on the low cliffs. For though it is early May, the dawn has begun late and so far nothing can be discerned across the water except the dull gleam of houses and surf and perhaps the sail of a clipper.

As the boat eased in its course, steadying itself against the wind, Claire walked back towards the young man and the girl, tying her cloak once more around her neck, and stopped before them. For a moment, she seemed a little self-conscious, as if they were strangers she had intruded upon, and so looked away awkwardly and concentrated intently on her gloves. Then, as the boat heaved once more and she had to steady herself against the bench, she reached out to touch the man's shoulder, hesitating only to glance at Mary to confirm that she still slept, then gently pulled up the collar of the greatcoat around the young man's neck. A small gesture, almost maternal (hand lifting up the collar, tucking it round before the closed eyes of the other girl, hand drawing away), but performed over-discreetly and almost with defiance. For a moment, the young man made no reaction, then slowly he looked up at the girl before him, looked up steadily at her face, and Claire turned away, moving to the rail and Mary woke up as the voice of a sailor was heard from below. 'Calais,' he called, 'Calais, quinze minutes. Quinze minutes ... C'est Calais.' They were almost there.

The motives which determined me to leave England & which I stated to you in a former letter have continued since that period to press on me with accumulated force. Continually detained in a situation where I esteem a prejudice does not permit me to live on equal terms with my fellow beings I resolved to commit myself by a decided step. I therefore take Mary to Geneva, where I shall devise some plan of settlement and only leave her to return to London and exclusively devote myself to business.

I leave England — I know not, perhaps, forever ...

At ten minutes past seven, in a cold May light, Percy Bysshe Shelley, his mistress, her sister, his child, walked down the gang-plank from the packet and set foot, at last, on the shores of France. A hundred yards away a carriage was waiting to transport them all, without delay, on the road to the south.

* * *

First, the eyes. Dark, almost black, set in shadow under heavy eyebrows; a Mediterranean nose eclipsing the mouth of a paranoiac, and hair that is over-long and styled, not according to the whim of the age, but more in the fashion of the hero of one of his employer's poems. The height is below average but the young man carries himself well (right hand within left, chin clear of cravat) and takes care, within reason, to be viewed from below. He is therefore to be seen more often than not on the back of a horse, on a neighbouring balcony, descending the stairs, arms akimbo before the mantel, reclining on the window-seat before a pretty second-cousin, or, as now, in the benched luxury of a carriage, parked one hundred miles to the east of the packet-boat at a point where the road north from Charleroi crosses the road from Nivelles. Outside, trees, the base of a hill, four or five men. 'Strangers, Florence, strangers,' Polidori wrote, 'in the affection of L.B., for he and I are like brothers, no longer employer and employee, but like one in blood. Since Ostend I have been by his side every hour of our journey — of which *more* tomorrow — and he has treated me always as a friend. So much so, that if I say I wish L.B. never to be granted perfect health, you will not think me callous or vindictive, for I am a spoilt physician now and cannot contemplate employment with any other. Oh, Florence, at *twenty*! Who would have thought it a year ago? Even dear Gilbert must be daisy-eyed in delight.'

After the eyes, however, the voice. Words tumble, scramble even, out of the mouth, without logic or forethought, and the voice rises higher, whining on, with the length of its crescendo in direct proportion to the interest of the listener. In conversation with John Polidori, one replies quickly when the voice is in the lowest register. A moment's silence and the words are above one, increasing in sound and height with awesome regularity. On a sober day, one might attribute this idiosyncracy to youthful eagerness, a naive anxiety to please, but if that is the case, the irritation is no less diminished. His skill in medicine, however, was, of course, undeniable, achieving his degree at Edinburgh at the surprising age of nineteen, after exhibiting such proficiency that his present employer had no hesitation in hiring him, after first reading a highly eulogistic recommendation from a notable hypochondriac. 'Hat in hand, knees like marrow-jelly, heart ricocheting around its cage, I met L.B. for the first time at Piccadilly Terrace. Outside, scandal, perdition, ranting women, but here, L.B. confabbing to us all. "I am going away," he tells me, "and I want you to attend on my health"—I am of course, by now, prostrate with disbelief. Remember my thesis?—"Patience is never a virtue of mine. However, if all goes well, you will remain in my employ for the whole journey. It may be three months. It may, then again, be the whole summer." Or, indeed, *more*, Florence. I understand L.B. is contemplating visiting Italy(!) after Geneva, and may well be there till next year. So far we have reached Brussels, then the village (headquarters, rotunda, boys with souvenirs) and are now here. Gentle plateau.'

At eleven o'clock, John Polidori was awakened from his day-dreaming by the arrival of a group of peasant children selling maps of the battlefield and rusted breastplates and one or two cockades. Unable to comprehend much of the language, however, as well as being, unlike Byron, reluctant to collect mementoes of the tour, the young physician pushed past the upturned palms and rode, with his employer and a guide, to the slopes of Mont St Jean in order to view the plateau from above, as Wellington had viewed it eleven months before, riding alone above the smoke in his grey-caped coat, a telescope under one arm.

* * *

Seeing the plains of Waterloo from a height, however, can be deceptive. The land looks abnormally flat, as if it had been rolled especially for the battle like an enormous green on which both sides were to play a pleasant game of bowls. It seems to set an air of politeness and gentility to the scene which is false, and the temperate air, as it was that day, and the mood of calm (the sheep, a small cornfield to the west, a silent row of Lombardy poplars), deludes the imagination and one is hard put to envisage this green plateau as the arena for the mass slaughter of sixty-five thousand men, and where in one small orchard, fifteen hundred English soldiers had died before it was even noon. One has to walk down into the grass itself to discover that what looked like a calm lake from above is in fact a turbulent sea, full of ridges and hillocks and sudden depressions, so that a man on tiptoe has at times a horizon of only a few yards. And this, too, in a brief moment of calm when there is no smoke and the sky isn't black with fire and the din of cannon.

A soldier of average height, for example, standing with his back to La Haye Sainte and facing the French cavalry in the south-east would perhaps see them four or five times as they charged towards him, even though the distance is less than six hundred metres and there is not a single copse or house or river bank between him and the enemy. He would see first the solid wall of blue as the grey horses began the canter, then the riders would disappear as if wiped out by an unseen hand, only to reappear, faster now, the gallop in its stride; and the bearskin caps and red plumes would be above the man for perhaps a full minute to become, once again, just a mirage. By now, the man is nervous, as his target constantly eludes him, and his ears are being deafened by the relentless and unseen thunder of hooves as four or five thousand horses, each weighing almost half a ton, career towards him. Cannon-fire, too, often within a few feet, grinds against his skull, threatening his hearing, and as he attempts to keep his ground he finds his ankles are now deep in last night's mud, his heavy scarlet coat is chafing his skin and his senses are being tortured by the screams of wounded horses and men and the smell of burnt flesh. His fear is enormous, he feels utterly alone and terrifyingly defenceless, and looking up he sees the enemy again and they are above him, almost suspended in the air, and then the explosion of sound breaks apart and he is under the hooves and lances of the horses and men. He wants to run, not so much from fear but from a bitter helplessness. He wants to turn and stumble, to have his back exposed and await the inevitable. But the man doesn't run, for his commander-in-chief has locked him into a pyramid of men and he cannot move. He is wedged between other soldiers, some wounded, some already dead who cannot even sink to the ground. He cannot think, either, for his mind is preoccupied solely with the loading of muskets (*Tear cartridge open with teeth, pour powder into firing pan, pour powder into muzzle, ram ball shot into muzzle, ram wadding into muzzle, aim and fire*), and if he breaks the routine for a moment his comrade behind him will almost certainly die, and he too, in his turn. Even when the enemy cuts through him and the bellies of the horses loom over him, he cannot move. He can only stand where he is and fire, despite it all.

During the battle our squares presented a shocking sight. Inside we were nearly suffocated by the smoke and smell from burnt cartridges. It was impossible to move a yard without treading upon a wounded comrade, or upon the bodies of the dead; and the loud groans of the wounded and dying were most appalling.

At four o'clock our square was a perfect hospital, being full of dead, dying and mutilated soldiers. The charges of cavalry were in appearance very formidable but in reality a great relief, as the artillery could no longer fire on us: the very earth shook under the enormous mass of men and horses. I never shall forget the strange noise our bullets made against the breastplates of Kellerman's and Milhaud's cuirassiers, six or seven thousand in number, who attacked us with great fury. I can only compare it to the noise of a violent hail-storm beating upon panes of glass.*

It is indeed a deceptive plateau when seen from a height on a clear sunny day in May, in a moment of peace.

On the summit of Mont St Jean, Byron dismounted and walked through the yellowing grass to the rim in order to gaze for the first time upon the fields below. He was bareheaded and dressed, despite the wind, in a thin olive-green coat and wore a white cravat knotted around the neck. He carried a swordstick as always, and a map of the battlefield bought an hour before in the village from one of the small boys. His curly, reddish hair, darkened by macassar oil, had already begun to recede slightly, though he was

* Captain Gronow, *Reminiscences and Recollections* (1862–6).

only twenty-eight, and he therefore wore it longer at the back, but not too long since he strove most of the time to keep a certain distance between himself and impropriety. Besides, his type of hair doesn't lie well when long and should be kept short, framing the head to follow, within reason, the contours of the skull. No side-whiskers, clean-shaven, well washed. 'Plenty of starch and clean linen', Brummell had said, and Byron had taken note.

His height, surprisingly, bothered him. Once, in a journal, he had assessed it as *5 foot 8½ inches* (rather coy emphasis on that half inch), and consequently he wore boots more often than not, fashioned carefully for him by a discreet Islington preacher. The man was indeed a craftsman, for the boots not only added an inch to the height, but they also disguised the deformation in the owner's foot, so that the lameness was hardly noticed except when the man walked, and even then the gait was smooth, slightly rolling and not unattractive. But it was not the feet of Byron one admired. It was the face. Handsome without a doubt, with no trace of effeminacy, except perhaps in the length of the lashes. A classical nose, straight in profile, set between dark, deep-set eyes under rather vain eyebrows. As one looks at the man, at the pale skin, the full mouth, the grey eyes and the broad-shouldered body, one doesn't find it hard to believe the stories of broken hearts and torn letters, and of one ex-mistress who was going slowly mad in the polite salons of Piccadilly, and of another committing suicide and being buried at a crossroads in Albania. Or of tales of another woman who had actually married the man and then turned overnight from a possessive lover into a harbinger of hate and scandal. Or even the small gossip concerning his most recent mistress, discarded like them all, who surrendered her virginity without question after a single evening's acquaintance, and who was now disembarking at this very moment on to the shores of Calais. *Do you know I cannot talk to you when I see you?* Claire had written a month before. *I am so awkward and only feel inclined to take a little stool and sit at your feet. This is how I always feel towards the person I love. When I behold them, nothing gives me half so much delight as to kneel down by them and hiding my head, to think about them.* Romantic words from a girl of seventeen, if not somewhat inhibiting. But if Byron himself thought of the one he loved at this moment, it certainly wasn't of Claire.*

'To your left, towards the east' — it is the guide, pedantic to the last — 'you can see the farm of Papelotte and the chapel of St Roch, where the First Corps of Prussian soldiers arrived under the command of Von Treskow and Von Lutzöw. Beyond that, if you follow my arm, you will see, just below the horizon, the place where Blücher himself arrived on the field of battle at four o'clock in the afternoon ... '

But Byron wasn't listening. He had returned to his horse, mounted, and had begun to descend the slope alone, back towards the plain. Half-way down, he eased up as he heard someone calling him and turned to see his physician, Polidori, hurrying after him, his face anxious, one hand holding his hat to his head.

'May I come with you, my lord? May I accompany you?'

Byron did not reply for a moment, although he realized that his hesitation was foolhardy, for already he saw his companion's eyes widening and the cheeks reddening and the mouth opening once more. He had learnt to recognize the symptoms well in the long tiring journey from

* For the sake of consistency the spelling *Claire* has been used throughout the book, though she often spelt her name and signed her letters *Clara* or *Clare*. At the risk of adding even more confusion it should be pointed out that these names were adopted and that Claire's real name was Mary Jane Clairmont.

Ostend, when mishap after mishap caused him to be thrown constantly into the company of this over-eager, tedious and yet rather sad young man. And yet Polidori did have the reputation of being a brilliant doctor and it was for this reason alone that Byron had hired him; but with luck he would never need him, and with more luck, he could, in time, send him away.

'I want to travel across the fields alone, Polly,' Byron said gently, and without waiting, rode on down on to the shorter grass of the plateau. A while later he glanced back to see Polidori still on the slope, not having moved, but staring in his direction, head down, like a scolded puppy.

It has been said that a month after the battle, hundreds of bodies were still lying on the field unclaimed and abandoned, and were slowly decomposing under the sun or were being picked at by crows and ravens and small ants. Shallow graves had been dug as a gesture of respect, but they had been opened by the rains, or by thieves, and small streams had been formed around the corpses and were flowing across the plateau. Apparently by mid-July, four full weeks after the armies had departed, little of the ground of the field could be seen at all, as it was littered by saddles and weaponry and dead horses. Only the smaller objects which were easy to carry and were ornate or shiny had been taken away, either by scavengers or by hordes of peasants who sold them by the side of the road to travellers and sightseers. It is also said that the valley was covered with the pages of books and diaries and old letters which the dead had abandoned, and which now flittered aimlessly across the dark grass.

By August, however, the authorities had been compelled to remove the bodies or bury them deeper in the soil in order to avert an outbreak of plague, since armies of rats had been seen invading the area. Most of the arms that could be carried or placed in a small barrow had already disappeared and were being hawked as far away as Ostend and Hamburg, so that people could buy them and place them in a drawer as a souvenir. Breastplates were the most popular items since they could be polished or fashioned into tea-trays (as many were), and were also easy to retrieve from the earth or off the bodies. But the supply was running out, for farmers from Waterloo and Quatre Bras were already ploughing up the valley for late planting, and were mending the hedges along the slopes around Plancenoit. By September, only the heaviest of cannon remained in the area, since they were too large to steal and too clumsy to sell, and so were left to rust in the woods or to lie in pieces in the ditches. But soon they too disappeared, and when autumn arrived, any remnants of the battle still remaining were only discovered by accident.

Then, as if to accelerate this process of obliteration, the grass began to grow thicker on the slopes and along the plateau, and birds began to return to the trees. Snow then fell and melted before November was out, and small rivers began to flow from Mont St Jean, cleaning out the ditches and making the soil ready for spring. It snowed again just before Christmas, more heavily this time, and the snow remained on the ground till the New Year and then late into February. By then roofs had been retiled, windows had been replaced and walls had been repaired. When the spring arrived, blossom appeared as usual in the orchards of La Haye Sainte and Hougoumont, and in the woods around Hubremont. Sheep were put out to graze once more, and in late April, when it was warm, families from near-by villages and even from Brussels itself took their children to the plateau for a picnic beneath the elms as they had done the year before and the year before that.

By May, to a visitor passing through, the fields of

Waterloo and Quatre Bras were indistinguishable from any other open land within a radius of a hundred miles or more, and only a scarred tree that had survived the winter hearth, or the glint of fresh plaster on a wall, betrayed the valley's recent history. A mere eleven months had passed. Eleven short months and almost all trace of one of the most horrifying battles in recent times had been wiped out. In the fields where an emperor had fallen, a farmer was planting corn, and only a small monument, bitterly self-conscious, in the corner of a field marked the spot where two hundred thousand men had waged war against each other for a few hours of the previous June. To Lord Byron, as he rode alone across the plateau, this almost callous apathy, this defiant indifference to what had gone before, produced within him such a painful and yet overwhelming sadness that he was moved finally to tears.

* * *

It was now almost noon and the men had driven the calèche from below Mont St Jean to the farmhouse of La Haye Sainte, and were now waiting by the gate of the orchard for Byron to return. They could see him walking his horse across the fields, leading it behind him and now and again resting to lean on his stick and gaze up at the slopes or to look back towards Plancenoit where Napoleon had sat, a folding table beside him, above the battle. Then, as Polidori and his companions watched, Byron mounted his horse and spurred it into a gallop and they saw him race breakneck across the open land, his body low around the neck of the animal, his back raised like a jockey. Not once did the horse stumble, though it had to mount the ridges and depressions without faltering, or without being allowed to ease the pace. At one point, the rider passed within fifty yards of the spectators and they could see

Byron's expression, calm, alert, utterly in control and yet strangely remote. Then he was gone and past them and had reached the copse beneath the village and was turning and heading back, increasing his speed.

In all, Byron crossed the valley three or four times, as if surprised to discover how small it was. Indeed, a man on horseback during the battle could leave the allied camp on the heights and by travelling south on the main road towards Genappe, bisecting the field, could be in enemy hands within eight or nine minutes at the most without tiring his horse. Four minutes and he would be on open ground below the muzzles of the French twelve-pounders. And if he urged his horse into a fast gallop, could be through the ranks of d'Erlon and Lobau and be behind French lines and in empty woods without covering more than fifteen hundred yards as the crow flies. Realizing this for the first time is unnerving, and one feels strangely disappointed as grand images of the battle are suddenly reduced to a field the size of a small race-course. Somehow, the dramatic charges of the Scots Greys or of Ney's cuirassiers seem easier to believe when seen depicted on grotesque canvases, rather than on the turf itself. It is as if nature had deceived one by refusing to imitate art.

When, after half an hour, Byron finally returned to the calèche, both rider and horse were exhausted. Dismounting, he leant against the stone wall, acknowledging no one, and gazed out across the trees in the direction of Genappe, his back to the carriage. After a moment, Polidori, hat in hand, found himself compelled to speak, and walking on tiptoe as if in church, approached his employer.

'My lord?' the voice began, low and tentative. 'Major Pryce Gordon suggested Hougoumont.'

There was no reply. Polidori glanced back at the major in question — a tall man who had been a friend of Byron's at Harrow and who had offered to show him Waterloo.

The endless anecdotes, however, had begun to tire after a while and Gordon, like Polidori at that moment, had found himself gradually ignored.

'My lord?' — voice a little higher — 'Major Pryce Gordon thought that no visit to Waterloo would be complete without him showing us Hougoumont ... '

There was still no reply. Defeated but not unbowed, Polidori walked quietly back to the other man, gave him a confidential smile and said, turning his profile, 'We'd rather not. Perhaps another time.'

The silence that then followed seemed so unbearable that once Polidori began to whistle, then realizing, apologized and wandered away into the orchard in order to peer into the windows of the house. When he was out of sight, Byron turned and walked back towards the calèche, stopping only to put his arm on the major's shoulder and say quietly, 'Let us go then, and see Hougoumont.' And then he opened the door of the carriage and entered, pausing only to add, 'I am not disappointed, Gordon. Not at this. I have seen the plains of Marathon and these are as fine ... I'm not disappointed.'

* * *

It was now in ruins. A year before it had been a large château, built in the eighteenth century of red brick and grey local stone, and with a row of bedrooms on the first floor facing east, so that the sun could light the windows in the morning. It had been set in the elbow of a hill so that it could be protected against the wind in winter, and one of the owners had planted an apple orchard in the west field. Around the house a wall had been built, the height of a man, surrounding the land and containing within it not only the château but a large kitchen garden, as well as a farmer's house, a gardener's cottage, some cowsheds, a barn and a single rather pretty dovecote. A small chapel had also been built under the very eaves of the house, with a small pointed tower on its slate roof, above a room no bigger than a farmcart. If there was ever a congregation of a dozen in the chapel, half of them would have been forced to stand outside because of the size.

It had been a fine house, belonging to a landowner of means, for carriage parks had been laid out to the south within the outer walls for visitors or relatives who might appear for dinner. In fact, visiting it would have been a pleasure, for the countryside around it was unusually diverse for that part of Flanders. Ideal for rambles and Sunday picnics, and yet safe for the children, for though the road to Brussels was near by, there was a wall, another wall and a row of elms between the house and any passing carriage. It had been a well-constructed château, too, set in deep foundations and designed to house families for generations without needless repair.

But then, in June 1815, it was occupied overnight by seven companies of Coldstream Guards, as well as six other allied regiments, and was chosen, almost by accident, as the first target of the battle. At 11.31 on the morning of the 18th, guns and infantry under the command of Jérôme Bonaparte began to attack the building. They were resisted, and what had begun as a minor skirmish developed gradually into a horrifying seige. After three hours, two thousand men were dead within its walls, and artillery was being used to burn out those still alive. When this failed, the French finally withdrew, exhausted, leaving a tragic Pyrrhic victory for the allies and the Château of Hougoumont in ruins. The next morning, only the chapel was found standing amid the rubble after the flames had finally died down.

It was still standing now. A small, semi-hectagonal

building with red scarred walls and a pointed grey roof with a ridiculously defiant tower on top. The house about it was gone, of course, though surprisingly a roof still clung to blackened rafters. In the orchard cows were wandering, and hay was stacked in the remains of the barn where the calèche waited. Polidori had at first been reluctant to tour the ruins since he had been forced to chase after the departing carriage on Byron's horse, and was now complaining of toothache. However, when no sympathy was offered he followed Gordon and Byron across the farmyard and over the shattered walls towards the chapel. Byron entered it first, alone, pushing open the wooden door and peering into the gloom. It was lit inside by two small windows in the roof but was still dark and little could be seen except the flaking white walls and the straw on the stone floor. He was about to leave when his eye was suddenly caught by the sight of a large crucifix still hanging on the north wall. It was perhaps five feet high and appeared to be made out of ivory, for it gleamed white and shining in the darkness. But on touching it, it was revealed to be wooden and highly polished. The face of Christ was badly designed but the overall appearance had a certain piety, especially here amid ruins and the ghosts of the dead. After studying the head for a moment, Byron turned away, but his attention was drawn back to it and he saw with surprise that the muscular naked figure on the cross didn't possess any feet, because the legs of the Christ terminated abruptly into charred stumps just above the ankles.

'It was the fire,' Gordon said, appearing at the doorway. 'When the men wouldn't surrender, the French set fire to the chapel.'

'But only the feet are gone,' replied Byron sadly. 'The rest is perfect. Untouched. Just the feet ... '

Then, shivering, he turned and hurried out of the chapel

into the fresh air. After a moment, he returned with a knife and knelt down before the statue and carefully carved his own name in the space where the figure's feet would have rested. Then he left, closing the door, and rejoined the others without glancing back.

Later, Gordon took them on horseback across a ploughed field to a small hill marked by two trees near the woods of St Lambert.

'There were *three* trees here once,' Gordon told them, 'but one was cut down. If you look, you can see the roots.'

He then dismounted and crouched on the earth and pointed to the remains of the third tree, overgrown now with weeds.

It was the spot where Colonel Howard, my friend's cousin was buried before being carried to England, wrote Polidori in his Diary that evening.

Byron had said nothing when first shown the site, but nevertheless was reluctant to leave, and asked to be left alone. The other two men returned later and found that he hadn't moved and was still on horseback, staring at the ground. But, on hearing them approach, he suddenly rode away fast as if avoiding them, so that they had to gallop in order to catch him up. And then, when they drew near to him again, they discovered to their surprise that Byron's mood had changed and that he was smiling and asking them how they were and where they had been so secretively. Startled, Polidori began to answer but before he could open his mouth, Byron laughed and rode away again across the plateau. But he didn't ride fast, as though encouraging them to follow. However, when they were within a few yards of him, they realized that he was singing, very loudly and with great enjoyment. It seemed to be a Turkish song, but at that distance, could well have been Greek.

When they made their way back to Brussels a few hours later, it was already evening, though still light. Polidori rode ahead with Gordon, leaving Byron alone inside the carriage, staring out at the dense woods around Soignes. The visit to Waterloo had made him tired and introspective, and he was grateful for the temporary solitude. It had been eight days now since leaving England, and his depression instead of being alleviated had steadily increased.

More last words — not many — and such as you will attend to; answer I do not expect, nor does it import. But you will at least hear me. I have just parted from Augusta, almost the last being whom you have left me to part with.

Wherever I may go — and I am going far — you and I can never meet in this world, nor in the next. Let this content or atone. If any accident occurs to me, be kind to Augusta; if she is then also nothing — to her children. You know that some time ago I made a will in her favour and her children, because any child of ours was provided for by other and better means. This could not be prejudice to you, for we had not then differed, and even now is useless during your life by the terms of our settlements. Therefore, be kind to her.*

A mile from the centre of Brussels, the carriage suddenly stopped and Polidori's face was seen at the window, peering into the gloom.

'It is beginning to rain, my lord,' he called out, clambering into the calèche and shaking a wet hat against a seat. 'It is beginning to rain.'

There was no reply from the figure opposite him, slumped on the cushions in the corner, as the carriage

---

* Byron, letter to Lady Byron, April 1816.

started off again to resume its journey. Puzzled, Polidori called out his employer's name, leaning forward to see any reaction. There was none. Byron had fallen asleep.

* * *

The Shelleys, as Polidori tactfully described them, even though only one of them was a Shelley as yet, were approaching Paris. There had been no incidents of note, except that Claire had been sick three mornings in a row. When asked, she had dismissed the occurrences, attributing them to the spices in the cuisine. She did not, however, dismiss the thoughts of her lover who had apathetically agreed to meet her in Geneva. Consequently, when her companions were asleep, she retired to her room and wrote a rather nervous and secretly anxious letter. It begins strongly, chin high, stating its somewhat incredible terms with a flourish: *I have no doubt you think my affection all a pretence. Or that you are handsome and my passions are excited. First, I have no passions; I had ten times rather be your male companion than your mistress.*

Perhaps; but emotion takes over and Laertes exits to reappear, more naturally, as Ophelia: *I know not how to address you ... I cannot call you friend, for though I love you, yet you do not feel even interest for me. Fate has ordained that the slightest accident that befell you would be agony to me: but were I to float by your window drowned all you would say would be: 'Ah, voilà' ...*

If Byron, at that moment, did feel any interest for Claire's affections, drowned or not, he did not announce it, for he never replied.

* * *

Seven days after these events, on a Thursday in May, a

man of thirty-seven sat down to dine in his apartments in Chapel Street, London. There was nothing remarkable in the meal itself, even though the cold fowl had been ordered direct from Watier's and the claret was the finest in the owner's cellar. True, it was served on the most expensive Sèvres porcelain, but such minor extravagances were not uncommon to the diner, for over the years he had acquired a taste for only the best in life, much to the chagrin of his creditors. His fondness for the social life was legendary, and for a brief while none would have it otherwise. This evening, however, he had chosen to shun the clubs and to eat alone. He had also chosen to go to the opera, and so, after the meal was over, went upstairs to change into suitable clothes for the occasion. The clothes were chosen with care (blue coat, white waistcoat, black pantaloons and opera-hat), for the man had acquired a worthy reputation for dressing very simply and without fuss. *The severest mortification which a gentleman can incur*, he had once announced, *is to attract observation in the street by his outward appearance.*

At the opera he took his usual place in a box, but seemed to show little interest in the performance, and finally left early by the back stairs. In the street below, in the darkness, a chaise was waiting for him, which he entered, and was taken through the darkest lanes to a crossroads just outside the edge of the town. As was arranged, his own carriage attended him there, complete with fresh horses and a trunk containing the man's most precious possessions. Without delaying for a moment, he entered his carriage and urged the horses fast towards the road to Dover, stopping only to thank one or two servants who had arrived to wish him farewell. By dawn, after driving all night, he arrived at last at the English Channel and boarded a small boat, which set sail immediately for the coast of France. It was May 16th, and a fine morning, and the man, like Byron three weeks earlier, was turning his back on England for ever. When London awoke that Friday it discovered all too soon that George Bryan Brummell was no longer at home. The Beau, outcast and penniless, had chosen, at last, to leave the arena.

[2]

BILLETS-DOUX

For the fashionable Englishman at home, it was the best of summers. For the fifteen years of the century his education and his pleasures had been severely restricted by the coast-lines of his country, and he was anxious, now that Napoleon had fallen, to move abroad once more. Anxious, too, to rid himself of the boredom of domestic affairs, for it had been a long hibernation.

In those tiresome years of his confinement he had been obliged to linger in his own land, picnicking with his second cousin in Wiltshire or hunting the fox in Derby. His life had been restricted to the trivialities of the Court and the dispatches from the war, and the monotony of it all was beginning to tire. If he was unable or unwilling to make his mark on the battlefield, he found himself compelled to shine in the salon. He talked and drank like Sheridan, dressed like Brummell and condemned them both. He painted his grass green in order to attract attention, and when that failed to stir the nation he jumped off Beachy Head. He attended a hanging on Tuesday, and shot himself on Wednesday because he was *tired of buttoning and unbuttoning*. During the day he paid homage to Prinny, and during the night to Harriette Wilson. His friends dined with the Duchess of Devonshire and Lady Jersey, his servants were slaughtered in the mines and his youngest son was beaten daily by Dr Keate at Eton.

He read Creevey and *The Times*, contracted small-pox

while hiking, gambled at White's, danced the new waltz at Almack's, and was shot to death on Hampstead Heath. His sister was painted by Romney, his mother by Lawrence and his house by John Nash. He was warned that his maiden aunt (on his mother's side) was reading Mary Wollstonecraft and Hannah More, and his younger cousin had acquired a mild penchant for landscape gardening. In the spring he put his fortune to win on 'Vandyke', and lost it all in the winter in a single game of faro. He voted Whig, bathed at Brighton, conceived at Bath and went off his head at Bedlam. He became arrogant, promiscuous, fat, bigoted and ultimately very, very bored. The precious jewel was set too firmly in the silver sea and he was becoming claustrophobic. In 1815, the victory at Waterloo brought not only a cheer but also a long, exhausted sigh. *We had thought of France from youth as forbidden ground, as the abode of the enemies of our country. It was extraordinary. They absolutely had houses, churches, streets, fields and ... even children.** The Englishman was free at last. He could move and stretch his legs, and in the summer of 1816, he moved south. After twenty years of stagnation, the Grand Tour had begun again.

Such a dramatic occurrence did not, naturally, go unnoticed by the hoteliers of Europe. They knew from experience that though the Englishman might be a traveller by nature, he insisted on touring in comfort and in packs, and visited only the most respectable havens of disquiet on the Continent. They knew, too, that the Englishman never travelled alone, for that wasn't touring, that was *exploring*, and only the eccentric — and the exile — did that. And so the hoteliers made ready, competing in excellence, snobbery and *ton* for custom, and one of the

* Benjamin Robert Haydon, *Autobiography* (1927).

most enterprising of them all was a certain Monsieur Jacques Dejean of Geneva.

Pertinently conscious of the clientele he wished to acquire, he had christened (with somewhat modest unoriginality) his grand *pension* 'l'Hôtel d'Angleterre', and had advertised its oaken charms as far abroad as Calais and Ostend. It was well situated at Secheron, on the western shore of Lake Leman, and strategically placed outside the walls of Geneva, since the gates there closed at ten, impertinently imprisoning its citizens till dawn. Dejean's hotel was large, tiresomely clean and dull in the correct Swiss manner, and indispensable for any tourist travelling from Dover who demanded that his whereabouts be well known. Here he was sure to meet long-lost friends from Oxford, or hear news of a rich relative who had happily died. Here, too, he would lodge with the cream of London society and meet people as high-placed as the Breadalbanes and the Binghams and the Belgrays, as well as catching fleeting glimpses of Lady Dalrymple Hamilton (of all people) or perhaps even Lady Jersey herself. Without doubt, l'Hôtel d'Angleterre at Secheron was an ultimate necessity for the rich, the fashion-conscious and the social lamb.

Strange, then, that of all places it was chosen by Percy Shelley to stay when he arrived in the middle of May with his mistress and Claire. It was not surprising therefore that the poor, the unknown and the anti-social were relegated to the top floor and the attic, well away from the flora and fauna beneath. Monsieur Jacques Dejean of Geneva had a reputation to uphold, after all.

Shelley, Mary and Claire had in fact crossed France to Switzerland at record speed, being delayed only by the Jura Mountains (tall pines, dark menace, indifferent snow), and by the loss of an axle just before the frontier. They had arrived at the hotel on the 13th and perhaps the true reason for lodging there lay with Claire. It was no secret by now that she was hoping to meet her lover by the lake, and undoubtedly if Byron was going to stay at any hotel it would be at Dejean's. Even before she had left England, Claire had laid plans for the rendezvous in a series of hastily-written letters. *Think of me in Switzerland: the land of my ancestors. Like my native mountain I am tranquil and as they are tranquil so is my affection. One thing tell me; say that you go well and somewhat tranquil; and if you can, you say you think well of me, but not unless you do. And when you read this letter say in that most gentle tone of yours, 'poor thing' ... We shall meet again at Geneva; to me the most beautiful and endearing of words.*

Your most grateful,
CLAIRE

*Pray write. I shall die if you don't write.**

But he didn't write and she didn't die. Instead, she had written again, and again she had received no answer. She had attributed his silence to a delay in the postal system, consoling herself with the thought that she would see him waiting for her at Geneva. But at Geneva there was no one waiting for her. There wasn't even a note.

In the first few days after their arrival, Claire would leave the others and travel alone by coach to Lausanne, beside the lake, in the hope that Byron had taken residence there, or farther down beside the shore at Ouchy. But he was nowhere to be found. Some days she would travel even farther round the water to Clarens or Montreux and once she touched the borders of Savoy before returning, late, in the darkness to Secheron. No letter awaited her at the poste restante in any town, and in Geneva itself travellers arriving from Dover laughed scornfully when Byron's

* Claire Clairmont, letter to Byron, April 25th, 1816.

name was mentioned, and whispered among themselves. A popular joke was repeated out of earshot about an incestuous affair, and at one time a rumour spread through the restaurants that Byron had fled to Italy or Turkey surrounded by dogs and blackamoors and little girls with ringlets.

A week went by, then ten days. Claire's companions had tired of her and now spent the long days drifting on the waters of the lake, under the windless sky, accompanied by William, the child, and a small dog. *From the windows of our hotel we see the lovely lake, blue as the heavens which it reflects and sparkling with golden beams. The opposite shore is sloping and covered with vines, which, however, do not so early in the season add to the beauty of the prospect. Gentlemen's seats are scattered over these banks, behind which rise the various ridges of black mountains, and towering far above, in the midst of its snowy Alps, the majestic Mont Blanc, highest queen of all. Such is the view reflected by the lake; it is a bright summer scene without any of that sacred solitude and deep seclusion that delighted us at Lucerne.** The evening routine was invariably the same. Shelley, in a straw hat, open-necked shirt and nankeen trousers would sail the hired boat from the harbour at six o'clock, accompanied by Mary, and they would both allow themselves to glide over the surface of the water, hardly speaking. At ten o'clock they would return to Secheron, tired and relaxed, to be greeted by the sounds of grasshoppers and evening birds and the smell of wildflowers and new-mown grass. To both of them, this was all they desired to be happy, despite their impoverishment and the hostility of their relatives. Mary's half-sister, however, was far from content.

Each morning the dark-haired, distraught girl would hurry down from the top floor to the hotel desk, and each evening she would wait in the courtyard, peering into the

* Mary Godwin, letter of May 17th, 1816.

windows of passing coaches. Carriages appeared, tourists emerged, carriages moved on. By the 25th, all reason indicated that Byron, wherever he was, was not exactly rushing to Claire's arms. She had learnt in her brief idyll with him (a seduction in Dover Street, a dismissal, a haphazard desire to be an actress at Drury Lane) that Byron took his travels leisurely and refused to plan a single hour of his day in accordance with another's wishes. So, finally (another carriage passing by), Claire attempted to forget him and accompanied Shelley and Mary for walks in the hills, and now and again visited the town to buy a book from Chez Manget in the Rue de la Cité. She stage-managed the role of the tourist and spoke the little French she knew in a stoic effort to ignore the passing days. Then on the twelfth night at Secheron she went to bed as usual, wrote yet another note, and went to sleep. It was as she slept at last that Byron arrived in the dead of night, tired and in secret, and dismounted from his bizarre Napoleonic carriage* into the courtyard below her window, and hurried with his servants and Polidori into the foyer of the hotel.

The next morning (a Sunday), Claire hurried down to the desk as usual to discover to her delight that her hopes were not in vain. The register was clearly signed by Byron himself, though the details indicated that his mood had been somewhat threatened. When asked his age by a pedantic night clerk, he had written with cold humour: 100.

I am sorry you are grown so old. Indeed I suspected you were two hundred from the slowness of your journey. I suppose your venerable age could not bear quicker travelling. Well, honour and your sweet sleep. I am so happy ...

CLAIRE

---

* Lord Byron travelled in a huge coach, copied from the celebrated one of Napoleon taken at Genappe, with additions. Besides a *lit de repos*, it contained a library, a plate-chest, and every apparatus for dining in it. (Major Pryce Gordon, *Personal Memoirs* [1831].)

A new dress was taken from a chest and dark hair was waved afresh. Ringlets were rolled carefully down each temple and along the cheek to diminish the width of the face, and scent was sprayed in the mouth to sweeten the breath. The small and delicate hands were manicured and the eyes, dark as they were, were darkened even more, and Claire, a slight smile, moved on to the terrace to await the reunion. Perhaps she picked some flowers (one speculates now with care) or clutched a present bought in the town. But if she did, the gifts were never received.

Instead Byron made no effort whatsoever to rekindle a past affair, and studiously avoided her. While Claire paced the veranda, the English milord (gossip on the stairs, whispers in the pantry) swam in the lake. He arose while she dined and returned while she snoozed. In a hotel as large as the Angleterre it was not, of course, difficult for Byron to eat, sleep and walk without meeting a distraught mistress, and avoid Claire he did. In fact, Byron made no attempt to meet anyone, for he had other more immediate plans. He had arrived at the hotel, disliked it intensely, disliked its owner even more, and dreaded the fact that it was filled with the peripatetic remnants of a society he had just made every effort to abandon. He wanted to be alone. It was as simple as that.

And so another note. Another whine.

How can you be so very unkind—I did not expect you to answer my last note last evening because I supposed you to be tired. But this morning; I am sure you CANNOT say as you used to in London that you are overwhelmed with affairs and have not an instant to yourself. I have been in this weary hotel this fortnight and it seems so unkind, so cruel of you to treat me with such marked indifference. Will you go (tranquil mountain becomes officious mole) *straight up to the top of the house this evening at half past seven and I will infallibly be on the landing place and shew you the room. Pray do not ask any servants to conduct you for they might take you to Shelley which would be very awkward.*

Awkward it wasn't, for Byron never appeared. That he actually read the note is undeniable, for it was found in his possessions when he died. But the bribery had failed, and though he must have admired the writer's tenacity (he had succumbed to it before in the greenhoused cosiness of the Albany), he was not yet prepared to bow to it again. How long Claire hovered infallibly on the landing is unknown, but her ardour, despite it all, remained undiminished. Years later, when her passion as well as her notorious lover was dead, she described him as *the merest compound of vanity, folly and every miserable weakness that ever met together in one human being!** Perhaps she also felt as strongly about him then, for a brief moment, as she returned to her bed alone, on that May evening. But if she did, she had only herself to blame. Byron had never invited her to Lake Leman, nor had he even hinted that he wanted her to be there if she so desired. She had come despite it all, and had been temporarily rejected. A small cross to bear, perhaps, for a pretty girl of eighteen; except that Claire was not only blindly possessive, she was also pregnant.

* * *

'What do you think, my lord? What do you think? Last night when I couldn't find you, I reflected on our relationship and a singular fact struck me. Since the time that you so kindly asked me into your service, we have achieved three major things together, my lord.'

It is Polidori talking. We are in a carriage. The lake to our left.

* Claire Clairmont, letter to Mary Shelley on the publication of *Lodore*, 1835.

'We have ridden together across the fields of Waterloo. You and I. We have visited Churchill's tomb at Dover. You and I. And now, we have bathed and rowed together on the Leman Lake. You and I, my lord. I and you.'

We are passing through the gates of Geneva towards the southern shore. It is late afternoon and rather fine.

'Such events, my lord, occurred to me as being significant. Since a year ago, I would never have dreamed ... And so, my lord, without delay, you know what I did?'

'You put the damned lot in your diary, Polly. Word by word, to bore posterity.'

A silence.

* * *

A carriage leaving Geneva by the coast road approaches the villa from above. Overlooking the lake in the village of Cologny, the villa stands about two hundred yards over the water, with its main façade gazing out across the Leman towards the vineyards of the Vaud and the dark spine of the Jura Mountains beyond. Not an impressive house at first glance, and one is inclined to dismiss it as bourgeois, since the severe lines of the walls and windows are relieved only by a balcony hemming the first floor on three sides, and a row of pillars from grass to salon. It seems too heavy and solid and pedantic for the lissome beauty of the lake, and ought to belong to a financier in Highgate or to a rather tasteless Councillor in northern France. And yet it has — to scramble for a word — an *aspect*. For there is something reliably comfortable about its simplicity — cream walls, green shutters, twelve poker pillars supporting the wrought-iron veranda before the salon. A large garden, despondently landscaped, with grass rolling steeply down towards the shore — so steep in fact is the slope that one enters the villa at the back on the first floor, without even mounting any steps — and punctuated by a single row of chestnut trees, another larger chestnut to the south, an apple tree and a small stone fountain. A muddle of yew hedges surrounds a kitchen garden, and roses (red, yellow) cover part of the balustrade, attempting to a degree to alleviate the austerity.

To Byron, the villa was ideal. It was just large enough to accommodate any friends who might arrive from England (Hobhouse, say, or Davies), and yet not too palatial and cold. It stood conveniently on the quietest side of the lake, away from the crowd, and, since it had a reputation of once housing Milton himself, carried just the right literary image for an English poet abroad. The rooms were light, with enormous windows, and studiously decorated in a style which, if not quite over-ambitious in taste, was, at least, unobtrusive. Polite Louis XV decor in the salon, sculpted panels in the bedrooms (woodland motifs, squirrels and oak leaves), and an ante-chamber hung with dark paintings of fallen stags and forgotten battles. It was a solid house, warm and unpretentious, and was named, as is the custom on the Continent, after the owner not the locale; consequently, it was known as 'Diodati'.

It was also, of course, much too expensive. The rent, twenty-five louis a month,* was exorbitant, and no one with parsimony would accept it. Byron therefore regretfully turned away and planned to seek elsewhere. Diodati was not for him.

Without waiting even to argue, he hurried down the slope, through a small vineyard to the harbour below the house, followed by a breathless Polidori. It was a fine evening and it wouldn't be dark for an hour or more, and so they decided to row back to Secheron.

* * *

* The louis d'or was equivalent in value to just under an English pound of 1816.

At times, it seemed as if the boat was hardly moving. A small two-master, no more than fifteen feet long, drifting idly in the centre of the lake, with its two sails clinging to each other on both sides of the boat like a bishop's mitre, hovering inches above the water. Little of the shore could be seen, though the Alps were still visible to the east and the sky was still the colour of zaffre. The journey back was perhaps six miles in a straight route, and naturally tiring for the rowers if performed without a rest. In the prow of the boat sat Lord Byron, resting on cushions, and gazing back over the heads of the others towards the receding shore of Cologny and the final glimpses of the villa. The boat itself was moving slowly, barely disturbing the surface, and the only sounds were from the oars and the wind in the sails.

My dearest Augusta

What a fool I was to marry — and you not very wise — my dear — we might have lived so single and so happy — as old maids and bachelors; I shall never find any one like you — nor you (vain as it may seem) like me. We are just formed to pass our lives together, & therefore — we — at least — I — am by a crowd of circumstances removed from the only being who could ever have loved me, or whom I can unmixedly feel attached to.

Had you been a Nun — and I a Monk — that we might have through a grate instead of across the sea — no matter — my voice and my heart are ever thine. B.

'My lord, there is a woman waiting on the jetty. She has just waved.'

Claire waved again. A little shyly. A head turning over a frilly collar to Mary. A quiet smile, and Byron resolutely remaining with his back to her until the boat eventually arrived at the harbour of the hotel. There were in fact three people awaiting his arrival, two of whom he had met before and had little desire to meet again. The third member of the party, Percy Shelley, was however a stranger to him, and if he had not been introduced Byron could well have thought that the younger man had no connection with the two women whatsoever, but was merely loitering or perhaps daydreaming. *Getting out, L.B. met M. Wollstonecraft Godwin*, wrote Polidori in his Diary, *her sister and Percy Shelley*. Nothing more. A brief, silent encounter, ignored by the diarist, who preferred to remain in the boat, face up, feet to the tiller, *letting the boat go its way*.

In the foreground, a dark-haired girl of eighteen in a pale yellow dress looks away, one hand touching her cheek. She stands alone on a landing pier isolated from the two other figures in the background, and appears to be the subject of the scene, since she is painted with great care, barely revealing the brush strokes. One of the other figures behind her is an older girl, thin but not gawky, wearing a bonnet in ultramarine to match her shawl. Along the hem of her dress is a rather naive pattern of flowers (roses and pinks) which is also echoed in the sleeves. Next to her stands a young man in his early twenties, with long auburn hair and an almost translucent skin, who is posed awkwardly and seems, therefore, out of place. His reflection in the water below the jetty is unnaturally clear, and the head is turned as he glances at the fourth figure, of whom one can only see the back. The nature and character of this last person (a man) is uncertain.

The picture as a whole (it appears to be a lakeside scene) is tolerably well executed, though the artist has committed one grave error and introduced vermilion into the colouring of the mountains. To my knowledge, Nature herself has not seen fit to present such a colour in her landscaping, and consequently it would be well that the artist should remember such a fact in future. On the whole, though, it is a moderately fine study, though one is puzzled by the bottom left-hand corner of the painting, where it seems a fifth figure lies on his back in a boat and appears totally irrelevant to the main theme of the picture which is, as the title states, 'First Encounter'.

Her head moved round farther and her eyes were obscured, lowered, as Byron moved past, moving towards the hotel. He stopped only once, after the brief acknowledgments, to glance shyly at the other man, five years younger, who immediately looked away.

'Are you the Shelley who sent me *Queen Mab?*'

A nod. Yes.

Byron hesitated, glanced back at the two girls, then back towards Shelley, studying the youth's hair and clothes with mild disapproval. In the water, Polidori finds himself adrift.

'I read it,' added Byron quietly, almost as an afterthought. '*Queen Mab* ... '

Then he was gone, up the steps of the harbour and into the hotel, without looking back.

An hour later, an invitation was extended to join him for dinner on the terrace. It was delivered by Fletcher, his valet, to the Shelleys' room at about six o'clock and was accepted with surprise. However, Fletcher made it clear that his master was only inviting Mister Shelley and none other.

At seven o'clock, Claire and Mary dined alone.

[3]

ALIENATIONS

'Now I suppose I ought to make it clear immediately, Florence, that I have nothing personal against Mister Shelley. I have seen many types in my time and Mister Shelley is a type that is not uncommon. Naturally, I disapprove (and who wouldn't, may I say?) of his relationship with the Godwin sisters, especially as I know he has a wife in England with whom, I understand, he rarely communicates. Such irresponsible behaviour is not only unchristian, but in my opinion totally selfish. But then Mister S. calls himself a "free thinker" — whatever that is — though it seems to me that free-thinking is not so free when the price falls heavily on the innocent. However, I will refrain from judging him at first glance, for as a doctor I have been trained never to offer a diagnosis without a thorough examination, and this I will abide by. But may I say now, I am not at ease with such a man, nor would I seek his company. One is judged in this world by one's friends, and in the next by one's enemies, and I myself seek none of the latter. L.B. proffered the hand of friendship to Mister S. and I will set store by that.

'But to continue. My first impression of Mister Shelley was of a rather shy young man, who seemed to me to be consumptive by nature. He was very thin and rather tall, and held himself awkwardly as if attempting to protract his height. I have seen such deportment in many sufferers from consumption and so mentioned the fact to him. He denied the suggestion vehemently, and so I did not press the matter. I was not, after all, *his* physician, and by the shabby appearance of his clothes and hair, I am glad of it.

'He arrived for dinner on the terrace as L.B. had requested and immediately put us all on edge by excessively thanking my employer and comporting himself in such a sycophantic manner that I could hardly contain myself and made an apt remark. However, L.B. pretended to be flattered — being well bred — and soon put the other at ease. Such a talent for tolerating others is one of my employer's finer virtues, and one I have commented on before, Florence. It is done with great style and charm and it is no wonder that L.B. is such a success in company. Strange to say, though, he prefers to be alone. That, however, is another story, as I digress too much.

'As they were both vegetarians, we all dined very sparingly. Mister Shelley's diet, I understand, was philosophical, while my employer's — as he confided personally to me — was because of his weight. Apparently he has a tendency towards obesity, which I had suspected. I therefore prescribed a strict diet as follows: *A thin slice of bread, with tea, for breakfast. A light, vegetable dinner with a bottle or two, perhaps, of Seltzer water and a little dry wine; and in the evening, a single cup of green tea.* This particular day, however, the menu was relaxed. Unfortunately, the conversation was not, being dominated entirely by Mister Shelley, and was exceedingly tiresome. He seemed almost obsessed in his desire to convert us to his eccentric thoughts (most of which I refrain from mentioning here as they are impolite), and I myself took great exception to his constant defence of atheism. However, once again, my admirable employer tolerated the prattle and cleverly feigned an interest and in truth, said hardly a word all evening, allowing the other to talk incessantly. It is fortunate that Mister Shelley is a teetotaller, for his garrulousness coupled with wine would be too much to contemplate. It was myself and L.B. who needed the brandy!

'I will not attempt to set down here, Florence, all that transpired that evening since much of it concerned matters totally alien to me and in which I professed no interest. Fortunately, I was not asked to enter into the discussion, but kept a discreet silence, except of course when I felt my contribution was essential. My employer and Mister S. did discuss the Godwin sisters at some length and I learnt to my surprise that one of them — the younger and more ill-tempered of the two — had been the mistress of L.B. himself, during his latter months in London. Naturally, such personal matters had never been discussed with me and I must say I was somewhat amazed that my employer should mention the fact to someone who was not only a total stranger, but an atheist as well. It is not my role to moralize, Florence, but I cannot condone such a lax attitude to the opposite sex. As a Catholic, I am aware how divine in the true sense a woman is, though L.B. no doubt has a right to hold his own views, as he has told me often enough. I will say no more.

'Mister S. thankfully left early, though plans were arranged for a breakfast next day. My employer also suggested a boat-trip for the afternoon with Mister S. which upset me to some degree, since it had already been arranged that he would sail with me. I assume that he must have forgotten.

'With luck then, Florence, Shelley etc. will leave the area soon, for I do not see them being my employer's type. Besides, I know he seeks a villa for both of us, which will take him away from the hotel and the encroaching (!) guests.

'Have no impression yet on the canton, though I am impressed. The women, however, are less pretty than I have seen, though it is pleasing to think that my father's country is now so near.

'Will write soon. My love to Gilbert — is he still with you?

Respectfully,
J.W.P.

'Am contemplating a career as a writer (!). Much encouraged by Mr Murray's offer* and have talked of my aspirations with L.B. He promises to comment quite soon.'

* * *

It was a shy, reticent encounter between two men who were, by nature, ill at ease with strangers. The older man had, without doubt, the dubious advantage of being successful and well known, and consequently needed only to present himself on the stage, without a word or gesture, for the onlooker to be satisfied. His reputation had gone before him on a hundred distorted routes, so that he could only now confirm or negate the expectations of the other, if such was his desire. He was pre-judged, sight unseen, and for Byron, vain though he might have been, that was his bitterest enemy.

He was no doubt as cynical as expected, and yet as sentimental. His limp might perhaps be more pronounced, but so were his good looks. He was as conceited, generous, arrogant, moody, witty and affectionate as one had expected, and yet, at times, none of these. Everything public about the man was well known, and so were many things that should have been private. All his major agonies, passions and desires were now folk-lore, and all that

---

* John Murray, Byron's publisher, who offered Polidori the sum of five hundred pounds to keep a Journal of his service with Lord Byron from April 24th, 1816.

remained for the stranger to discover were the minor idiosyncracies of the man, for these were all that society had left untouched. And yet in a way these very things were the most fascinating and perhaps the most revealing.

To the world, he was a shadowy figure in a landscape they had created, who had slept with his half-sister, divorced his wife and had versified now and again. But to his few intimates, he was a superstitious hypochondriac, who went to bed with pistols under his pillow because he was afraid of the dark. He was a man who was almost miserly with money, and yet absurdly generous with his company, tolerating bores long after everyone else had gone home. He was a shy romantic who bit his nails, distrusted intelligent women, disliked children, and made friends with almost no one. He was publicly heterosexual, privately bisexual and the writer of *enthusiastic and stirring verse*. And yet he was adored, imitated, pursued and condemned, but never ignored. Above all, he was, next to Napoleon, the only man in western Europe to command the attention of every intellectual he encountered, and almost everyone else he didn't. Lord Byron was Lord Byron, and that, inevitably, was his tragedy. When Shelley first met him in these last days of May, he treated him with awe. After six years of friendship with him, his initial attitude hardly changed. For Shelley never learnt to separate Byron the Legend from Byron the Man. Nor, indeed, did Byron.

On the day after the first dinner, Percy Shelley put a straw hat on his head and went for a walk with his notorious companion in the hotel garden. It was a fine day, though rather windy, and so they wandered slowly under the trees, observing lizards on the southern wall, and made their way down towards the edge of the lake. Mercifully,

Polidori had gone to Geneva to breakfast with a fellow doctor, and so they were left alone. The conversation was self-conscious and polite at first, dwelling on casual topics such as the beauty of the Alps across the water or the dullness of the Swiss. Being near Geneva, the talk soon drifted to the subject of Rousseau, and Byron suddenly talked enthusiastically of *La Nouvelle Héloïse*, asking Shelley if he had read it. Shelley, regretfully, had not. The subject therefore was dropped, and nothing more was said.

They walked for a while in silence, observed from above by a dark-haired girl at the top-floor window. She watched them as they made their way beside a wall to the jetty, and then they were out of sight. The window was closed and Claire returned reluctantly to her book.

Strangely, it was Shelley's natural good manners that first charmed Byron, perhaps because they were an unexpected surprise. He knew from Claire's description in London that Shelley came from the landed gentry,* but his initial impression of the younger man was far from reassuring. Shelley's hair was too long, his clothes were too untidy and his voice was too high-pitched for comfort. He had a tendency to be over-dogmatic about his somewhat extreme views which at first irritated Byron, since he cherished a reluctance to preach. And yet this young poet with his defiant beliefs had an absurd charm which Byron could only envy. It rose from a natural honesty and integrity that was, if not necessarily rational, undeniably rare in a society that boasted neither.

Grateful at last to find a companion whose intellect almost matched his own, Byron suggested a boat-trip across the lake, where they could both talk in isolation, away from the prying eyes of passing tourist and expectant

---

* He was, in fact, the son of Sir Timothy Shelley, Baronet and M.P. for Shoreham. The Shelley estate was at Warnham in Sussex.

mistress, and where they could relax on cushions under the sky. It was agreed.

* * *

'I must admit, I rather despised my schooldays, especially when I was at Eton. I'm not really at ease in disciplined society and have a rather tiresome tendency to kick authority on the shins. To me, a career in the army would be nothing less than hell on earth, with myself desperately trying to play the Devil. As always.'

The boat was now halfway across the water, just north of Hermance, and drifting fast in the breeze. It was not warm enough to bathe or even laze with raised oars on the surface of the lake. And so both men sat opposite each other, across the tiller, hunched up against the wind, and reminisced in low voices about their adolescence. However, after a while, Byron preferred to smoke a cigar and listen while his companion, hat pulled down low over his forehead, chattered on in a hesitant tone, gazing out across the waves and stopping only to inquire politely if Byron perhaps might be bored.

'I suppose in a way I was responsible for my own misery, because I must have been rather unconventional to say the least. Everybody teased me, I remember, which was a little irritating, especially when it came to physical recreation. I'm absolutely useless at anything like that, so you can imagine how popular I was. At Eton, as well. I can't even swim. Not a stroke. Can you?'

'I once swam across the Hellespont.'

'Did you? I suppose I ought to be terribly impressed, but I can't honestly say I am. My respects go out, *sans réserve*, to Leander who was drowned, in an absurd way. One remembers, you see, the Greek who failed to swim it, but will we remember the Englishman who succeeded?'

A smile, as he looked at his companion and added, 'On second thoughts, I suppose we will.'

The boatmen now began to turn the boat away from the direction of the Rhône, and back towards Nyon and the west, cutting across the wind at an angle.

'I remember one awful day at Eton which I recall with embarrassment,' Shelley said quietly after a long silence. 'I tell you this in order to show you what kind of coward sits opposite you. I was once involved in a fight with a boy called Styles whom I disliked intensely. He didn't like me very much, and at the time I was inclined to agree with him. Anyway, a battle to the death was arranged on the playing fields at noon — dramatic hour — and I found myself up against a bully to end all bullies. At first, everything went well because he was shorter than myself, and I realized that as long as I kept hitting out madly in all directions he wouldn't dare approach too close. Unfortunately, he did dare, and I must admit that in no time I was black and blue. Then came the miserable *coup de grâce*. A blow like no other hit me below the belt and almost crippled me, and from then on, it was not my honour that was at stake, it was my life. So I ran. Would you credit it? I ran as hard as I could, pursued, need it be said, by the whole carnivorous pack, and never stopped till I reached Bethel's house. Bethel was m'tutor. I tell this tale in shame and add only the comment that from then on, these hands have devoted their energies solely to chemistry and the arts, and long may they reign.'

Byron smiled and said casually, 'When did you go to Eton? Ten years ago? Eleven?'

'Eleven. No. *Twelve* years ago. How time flies. Twelve years ago. 1804.'

'1804? Then perhaps we have met before. Or at least have seen each other.'

'Why? You weren't at Eton were you?'

'Regretfully no, but in 1805 I played cricket for Harrow in a match against your school. You could well have watched it.'

'Perhaps, but I doubt it. I didn't like cricket either.'

'Well, anyway, we were beaten.'

'Too bad. Too bad.'

'Though I did score eleven notches in the first innings and seven in the second, which was quite remarkable for Harrow.'

'If I had seen it, I would probably have cheered you out of spite.'

Later in the morning, it began to rain and the mountains were once more obscured in mist. The boatmen decided to head back for Secheron before their passengers were soaked or were thrown overboard by the rising waves. They reached the jetty by one o'clock to discover an anxious welcoming committee pacing up and down the shore, kicking stones angrily into the water.

'Don't look now, but Polly's returned,' Byron said, gesturing towards the beach.

'Polly? Oh, you mean him? Isn't he rather strange? Even for a Catholic?'

'Damned Murray's giving him five hundred pounds to keep a diary of our travels, so now he believes he is a writer.'

'Is he?'

'No, he's a doctor, and a meddlesome one at that.'

'I must say,' replied Shelley, smiling, 'he looks rather cross. Perhaps you ought to be violently ill in order to give him something to do.'

'I will be, Shelley. Never fear. I will be.'

After lunch, Byron and Polidori set out to look at some other villas around the lake, but none of them were suitable. Diodati was still vacant but still as expensive, so Byron, once again, decided to look elsewhere. All in vain.

Later, Shelley invited them both to dinner with Mary and Claire, but was refused because of a previous engagement in Geneva. It was a polite soirée at the home of Madame Einard, decorated by one or two local celebrities whom Byron rather liked, including Charles Victor de Bonstetten who had known Gray and Rousseau and had taken tea with Voltaire. Polidori on his part cornered and talked in his native language with a fellow Italian, Pellegrino Rossi, who made a great impression on the doctor, since Rossi was well known as a liberal, a lawyer and an economist. Consequently, the dialogue between them was profound: *Rossi told me*, Polidori confided in his Diary that night, *that Geneva women were amazingly chaste — even in thoughts.*

In the carriage back to Secheron, Byron was silent, staring out at the dark sky and the dense frieze of mountains above the lake. Across the water he could see the greyish-blue haze of the vineyards above Bellerive, and the blur of a sail idling in the distance. There was no sound except the dull rattle of the carriage, and the night insects in the trees above the road. The air outside was cold, restless, and yet local farmers were preparing for thunder, and warning flares had been set out along the coast just east of Lausanne. Moreover, it had been noted that Mont Blanc had not been visible for three days, which was rare and somewhat ominous for the end of May.

Opposite Byron, in the facing seat, Polidori seemed unusually subdued, partly because of his companion's introspection and partly because of the wine, for he sprawled inelegantly across the carriage, chin on hand, eyes half shut under heavy eyebrows. His companion glanced at him, thinking that the doctor might be asleep, and immediately Polidori opened his eyes, gave a half smile (upward glance, finger scratching ear), and looked away. He was, in truth, quite a handsome man in repose, especially as now his Latin features had been heightened by a deep tan acquired during the long days of travel.

'Rossi's a remarkable man, don't you think, my lord?' he said after a while.

Byron nodded abstractedly and took a cigar from a box behind him.

'He speaks well,' Polidori continued. 'Speaks well. I admire that kind of man. Bright mind. He has a bright mind, my lord. Good family. That man I can talk to.'

No answer. Above them, the driver was heard to call out a greeting to a passing coach but the words were lost in the air.

'And Bonstetten, too. Grand old man. Don't you think? My kind of society. It's my kind of society. People like that. People like ... The women are chaste, though. Oh yes. Plain and chaste. Don't you know, my lord? Shall we visit there again, my lord?'

'What did you say, Polly?'

'Shall we visit there again, my lord? We were asked ... '

'No, Polly. Not I. You go on your own.'

'Oh ... ' (a pout, a shrug). 'Well, I will decline then, my lord.'

'As you wish.'

Byron closed his eyes, pulling his coat closer to him. It was about half past ten and yet he felt tired. Tonight, however, he planned to write.

'My lord?'

'Polly, I'm tired ...

'My lord, I must tell you. I have begun my tragedy.'

'I'm sorry to hear it. But you look well enough to me.'

'No, my lord. My *play*.' The voice was beginning to rise. 'I told you of the play I was writing. Well, I have begun it. And I am surprised, my lord, how simple it is to write. As a profession, it is a child compared to medicine. I believe already that I can master the art tolerably well and know you will be impressed by my writing, my lord. It will give you ideas, I'm sure. The rhetoric is fine—'

As for Polidori, may I say I never was much more disgusted with any human production than with the eternal nonsense, and tracasseries—

'—and I have begun in the Grand Manner with a masterful speech, which I believe, my lord, could only be performed by Mister Kean—'

—and emptiness and ill-humour and vanity of that young person.

'—who, since I know of your connections at Drury Lane, I will of course entreat to you. However ... '

'However what, Polly? However what?'

'However ... '

'May I remind you, Polly, that I have hired you—and pay you excessively, may I add—because of your reputation as a doctor, not as a dramatist. I want you to administer me with physics, not blank verse. If you persist in devoting your energies to writing, I will be obliged to turn to Shelley when I am ill. Or the gardener. Do you understand me, Polly?'

'That is unfair, my lord. Just because—'

'Just because nothing. I will not tolerate your damned scribbling while you are in my employ.'

'But my lord—'

'Let that be an end to it, Polly,' replied Byron angrily. 'I do not wish *your* tragedy to be mine.'

* * *

'Dear Florence. I am in despair. This very night I contemplated the ultimate act, and deferred only with reluctance. The poison was in my hand but finally I refrained. I know not why, *for I could see no happiness in this world for me. My employer is jealous of me and my aspirations. He is bitterly envious of my talents and in short, has said so. I believe also, that this painful attack has been inspired by another who has shown all too well how much he too is jealous of me. I will say no more. But, Florence, I am in despair.*

'*My best to Gilbert. You are the only friends I now have.*
                                                      '*P.*'

* * *

An hour after arriving at the hotel, Byron visited Polidori's room and discovered him at the writing desk. A polite comment was made about the weather, but the doctor didn't reply, stubbornly keeping his back to the visitor. Puzzled, Byron remained silent and casually studied the books (a dictionary, a sketchbook, Tasso) on a table below a window.

'I do not intend to prevent you from writing, Polly, do not think that. If ... that was my impression, forgive me.'

The younger man made no reaction, though his ears were now red. Outside, it had begun to rain but without force.

'You are hired by me as a physician,' Byron continued wearily, 'and that must come first. My health and your passion are not good partners, Polly. Not in any way.'

A momentary silence, and then Byron walked back to the door, stopping only to place a book on the mantel.

'If you wish to write, Polly, you must also wish to read. So I have brought you a book. A book to read. Read it and learn. It is called *Queen Mab.*'

The door was opened and Byron left hurriedly, pausing only to add, 'It was written by Percy Shelley when *he* was your age.'

The door was closed quickly and he returned to his

room. On the way, Byron heard a crash and the sound of breaking glass from Polidori's room. Later, however, the book was retrieved from the rhododendrons, dried before the fire and read till dawn. The reader was grudgingly impressed.

[4]

REMINISCENCES AND RECOLLECTIONS

It was to be expected, of course. The season had begun as usual, and the young girls were as pretty as they always were. The clubs were as crowded and the stakes were as high, and the evenings at Carlton House were no less spectacular. The elite still rode in Hyde Park as they had done before, and took tea at Kew. The gossip was just as barbed, and infidelity was just as fashionable, and yet, despite it all, the arena seemed tamer, less inspired, as if it had lost its ability to surprise. The game seemed to have gone sour, and the players were obliged to wander aimlessly about in search of a leader.

After a month, they had realized that there was none to be found amongst them, for poor Sheridan was dying at last, Alvanley was silent and Prinny was finally beginning to bore. The social lions had fled to the Continent, and it was the society who had cast them out who were the first to mourn their departure. The bay window at White's was empty and the voices at Devonshire House were subdued. And so, bored and restless, the players found themselves obliged to pursue the fugitives, in a vain attempt to relieve the ennui they had created, sadly blind to the fact that their efforts would be far from welcome.

Brummell was now in Calais, but he had locked himself in a hotel and would see no one, least of all the English. In time, the visitors tired of staring at a closed door and went on their way, travelling south in the wake of the more notorious exile.

They found him at Secheron, at the end of May, and spied on him from balconies, squabbled to acquire a room next to his, and accosted him in the garden. At first, Byron attempted to be polite and signed their books and posed for their sketches. But by the end of the month, the routine became unbearable. Bolstered by his initial amity, the visitors followed him in droves, plaguing him with questions, and little children of four were sent to ask him to tea. When he ignored them, they stared at him silently, whispering among themselves; and when he spurned them, they began to hate him and sent malicious gossip back to England, embroidered by innumerable maiden aunts into a vicious sampler. He was accused of every sexual vice they could imagine, and even Polidori, in his simplicity, was labelled a catamite. Byron's letters were opened, his carriage was mutilated for souvenirs, and his servants were bribed. By the 30th, the situation had become intolerable. *Switzerland is a curst, selfish, swinish country of brutes, placed in the most romantic region of the world. I never could bear the inhabitants, and still less their English visitors ... I know of no other situation except Hell which I should feel inclined to participate with them.** But then, it was all to be expected.

There was only one solution, and that was to move out of Dejean's hotel as soon as possible and find a villa to shut himself from the world. But villas in Geneva were hard to find. Most of them had already been taken, and the ones that remained were either too large, too small, too noisy or too expensive.

On May 29th, he toured the eastern corner of the lake where the Rhône thundered in to the Leman from the Alps, but neither he, nor his banker, Hentsch, could find a

* Byron, letter to Thomas Moore, September 1821.

desirable residence. The situation was slowly becoming a nightmare. Moreover, Shelley was also anxious to quit the Angleterre, since he was now in debt, and Dejean was not renowned for his tolerance. 'Perhaps we could share a house together,' Shelley had suggested at breakfast. But Byron had politely declined the idea, since he preferred to be alone — away not only from the other guests, but also from Claire. Mercifully, in the past two days she had avoided him, sulking in her room. She had not, however, forgotten him. She was merely marking time and carefully, and rather pedantically, changing her tactics.

* * *

The next afternoon, an excursion took place on the lake. It had stopped raining and the sun had appeared and coats had been removed, folded and placed at the bottom of the boat. Across the water, in the direction of Vaud, women could be heard singing in the vineyards, and young boys in breeches were fishing from the jetty at Evian. The sky was Wedgwood blue, the wind was temperate and the lake was still. In the prow of the boat (a small sailing dinghy) Shelley was sitting, wearing a white open-necked chemise tucked into honeyed trousers, a book at his feet. On his head was his straw hat, slightly frayed around its edge. At his elbow reclined Polidori, all in black, with *Queen Mab* (pages still damp) in his pocket. His employer sat opposite him and appeared to be asleep, but in fact was merely daydreaming. There were no women with them for the Godwin sisters had gone to Geneva to shop and visit the statue of Rousseau in the Plainpalais. Except for the boatmen, therefore, the three men were alone. The conversation that took place between them, however, was far from tranquil, despite the mood, though it began pleasantly enough. Polidori was the first to speak.

'I am much impressed by your *Queen Mab*,' he said suddenly, pulling the book from his pocket and holding it up. 'It occupied me the whole night. The more I read it, the more beauties I find.'

'You are very kind,' Shelley replied, and added politely, 'Byron tells me you are *also* a writer.'

Polidori glanced self-consciously across the boat, but made no reply.

'Well ... ' Shelley continued, 'perhaps one day you will read your work to us.'

'Well, I ... '

'We will look forward to that,' Byron said quietly, his eyes still closed. 'Won't we, Polly?'

'Yes, my lord.'

A silence. Then, 'Do you agree with all of it, Polly?'

'All of it, my lord?'

'All of *Queen Mab*?'

Byron then took the book and opened it. 'This, for instance. "A husband and wife ought to continue so long united as they love each other. Any law which should bind them to co-habitation for one moment after the decay of their affection would be a most intolerable tyranny ... Love is free." Did you read that? *Love is free.* And what of this? "A system could not well have been devised more studiously hostile to human happiness than marriage." Is that your view, too, Polly? Do you believe in free love like Shelley here?'

'Well, my lord ... it depends on what you mean by —'

'I mean what it says. Do you agree with marriage?'

'As a Catholic, I must.'

'I am not seeking an excuse from you. I am seeking an opinion. Are you anti-marriage?'

Polidori was unsure and looked away. A self-conscious smile. 'I feel I am in favour of marriage, my lord ... because —'

'I am not,' Byron replied emphatically. 'My God, *I* am not.'

'But my lord, do you attack marriage in general or marriage in particular?'

'Both. I despise the general and am mercifully separated from the particular. Lady B. has stung me enough, and with the grace of God I will not see her again in this world. With the grace of the Devil, I know I will not see her in the next.'

Next to him, Shelley began to laugh, his cheeks flushed. He had been silent throughout the discussion and had quietly watched Polidori's face with interest.

'You are a Catholic, I understand,' he said quietly to Polidori. His voice was polite but the implication was there.

'Yes,' replied the doctor warily.

'Where were you educated?'

'At Ampleforth.'

'Ah, Ampleforth,' repeated Shelley, savouring the word. 'Yes, Ampleforth. That dungeon of insight. That, I suppose, accounts for it.'

Byron smiled and both men stared at Polidori, who found his face reddening.

'Ironic is it not?' continued Shelley, 'that it is the celibate who preaches the sanctity of marriage. I feel it is rather like a mole lecturing on the techniques of flying.'

'I resent that, sir,' Polidori shouted suddenly, his voice high. Opposite him, Byron folded his arms and watched. 'I resent that. I, at least, sir, do not cohabit openly with a mistress. I, at least, would marry her.'

'What? And be a bigamist? I *am* married already, Doctor, but not alas to Miss Godwin. But even before I married Harriet, I could not endure the bare idea of marriage. I found it hateful, detestable. A kind of ineffable sickening disgust seized my mind when I thought of that most despotic, most unrequired fetter which prejudice has forged to confine its energies. Yet this is Christianity — and Christianity *must* perish before this can fall. I do not even speak of Christ as Christ *is*, but as the world would have him. For anti-matrimonialism is as necessarily connected with infidelity as if religion and marriage began their courses together. For God's sake, Polidori, if you want more argument read the marriage service before you *think* of allowing an amiable beloved female to submit to such degradation.'

Polidori knew he was outnumbered. He knew also that he had neither the wit nor the confidence to retaliate. He could only lash out ineffectually, like an aged prizefighter, hoping that one of his blows would wound. He had begun the excursion with an amicable, if self-centred, affection towards Shelley, but now his sympathies had been betrayed. Tonight, he reflected, *Queen Mab* was returning to the rhododendrons.

'Then why did you marry, if that is how you feel?' he snapped at the man at the prow. 'You preach but you do not practice.'

'Why I married, Doctor, is still an enigma to me. Perhaps I can say that marriage to Harriet brought me some well-needed money, since I had none. Or that I married her because I was naive, or because it was her wish. Whatever the reason, the relationship was hellish. Because of it, I almost lost a friend, I was disowned once more and I found myself linked, chained to a woman who was unfaithful not only in body but also in soul. The only blessing was that because of it I met Mary. If it was not for her, I would have died. Believe me, death was often a great comfort. It ... '

Shelley then hesitated as if about to add a confidence, but stopped and turned away. His companions were silent, avoiding each other's gaze. They began to be aware once more of the boatmen and the water and of their position in the lake, and realized with surprise that they were not far from Lausanne.

'What has been achieved by it all?' Shelley added, turning back to the others. His voice was now nervous and shrill. 'Harriet is still my wife and remains miserable and wretched in England. I am obliged to elope with another woman like a thief, so that in order to prevent myself hurting the former whom I abhor, I hurt the latter whom I love. Consequently, all three of us are now unhappy, and for why? To please the bigoted laws of churchmen like you. It is a miracle none of us has not ended it all. Marriage, Doctor, should be based on love and love only. When the love ends, so should the contract. That is the sum of it, and that is the very thing you and your Church ignore, and God, I am sick of it. Sick of it ... '

His voice breaking, Shelley turned suddenly away and turned on to his stomach and lay down with his shoulders and arms over the bow of the boat so that his hands drifted into the water and his face was hidden from sight, upstaged by the breadth of the hat. Behind him, the young Italian was still and quiet, eyes lowered, cheeks scarlet. Opposite him, his employer had closed his eyes and folded his arms and was idly chewing a wad of tobacco to stave off his hunger. There was a long silence, which was broken suddenly by a piercing scream, barely human, that soared into the air without warning, then levelled out tonelessly to incorporate three or four guttural syllables of obscure origin. Both Polidori and Shelley looked up in horror, fearing the worst.

'It's a folk chant,' said Byron casually, smiling at his companions. 'I learnt it in Albania.' Then, laughing at the stunned faces around him, he repeated the cry, standing up in the boat and shouting it interminably across the water over and over again, stopping only when the boat and its dazed passengers had finally reached Secheron.

An hour later, Byron disappeared. When inquiries were made, it was discovered that he had been suddenly overcome by a severe fit of depression and had wandered off alone into the vineyards above the town, taking with him only his walking cane and a letter he had just received from London. When he finally returned, the hotel was in darkness.

* * *

Polidori was alone once more. It seemed months, not weeks, since he had written in a letter to his sister, Fanny: *I am very pleased with Lord Byron. I am with him on the footing of an equal—everything alike.* But no more. Now everything was different, for he had been pushed aside like one of the servants, like Fletcher or Berger or the maid on the stairs, to appear only when summoned and to speak only when asked. He felt an outsider, superfluous, relegated to the wings now that others had entered the stage. He was alone once more, his vanity wounded, and he could only reminisce on the days, so recently past, when it was only he and Byron together, crossing the flat plains of Flanders, visiting the art galleries, or collecting souvenirs in Morat, and when he was his employer's sole companion and confidant. But now, when meeting Byron on the stairs or waiting for him on the shore, he was dismissed with a polite but brief 'Good morning' or 'Good evening', as if he were a distant relative with whom the other had neither the time nor the inclination to linger. At breakfast, he was ignored, and at dinner, it was Shelley who sat on Byron's right.

In his letters to Florence he tried to ease his bitterness by speculating that Shelley would soon leave, or that his employer would soon tire of the younger man's company;

but the doubts were there. In the past week, even his Diary had begun to lose its charm despite the five hundred pounds and the lure of fame, for the entries of late were no longer as detailed or as enthusiastic as they had been at the beginning. Where the events of Waterloo or Cologne demanded, and received, no less than four, perhaps five pages of script, the events at Secheron were often scribbled hurriedly in a paragraph or even a line, and a form of shorthand had even been adopted to ease the task. In time, he knew, he would abandon the Journal altogether, without regret.

On May 31st, he thought of leaving Switzerland once and for all, and setting off on his own, pride intact, towards Italy; but the idea was rejected, for he knew, despite it all, that he would rather be a lackey to the celebrated Lord Byron, no matter how humble the role, than be alone, an anonymous being, without any claim to fame of any kind. And so he remained, harbouring his resentment, and planned with renewed determination to finish a tragedy that would not only put *Queen Mab* in the shade, but its author too. He would write through the night, eating alone within his room, and would leave only to collect his thoughts, stretch his legs or post a letter to England. And so, on that last day of May, he locked himself in his room and wrote all afternoon, and would have written all evening except for an unforeseen encounter from an unexpected source. He had lain down his pen for a moment and had gone to close the window since the light in his room had begun to attract mosquitoes, and had suddenly seen her in the garden below.

He had seen her often before, of course, as she walked in the orchard, always with a book, or sitting on the terrace with her half-sister, and once he had inquired after the child. On this particular evening however, she was walking alone in the garden below his window, a rolled parasol (white with blue ribbons) in one hand, eyes lowered towards the pages of a novel. From the window, his shoulders against the shutters, Polidori could see only the top of her head, her fair hair tied in a chignon above a long neck, rising from a square-necked gown. Thin shoulders, narrow waist. She was merely walking up and down on the short-cut grass, disappearing now and again out of sight as her movements were temporarily obscured by the leaves of a lime tree, then reappearing directly below, pose unchanged, to turn at the edge of a small bed of roses. Now and again, she would stop and stare ahead of her, pensively, then hurry to a larger book lying on a garden seat which seemed to be a dictionary, for she would turn over the pages agitatedly, stop, hover an index finger over a selected word, then return to the novel and the slow stroll up and down the lawn. Polidori watched these actions with interest for some time, until the girl below became aware of his gaze and looked up suddenly, her right hand raised to her eyes. Realizing it was too late to duck back out of sight, he stared down at her and gave a self-conscious smile. To his surprise, the smile was returned and so, impulsively, he called out, 'What are you reading?'

He saw her hold up the book and call out a title he couldn't hear. It was repeated.

'In English?' Polidori asked.

'No, in Italian. I'm trying to learn it,' and then, her voice louder, 'I *must* learn it.'

The opportunity was there. Two minutes later, he was walking beside her; and within half an hour he had offered and been accepted as Mary Godwin's new Italian tutor.

There was to be no fee.

* * *

'She is perhaps five feet three inches, or five feet four

inches but no more, and has a good carriage, unlike many English women of her class. Her hair is light and fine and is swept away from a broad, untroubled brow to frame a thin and rather pinched face. Observing her from a distance, as I have only achieved before, one has the impression of a thin, well-collected young girl of temperate ways, and she puts one in mind of a fine, well-trained chestnut—I refer of course to the horse, Florence, not the fruit! Her eyes are unnaturally fine, being generously large and oval, and are the colour of dry sand. I was much taken by such eyes, for they reminded me of the eyes one sees in a Renaissance fresco or in the face of a Muse by Lorenzo Lotto. The face is well redeemed by such a feature, for the mouth alas is thin and tight and implies a meanness and an acerbity which is not flattering in such a young person. However, I found her manners charming and her initial behaviour towards me, as we walked in the hotel garden, very comforting. She is the daughter of that notorious woman Wollstonecraft,* whom you so much admire, and also of that boor Godwin whom *I* so much despise.

'On this particular evening, Mrs Shelley and I (I call her "Mrs Shelley" euphemistically on the grounds of propriety and with the sole desire to placate *her* good name, not his) took a stroll along the lake shore in order to discuss my future role as tutor of Italian studies. It is a role I welcome, since my work of late (except for my tragedy) has been somewhat overlooked, as you are no doubt aware.

* Mary Wollstonecraft, authoress of *Reply to Burke* and the *Vindication of the Rights of Women*. In a short, tragic life, she was the victim of a series of bitter love affairs, notably with the painter, Fuseli, and the American, Captain Gilbert Imlay. By the latter, she gave birth to a daughter, Fanny Imlay, but on discovering that her lover was living with an actress, attempted suicide by throwing herself into the Thames. Saved from this fate, she met and married William Godwin and died in childbirth at the age of thirty-six, in September 1797. Her fame rests on her unselfish fight as a pioneer for women's emancipation.

'Then, however, as it grew darker (there being almost no twilight here), our conversation turned to other subjects, some, may I say, quite sinister. Mrs Shelley seemed to be in a talkative frame of mind, no doubt because she had been neglected of late by S., and told me much of her history, of which I will relate briefly. Her mother it seems had an unhappy life and once attempted suicide by jumping off Putney Bridge, but was saved in time and eventually married Godwin, which seems to me to be a fate far worse than drowning. However her misery was to be spared, for she died not long after whilst giving birth to this young woman who accompanied me beside the lake. She also left another daughter, Fanny, who is her natural child and is well-loved by all, but seems to be a melancholy girl. The third sister, Miss Clairmont, is of no relation, being the daughter of Godwin's second wife by her first marriage.

'Having exhausted the subject of domestic relations, we began to walk away from the shore on to the slopes of vineyards that lie above the village. It was a still evening, very quiet and unnaturally dark, and I myself felt somewhat ill at ease, as if about to witness something evil. I brushed aside such idle emotions, attributing them to my own melancholy, but I couldn't completely erase my sudden nervousness, and so I attempted to rationalize it. As you well know, Florence, I am not in any way inhibited by the dark or by the night, unlike L.B., and so could not understand why such an hour troubled me. It was, without doubt, a starless sky, *sans lune*, but there was still some light from the west, and the weather was not intemperate. Then, as we made our way along the narrow stone paths that separate the vines, I realized with a sudden horror that my nervousness was created by my companion herself. It was she, this young girl, who disturbed me. I cannot explain why, and perhaps it was her conversation (which was now quite macabre) that disturbed me. Whatever the reason, I began to feel a little afraid!

'We had now reached the top of the highest slope and were totally alone. Below us was the lake, a large, dark crescent disappearing to the east in the direction of Montreux. A few flickering lights could still be seen, but they were now far away. About us were only the dark shadows of trees and vines, relieved briefly by the green gleam of a glow-worm on a wall or by the sudden appearance of a bat. We were alone.

'At first, we had discussed Switzerland and had chatted politely about its features—may I note that conversation with Mrs Shelley is almost always *polite,* no matter what the subject. She told me of an earlier visit she had made to this country in the company of Miss Clairmont and Mister S., and related many interesting anecdotes, including one about her carrying a donkey which amused me. I, on my part, was encouraged to discuss my own life, which I did, naturally, with some reserve. I told her about my connections with Alfieri* and of my career in Edinburgh. The latter seemed to interest her greatly, for she began to plague me with many questions about my profession, asking me about illness and disease and about the dying. It was not a subject I cared to discuss with a lady, but she insisted so vehemently that I found myself confabbing about death, which to her was the end of life, not the beginning. Then, quite suddenly, without warning, I felt her touch my hand. At first, because of the darkness, I imagined it to be a bat or perhaps a leaf on a tree that had brushed against me, but it was repeated. There was no intimacy implied, I hastily add, in the gesture, nor would

---

* Vittorio Alfieri, Italian poet and dramatist, author of *Della tirannide*, *Saul* and his own *Vita*. Polidori's father, Gaetano, was secretary to Alfieri for some time, and Mary Shelley in later years was interested in writing a biography of the man.

I seek it, for the hand that touched me was as cold as winter. It was like the hand of a corpse. Now, I know you think me to be fanciful, but that was indeed the impression I received. Immediately, I drew away and asked her if in fact she *was* cold. There was no answer. Instead I watched her walk away from me towards some trees, black against the sky, pulling her woollen shawl around her.

'I hesitated, Florence. I hesitated with discretion, then approached her again and discovered that she was talking to me. The words were indistinct at first, but on drawing nearer, I realized she was describing the death of a baby. It was, in truth, her own. You can imagine how I felt. I attempted to be sympathetic, though she seemed to be in no way distraught by the tragedy she was relating. However, she then began to talk once more of drowning and quoted Ophelia, and described to me in great detail the construction of an infant coffin. Such talk from this girl was now unnatural and I was anxious to leave, but she took hold of my arm and asked me if I had ever attended a post-mortem and to explain the process to her. I refused politely, pretending that I was ignorant of such matters, and this seemed to satisfy her, for she released her grip and began to walk down the slope towards the hotel. Of that, at least, I was relieved.

'But the dialogue was not yet over. I now learnt that she had first made love to Mister S. in a cemetery! May I say now that such confessions embarrassed me greatly, but she appeared to be unconcerned. *It was in a cemetery,* she told me, *upon my mother's grave.* And then she asked, *Do you not find graveyards very sensual, Doctor Polidori?* Of course, I refused to answer and pretended not to have heard. But she seemed obsessed by the idea for she repeated the question and talked endlessly of the cemetery at St Pancras where her mother was buried, and where she used to spend the night alone. I could bear no more and so made my excuses to return quickly to the hotel, which I did, leaving her alone. It was irresponsible of me, I realize, Florence, but I could take no more. I fear for that woman, believing her to be corrupted by S., and have resolved not to walk at night with her again. However, she needs comfort and I will do my best to befriend her, in the vain hope that I can help. By day, fortunately, she is seemingly very pleasant, but this dark side belongs to the Devil.

'It has been a solemn two days altogether, for another incident occurred yesterday that saddened me greatly. It rained once more in the morning, but had cleared temporarily by noon, and so I decided to take a stroll along the beach after shopping in Geneva. It was while I was nearing the outskirts of the village that I saw a group of people standing at the water's edge, assembled around an object on the sand. My natural curiosity drew me towards them. Reaching the source of interest, I peered over the onlookers' shoulders and saw the focus of their attention. It was the body of a girl lying in the tide who was no more than eighteen years old and very handsome. She was also totally naked, and strangely I felt more sadness for her because she was thus exposed than because she was dead.

'Assuring everyone of my profession, I knelt down in the wet sand beside the body and examined it as decorously as possible, and soon ascertained, much to my dismay, that she was indeed no more. Believe me, Florence, my heart wept to see such a tragic sight, for the dead girl appeared, in her final repose, to be so helplessly frail. Immediately, I covered the body with my coat, shielding her nakedness from the prying eyes, and waited till a wagon arrived to take her away. Without doubt, she is yet another suicide, a fate that has regrettably become so common lately amongst young women.

'When the body had been taken away, I found I had to walk for a full hour to relieve my depression. I understand that she is to be buried today on the edge of town and will go there to pay my last respects to this pitiable stranger.

'I close now. Forgive the sombre mood of this letter.

To Gilbert, as always.

P.

'Good news! The Shelleys are leaving the hotel! I was informed of this this morning. They are preparing to depart this moment and are moving to a house on the other side of the lake. I am, of course, delighted. Wouldn't you be?'

[5]

ALARUMS AND EXCURSIONS

You will perceive from my date [June 1st], that we have changed our residence since my last letter. We now inhabit a little cottage on the opposite shore of the lake, and have exchanged the view of Mont Blanc and her snowy aiguilles for the dark frowning Jura, behind whose range we every evening see the sun sink, and darkness approaches our valley from behind the Alps, which are then tinged by that glowing rose-like hue which is observed in England to attend on the clouds of an autumnal sky when daylight is almost gone. The lake is at our feet, and a little harbour contains our boat in which we still enjoy our evening excursions on the water.*

It was a small, square two-storey house, totally devoid of charm, but pleasantly situated on the slope of a meadow beside the harbour of Montalegre. On the western side, four windows faced the lake and the setting sun, and on the eastern side, a small vineyard separated it from another building, now quite familiar, which stood no more than two hundred yards away on the hill of Cologny.

Perhaps it was mere coincidence that prompted Shelley to choose a house so close to the Villa Diodati, but their proximity could not be ignored either by Claire, or, indeed, by Polidori. And yet, paradoxically, Byron still had not decided on Diodati as a residence when the Shelleys took the small house below. In fact the situation was quite the reverse. He had actually preferred to stay in the public arena of the Angleterre rather than pay the rent for such

* Mary Godwin, letter of June 1st, 1816.

an edifying but expensive villa. Perhaps it was coincidence then, indeed; or was it perhaps that Claire (lately a mere handmaiden to the activities) optimistically hoped that her former lover might change his mind, forego his natural antipathy to extravagance, and hire Diodati despite everything, just to be near Shelley and privacy.

If that was indeed Byron's wish, he made no indication of it, choosing instead to remain with Dejean and the gawpers, and to row across the lake each morning and evening in order to converse with his new acquaintances. Moreover, at the hotel he could at least lock himself in his room to concentrate on his writing, blessedly free from the more familiar interruptions, of which there had been many. One incident, in particular, serves perhaps to illustrate several.

It took place on the day Polidori had journeyed to Geneva to attend a funeral, leaving Byron alone at the hotel, alone that is as far as his more familiar companions were concerned. Earlier, he had seen Mary and Shelley take the boat from the harbour and set out across the lake, together with William, William's wet-nurse and a large hamper. Everything indicated that an excursion and a picnic were planned and that the party would not return till late. Byron therefore was alone for a few hours and not disappointed by the prospect. Consequently, after writing in his room for some time, he decided to take a stroll in the hotel garden and along the shore, to exercise not only his own legs but also those of a dog he had recently seen and bought. It was a casual promenade (three hundred yards, no more) taken at a leisurely pace, even for Byron. Suddenly however it was interrupted by the awareness that the walker was being followed. Footsteps had been heard, a rustle of skirts, a face ducking out of sight behind a tree or a wall, to reappear sulking and pouting at the gate to the hotel garden.

Caricature for Albé (Byron): He, sitting writing poetry, the words 'Oh! faithless Woman' round the room, hearts are strewed, inscribed, 'We died for love of you.'*

The exchange that then took place in the garden was familiar by now to both protagonists, since it was not the first such incident.

'I did not ask you to follow me eight hundred miles,' was Byron's onslaught, delivered very loudly and with great force. 'If you insisted on chasing across France — and *France* of all places — in pursuit of a man who neither wished your appearance nor relishes it now that it is here, you must not weep and scratch if he cuts you now. I do not like to be pursued by a woman. It puts me at a disadvantage and inhibits me.'

To this, Claire's sally would be predictable, shouted equally as loud and with complementary venom. To her, Byron could not excuse his coldness on the grounds of apathy, since he had willingly seduced her and had not yet abandoned her.

'Furthermore,' Claire added, 'you did not exactly *deny* me the right to follow you here. You gave me your address. You knew I was journeying here—'

'You may journey where you wish, but do not make *me* your excuse.'

'Excuse or not, I am here. How can you be blind to—'

'I am blind to you. And will be blind to you until you return to England.'

'Return? You would cast me out?'

'If that is the phrase you choose to use, then yes, I would cast you out.'

In a second caricature, suggested by Claire four years later, Byron is portrayed sitting drinking spirits, with his mistress, Fornaria, sitting opposite him drinking coffee.

* Claire Clairmont, one of a series of caricatures of Byron suggested by her in November 1820.

Fumes appear from Fornaria's mouth, over which is written 'garlick', *these curling, direct themselves towards the English footman who is just then entering the room and he is knocked backward.* Lord Byron is writing and saying, 'Imprimis, to be a great pathetic poet. First prepare a small colony, then dispatch the Mother, by worrying and cruelty to her grave; afterwards to neglect and ill-treat the children — to have as many and as dirty mistresses as can be found; from their embraces to catch horrible diseases, thus a tolerable quantity of discontent and remorse being prepared, give it vent on paper, and to remember particularly to rail against learned women. This is my infallible receit by which I have made so much money.'

Fornaria, Claire wasn't, nor, as far as Byron was aware in this month of May, was she the Mother. But Mother or not, she was dispatched nevertheless, spared at least from being cast in those seemingly vile roles of *dirty mistress* or, worse, *learned woman*. Dispatched and sent away in full view of a garden of spectators, pushing each other aside to see the quarrel and to witness Claire, hair loose, hurrying in tears back into the hotel, not to reappear till morning. It was on that day that she left with the Shelleys across the lake to Montalegre to lodge with them at Maison Chappuis. The distraught admirer was at last away from the great pathetic poet.

On the day of the Shelleys' departure, Polidori himself was hard put to disguise his delight at the events, and was seen eagerly helping the porters load the sailing boat with luggage, and clamouring to assist in any way. Finally, overcome with fine deeds, he offered to take the child William to be vaccinated, 'since I knew they would have neglected to perform such a necessity', and set off in the middle of the morning towards Geneva. With him in the carriage was the Swiss maid, Elise, as well as William, whom Polidori had promised to return later to Maison Chappuis. It was a warm day and they were in no hurry, so Polidori put his feet up on the opposite seat, lit one of Byron's cigars and allowed himself to be taken slowly along the shore to the capital. For him, as well as for his employer, it was, after all, a day of blissful farewell.

* * *

When the diarist John Evelyn visited Geneva in 1646, he saw a crocodile hanging in chains outside the Town House, and seven judges without hands painted on one of the walls. Times however had changed. The two bridges across the Rhône, bisecting Geneva, were then made of timber and were covered with water-mills and small shops belonging to smiths and cutlers. Between the bridges was an island on which stood a tower built apparently by Caesar himself, as well as the Mint and a small sun-dial. When Evelyn walked through the gates of the town, he found himself on a large field which had been named Campus Martius in the Roman manner, and where he witnessed the youths of the town competing against each other with guns and crossbows and swords, as they did every Sunday after evening devotions.

He also observed, like Polidori 170 years later, that the Swiss women were far from being the prettiest in Europe, by any means. Their necks were too thick and they had the 'faces of puddings', but apparently were a little less chaste than their descendants, since adultery had become so common in the seventeenth century that it was punishable by public execution on the Campus Martius itself. By 1816, such entertainment had declined and the field was no longer in use. Little else, however, had changed. Geneva was still a fortified town, in which the houses were tall and cramped in narrow streets, many of them on a slope, and where the architecture was noted for its tastelessness. It was a town of booksellers and watchmakers and bankers, and where the gates in its walls were closed regularly at ten o'clock each evening, sealing off its snoozing inhabitants and their plain wives from the world. A promenade, however, had been added in the past few years, below the south wall, and was called Plainpalais. Here a small obelisk had been erected to Rousseau, *Citoyen de Genève*, where all but magistrates were encouraged to walk and picnic beneath the poplars. Here, too, Polidori arrived with Shelley's baby, and discovered, it being Sunday, that the gates were shut and that he was locked out.

Driving around the wall he reached the second gate and was told that the gates would remain shut till the services at St Peter's (a spacious Gothic fabric) were over. Irritated and hot, his loathing for the Swiss rekindled, Polidori urged the driver to take the carriage for a slow ride around the outskirts of the town, in the hope that they might encounter an inn where they could find something to eat or drink. At midday, they arrived (William now in tears) at a small village to the south of Geneva, where they heard music. Stepping out of the carriage, Polidori and the maid found themselves in the middle of a local fair.

A small rostrum had been set up before a livery stable, covered in ribbons and flags, and half a dozen men, members of a band, were playing a waltz. Across a level, men and women were dancing, most of them youths and girls with red cheeks from the village. *Saw a village where lads and lasses,* wrote Polidori in his Diary, *soubrettes and soldiers were dancing, to a tabor and drum, waltzes, cotillions etc.* The lads and, no doubt, the lasses, kept Polidori at the village for two hours or more, so that it was late afternoon (William duly vaccinated) when he finally arrived at Shelley's new house at Campagne Chappuis. The child was duly exchanged for a gold chain and seal as a payment for services, and the doctor was guided breathlessly around the house, stage-managing enthusiasm as windows were opened and closed for him, cupboards were revealed and paintings were removed from walls for closer inspection.

Later still he was taken for a sail on the lake, and was asked to describe the vaccination and the fair and was listened to attentively as he did so. It was a pleasant evening for him and for a rare moment his Diary rises to detail. *The sunset, the mountains on one side, a dark mass of outline on the other trees, houses hardly visible, just distinguishable, a white light mist, resting on the hills around, formed the blue into a circular dome bespangled with stars only and lighted by the moon which gilt the lake. The dome of heaven seemed oval.*

Later even still, as it grew cold, all returned to Maison Chappuis to drink green tea and to talk till the early hours. 'It was during those long nightly conversations that I felt that I was an intruder more than at any other time,' Polidori wrote to Florence. Whatever the subject, they were usually too esoteric or too personal to include him, and eventually, after half an hour of passive resistance, he would get up from his chair and leave the house to walk alone along the beach, or retire to another room to continue writing his tragedy. More often than not, his departure was unnoticed. Regretfully, he realized on this first night at Montalegre that nothing, after all, had changed. The Shelleys had moved across the lake, but instead of Byron spending less time with them, he spent more, since the effort of visiting demanded that he stay in their company longer. After that initial evening—four hours of conversation ranging from anecdotes of Grattan and Curran to the philosophy of madness (a popular item) —Polidori resolved to pursue another course of endeavour. If he was denied the intimacy of one society, then he would find another.

He had always liked music. Music, he felt, was in his blood, partly because of his nationality, and partly because of his father's influence over him as a child. Memories of long musical evenings in the drawing-room (John W. on the viola, sister Charlotte at the piano) and innumerable visits to the opera had shaped his musical knowledge to a level that was considered quite exceptional in such a young man. Though his actual ability to perform the music he enjoyed was somewhat limited, he did possess a tolerably tuneful voice, and could sing, under pressure, in two languages. At Ampleforth, as a ruffled chorister, he had, in fact, added a third, contributing a querulous Latin falsetto to Vespers and High Mass.

Consequently, on the evening of June 4th, Polidori, in a freshly starched cravat and raven-black suit, attended for the first time, at the recommendation of de Roche, Madame Odier's Musical Performance And Appreciation Society (Refreshments Served), which took place in Geneva each Wednesday evening from seven till ten. It was hardly an explosive affair, and yet the genteel society of a dozen devotees (mostly English) sitting politely, knee to knee, in the salon listening to a local widow entertaining on the 'cello, or nodding to a lecture on tonal aesthetics, was refreshingly pleasant after the green-tea discourses at Secheron and Maison Chappuis. Polidori, in truth, was enchanted. He was welcomed like a brother, especially as the members were mostly physicians like himself, and introduced to a whole new stratum of open-minded, uncomplicated people. He was once again his companions' equal. Moreover, there was the added attraction of the female members of the society, notably saffron-haired, willowy-waisted Mademoiselle Odier, the doctor's daughter, with whom Polidori promptly fell in love, moving his chair near her piano stool as she sang 'Ranz des Vaches' especially for him. Afterwards, tea and cakes.

At 8.30, the Appreciation Society adjourned to a larger room where dancing began, mostly French country dances and cotillions. Intoxicated by the occasion, and also by the brandy that was now being secretly passed around amongst the gentlemen, Polidori awaited his opportunity to take the delectable Mademoiselle Odier on to the floor. The opportunity soon came. Blissfully unaware of the English members' disdain of the new dance that was sweeping the ballrooms of Europe, the musicians boldly struck up a waltz. Immediately, the floor was cleared, leaving only one or two defiant Swiss to lead the dance, as the English retired arrogantly to their corners, and the ladies found themselves still sitting on the chaise-longue long after the first few bars were over. By the window, Mademoiselle Odier contemplated her fan.

'Mademoiselle, permettez-moi.'

She looked up, cheeks reddening, one hand resting on her bare shoulder, to see Polidori standing above her. With a smile he gestured towards the floor, bowing slightly, then took her arm and led her into the waltz. 'For the first time since arriving in Geneva, I felt at ease. The assembly was charming, I was accepted without rancour and my companion in the *valse* was nothing less than exquisite.' She was also only fifteen, in love with another, and politely unimpressed by the doctor's bravado. After that first waltz, there was to be no other. Strangely apathetic towards her partner's boast that he was the friend and companion to the sixth Lord Byron himself (though her mother almost fainted with curiosity), Mademoiselle Odier returned to her window-seat after a muttered 'Merci' as the music stopped, sat in profile and resolutely declined all other offers for the rest of the evening. Nevertheless, Polidori was not dismayed. He had found his nirvana, modest though it may be, and by the end of the soirée had not only made an introduction into

Genevese society, but had also resolved to return the following Wednesday. Madame Odier's Musical Performance And Appreciation Society (Refreshments Served) was, to him, an unqualified success.

At ten o'clock, he and Doctor Gardner, an Englishman, left hurriedly, having forgotten the time, and just managed to leave the town before the gates were shut. Reluctant to end the jubilant mood so early, a bottle of brandy was bought, and the two men wandered aimlessly along the outskirts of the wall, drinking constantly and discussing with great enthusiasm the new-found charms of La Belle Genevoise. Polidori was told of other soirées and of other women, some more accommodating than sweet Miss Odier, and both men resolved to meet again in the near future with the strict intention of introducing the younger doctor to the more fundamental aspects of Genevese life. At eleven o'clock, Gardner abruptly collapsed in a drunken faint, and Polidori, only a degree soberer, found himself obliged to hire a calèche in order to carry his companion home. When he himself finally arrived, staggering joyfully along the shore to Maison Chappuis, it was past midnight and he was confronted, pacing up and down the harbour, by an angry and very sober employer.

'Polly!'

The voice was incisive and unexpectedly bitter. Polidori stopped and waited as Byron limped slowly towards him. On his right, through the trees, he could make out the shape of Percy Shelley standing by the door of his house, watching the two men.

The subsequent events that immediately followed are, on the surface, obscure. Polidori himself, naturally, makes no mention of them in his Diary other than that a 'quarrel' ensued, but other witnesses, notably Mary Godwin, reported later that it was much more than just that. Certainly a quarrel took place, but quarrels and Polidori were by no means strangers. On this particular night, however, not only was he drunk, but he had also apparently incurred the temper of his employer.

'Polly! Where have you been?'

The question was repeated perhaps three or four times, until the doctor, angered that the mood of the evening should be so abruptly shattered, replied angrily, 'I have been to Geneva. Am I not entitled to do that, at least?'

'No,' shouted Byron, stopping a few feet away. 'Not when you ignore my demands.'

'What demands? Am I to be chained to you hand and—'

'You ask my permission before you disappear.'

'I did not disappear. I went to Geneva.'

'I beg your pardon, Polidori, but you disappeared. You are in my employ as a physician and you are paid to attend my needs.'

'What needs are these?'

'What needs, for God's sake, does one hire a physician for?'

'Oh, I see. You refer to sickness.'

'Of course, I refer to sickness.'

'Oh. Well, when you are ill, I will attend to you.'

'When I am ill, Polidori, you disappear.'

'I beg your pardon, my lord, but I have never disappeared when you have been ill.'

'I have been ill *tonight*, damn you!'

A silence. Near by, Shelley moved closer, walking on tiptoe for fear of disturbing the mood. On the quay, Polidori neither moved nor looked away, but stood rather unsteadily, staring at the other man. He made no attempt to reply.

'I was ill tonight, Polly,' Byron said finally, his voice lower and more controlled. 'Are you not aware that my stomach needs constant attention?'

Polidori's immediate laughter startled even himself. The situation seemed suddenly absurd, but the laughter was regretted. However, it was too late. He attempted an apology but his efforts were squashed by the arrival of Shelley.

'I think he's drunk,' Shelley said quietly. 'I do believe your doctor is drunk.'

But Byron didn't hear, for he had turned and walked away, bored already by the situation, and stood now alone beneath a shadow of some chestnut trees. A few yards away, a dog had appeared and was sniffing along the edge of the water.

Polidori, now relieved from one assailant, raised his head and turned slowly towards the other. 'What did you just say?'

'I said I thought you were drunk,' replied Shelley, smiling, but without malice. And then added politely, 'Aren't you?'

Polidori was certainly drunk, though rapidly becoming sober by the second, but unlike Gardner, alcohol did not affect him wilfully. Instead, he became calmer, more rational and much more confident. Indeed, confident enough not to be cowed by Byron, nor, more especially, by Shelley.

'I am not drunk,' he said slowly, looking up steadily at Shelley, 'nor am I incapable. And I will prove so. You boast often of your prowess as a writer and I will challenge you to that quite soon. But you also boast of your skill with a boat, do you not?'

Amused and puzzled, Shelley replied, 'I hope I do not boast of it.'

'But you consider yourself skilled?'

'Yes ... but not as skilled as Byron or Maurice —'

'And you would say,' interrupted Polidori, 'that such skill demands concentration, would you not?'

'It depends. Some times more concentration than others. In a squall, for example, or on a windy day—'

'Like tonight?'

'Yes. Like tonight.'

Shelley smiled, looking at the doctor with bewilderment, and glanced back to see if Byron was listening. He was.

'And you would say, Shelley, that such skill on such a night is beyond the capabilities of a drunken man? Since sobriety and concentration are of the essence?'

The light was seen for the first time, and Shelley laughed. 'Are you challenging me to a boat-race, Polidori?'

'I am.'

At this moment, even Byron laughed, stomach forgotten, but Polidori's expression revealed that he was in earnest. 'Do you accept, sir?' The question was emphatic.

'Yes,' replied the other. 'Yes, I do. If that amuses you ... '

It did. Within minutes, two boats in the harbour were made ready—one owned by Shelley, the other hired by Byron. The race was to be to a near-by headland, no more than a mile away, just west of Bellerive, and back again. Then, watched by Byron and Mary from the jetty, and by Claire from her bedroom window, the two contestants (jackets folded on the pier) set off, heading out of the harbour, around the stone jetty and out into the lake in an easterly direction. It was, by all reports, a miserable race.

If Polidori had any knowledge of sailing he didn't reveal it now. Instead, his boat, a two-master, allowed itself to be caught by a cross-wind, was spun around and finally keeled over, its occupant clinging grimly to its side, a few yards outside the harbour. Ahead, Shelley's boat could be seen skimming across the waves in a direct line for Bellerive. Fifteen minutes later, he returned to an appreciative audience and the unabated fury of his competitor.

What had begun as a humorous diversion now collapsed into a farce.

Once, when Byron was asked to describe Polidori, he replied uncharitably that he was *exactly the kind of person to whom, if he fell overboard, one would hold out a straw to know if the adage be true that drowning men catch at straws.*

Though Polidori did not drown to prove the adage on this particular evening (he was, in truth, a fair swimmer), his humiliation was such that he was prepared to die to reclaim his honour. In short, he challenged his triumphant competitor to a duel.

Shelley's reaction was to laugh at the Romantic absurdity of such a gesture and consider it as no more than a vain boast from a very vain young man. Byron, however, was not so unrealistic, since he himself had been challenged by the doctor less than a few weeks before.* Stepping immediately between the two men, he turned to Polidori, seizing his shoulder.

'No more, Polly. No more. It is over.'

'It is not for me. That man refuses, my lord.'

'Yes, he refuses,' Byron replied, gesturing to Shelley to leave. 'But recollect that though Shelley has some scruples about duelling, *I* have none, and shall be, at all times, ready to take his place.'

The implication was too obvious for Polidori to ignore, and so he turned away, unable to contain himself any longer, and burst uncontrollably into tears. Behind him, Shelley returned quietly and solemnly to his house.

* The incident took place in April of that year while Byron and Polidori were touring the Rhine. Though not strictly a challenge, Polidori, after reading much of Byron's works, turned to him and said defiantly, '*Pray, what is there excepting writing poetry that I cannot do better than you?*' Byron had replied that there were three things, '*First, I can hit with a pistol the keyhole of that door. Secondly, I can swim across that river to yonder point — and thirdly, I can give you a damned good thrashing.*'

Polidori, it is reported, meekly left the room.

'Go home, Polly,' Byron said quietly, taking his arm. 'Let Maurice take you home. Tomorrow we must go and see Hentsch about a villa for ourselves. Go home now and I will see you in the morning.'

The younger man hesitated, hiding his head as his employer turned to Maurice, his boatman, and told him to take the doctor back to the hotel.

'Come back for me in an hour,' he added. 'I am too restless to sleep just yet.'

Slowly, Polidori allowed himself to be led on to the boat and was taken back across the lake to Secheron. Byron watched the boat until it was hidden by the darkness, then turned wearily away and began to walk slowly along the beach in no particular direction. He suddenly felt very alone.

I am a lover of Nature and an admirer of Beauty. I can bear fatigue and welcome privation, and have seen some of the noblest views in the world. But in all this — the recollections of bitterness, and more especially of recent and more home desolation, which must accompany me through life, have preyed upon me here; and neither the music of the Shepherd, the crashing of the Avalanche, nor the torrent, the mountain, the Glacier, the Forest, nor the Cloud, have for one moment lightened the weight upon my heart, nor enabled me to lose my own wretched identity in the majesty, and the power, and the Glory, around, above, and beneath me.

I am past reproaches; and there is a time for all things. I am past the wish of vengeance, and I know of none like for what I have suffered; but the hour will come, when what I feel must be felt, and the **** but enough.

To you, dearest Augusta, I send, and for you I have kept this record of what I have seen and felt. Love me as you are beloved by me.

Two months had now gone by since leaving Augusta in London, but unlike Childe Harold, he was no longer a pilgrim, for his thoughts turned back to the past not to the future. His natural melancholy had grown deeper, and though in England he had preferred solitude to society, here it only encouraged him to reflect on what he had lost for ever. He was restless, bored, and ultimately, disenchanted. *If I could explain,* he was to write later,* *at length the* real *causes which have contributed to increase this perhaps natural temperament of mine, this Melancholy which hath made me a by-word, nobody would wonder; but this is impossible without doing much mischief. I do not know what other men's lives have been, but I cannot conceive anything more strange than some of the earlier parts of mine. I have written my memoirs,† but omitted* all *the really consequential and important parts, from deference to the dead, to the living, and to those who must be both.*

Leaving the beach, he walked, aided by his stick, the dog at his heels, into the dense woods that descended to the water itself along the slopes of Cologny. The night was humid yet clear, though storms were forecast. Soon, walking became difficult and tiring, the shadows became unnerving, and so he returned towards the lake, oblivious of time, to discover that his boat had returned, found him absent, and departed. He had been away for almost two hours.

After waiting for a further half hour, he suddenly became nervous of the darkness and hurried to Maison Chappuis, climbed the narrow staircase and went to bed with Claire. The affair, for whatever reasons, was at last resumed.

I was not in love [he was to explain to Augusta], *nor have any love left for any, but I could not exactly play the Stoic with a woman who had scrambled eight hundred miles to*

* Byron, *Detached Thoughts*, October 15th, 1821.
† At Byron's death, the Memoirs were given to John Murray, his publisher, who burnt them in his grate. The contents were never disclosed.

unphilosophise me, besides I had been regaled of late with so many 'two courses and a dessert' (Alas!) of aversion, that I was fain to take a little love (if pressed particularly) by way of novelty.*

It was a novelty that was to cost him dear. If it was indeed just sex he was after, it was far from being unavailable in the neighbourhood villages or the salons of Geneva, and certainly there were women who were not only prettier and more experienced, but also more discreet. And yet, hand on heart, he claimed to have denied them all in favour of a stocky, eighteen-year-old English girl whom he openly cared nothing for.† Love it certainly wasn't — at least not the intensity of love he reserved for Augusta or for himself — though resigned affection (plus an abject laziness) may well have re-stimulated a seduction so perilously close to home. But once again, whatever the reasons, the affair had re-commenced. By Miss Clairmont, at least, he was welcomed with open arms. She had finally regained her celebrated lover. But it was to be a bitter success. The portents were already there.

---

* Byron, letter to Augusta, September 8th, 1816.
† *H. has told me all the strange stories in circulation of me and mine — Not true ... As to all those mistresses Lord help me — I have had but one.* (Letter to Augusta, September 1816.)

[6]

VICTIMS

JUNE is not a predictable month in many ways. It seems to sit like a reluctant watershed between spring and summer and often has neither the freshness of the former nor the heat of the latter. It is an indecisive month, and nowhere more so than in Geneva in 1816 when it was a month of storms. It was a month of storms and rain and sudden squalls, so that sailing was dangerous, swimming was discouraged and inhabitants around the lake were obliged to remain indoors for days on end. If the rains were unseasonal and depressing, the storms themselves were often spectacular displays of natural pyrotechnics, exhilarating to watch, especially for the occupants of Maison Chappuis. *We watch them as they approach from the opposite shore of the lake, observing the lightning play among the clouds in various parts of the heavens, and dart in jagged figures upon the piny heights of Jura, dark with shadows of the overhanging clouds, while perhaps the sun is shining cheerfully upon us.**

On the other side of the Leman, Byron was also undismayed, and recorded much of the splendour in his writing,†

* Mary Godwin, letter of June 1st, 1816.
† The sky is changed!—and such a change! Oh Night,
And Storm, and Darkness, ye are wondrous strong,
Yet lovely in your strength, as is the light
Of a dark eye in Woman! Far along
From peak to peak, the rattling crags among
Leaps the live thunder! Not from one long cloud,
But every mountain now hath found a tongue,
And Jura answers, through her misty shroud,
Back to the joyous Alps, who call her aloud!
(*Childe Harold's Pilgrimage*, III. XCII.)

obviously preferring the storms outside to the ones that constantly raged within his room. Polidori, however, was becoming less of an irritant than in earlier days, since he now found, more often than not, his amusement with the new acquaintances in Geneva. Moreover, the nocturnal visits by Claire were now an embarrassment to him, especially as she made her disapproval of his presence repeatedly clear. *Pray if you can*, she wrote to Byron, *send M. Polidori either to write another dictionary or to the lady he loves. I hope this last may be his pillow and then he will go to sleep for I cannot come at this hour of the night and be seen by him. It is so extremely suspicious.*

Without doubt, Polidori would have been the first to take a lady-love as a pillow if he could find one, but so far his only contact with women was the pretty little Mademoiselle Odier, and clearly he had to seek elsewhere. Now that both Shelley and his employer were suitably serviced, his own empty bed seemed colder than ever, especially for a handsome, twenty-year-old youth on a night of storms. So accordingly, on the very next day following his debut at Madame Odier's soirée, he returned to Geneva and found himself immediately involved in a ponderous discussion on somnambulism with Doctor Odier. However, it was a subject that fascinated him (and lately, according to Claire, *occupied* him), for he had made sleep-walking the basis for his thesis at Edinburgh in 1815.*

The dialogue was endured for as short as possible before he was released to hurry upstairs where the ladies were settling down for dinner. One glance showed him, heart sinking, that the choice was thin. What appeared before him were half a dozen middle-aged dowagers from the east side of town (narrow mouths, cherried breasts, the voice of Hector), who studied him with disdain, since he was neither English nor Genevese, as well as two

* Polidori, *Disputatio Medica Inauguralis de Oneirodyniâ*.

spinsters, the eternal Madame Odier (sans fille, hélas), and a distant aunt. There was indeed only one female under thirty, who unfortunately possessed the shoulders of a well-trained basset hound and who, despite Polidori's desperate overtures, retained the facial animation of a Court card. Otherwise, there were only the English, *speaking amongst themselves, arms by their sides, mouths open and eyes glowing. Might as well make a tour of the Isle of Dogs.* The phrase was apt and Polidori, hopes shattered, left in despair.

That night was spent in a celebrated house on the corner of the Rue Basse. It was an expensive gesture, but the room was clean, as was the girl, and it was a small comfort after a wretched week.

The next day, he returned to the hotel to discover that Byron had renewed his interest in the Villa Diodati, encouraged, no doubt, by Claire. The villa was still for hire, though other offers had been made, and its attraction as a haven of quiet was becoming more desirable every day. The 'staring boobies', as Byron politely dismissed the English tourists who still plagued him, were now more bothersome than the mosquitoes, especially now that a mistress had been introduced into the proceedings. Despair weakened his natural parsimony, and so on June 6th, he took Polidori with him to re-visit the villa. Waiting for them on the lawn was Hentsch.

'I think I can get it for you for 130 louis for five months. Perhaps 125,' he told them as they walked once more around the pillared façade.

'One hundred and twenty-five is the most I will pay,' Byron replied. 'Besides, I am not sure whether I want to stay that long. Five months? It will be winter.'

'It will also be cheaper on such a basis. If you agree, I can prepare the papers immediately.'

It was agreed. If there was any hesitation it was quickly

erased the moment the prospective owner stood on the balcony and gazed across the lake at the magnificent view before him. Here, at last, he could work in peace. By dinner-time, he was formally the master of Villa Diodati,* and four days later the servants, Fletcher and Berger, packed the possessions and the entourage set off for their new home.

I have taken a very pretty little villa in a vineyard, with the Alps behind and Mount Jura and the lake before—it is called Diodati, from the name of the proprietor, who is a descendant of the critical and illustrissimi Diodati's, and has an agreeable house, which he lets at a reasonable rate per season or annum, as suits the lessee. When you come out don't go to an inn, not even to Secheron; but come on to headquarters where I have rooms ready for you and Scrope, and 'all appliances and means to boot'.†

The vineyard he mentioned was that same vineyard that flanked Shelley's house, who was now his only neighbour. It separated the two houses by about two hundred yards and also served to isolate both, so that Byron's seclusion was complete. One approached the house along a tree-covered drive to arrive at a large oak door set in the southern wall, in the shade and away from the lake. Since the villa was set on a slope, one walked from the door along a darkened hallway to appear on the balcony, the *rez-de-chaussée* beneath one, and the lawn below, descending steeply to the harbour. Standing here, on the north balcony, above the lake, one's back was to the grand salon, the largest room in the villa, lit by five tall windows on three sides, and decorated in pale yellow. On the right of

---

* By coincidence, it was at a house owned by a Diodati that John Evelyn visited while he himself was in Geneva in 1646. *The next morning having a letter for Signor John Diodati, the famous Italian minister and translator of the Holy Bible into that language, I went to his house and had a great deal of discussion with that learned person.*

† Byron, letter to Hobhouse, June 23rd, 1816.

the salon was the dining-room, and across the hall was the rather narrow room adopted by Byron as his bedroom. It too had access to the balcony. Above this floor was Polidori's room, which he described thus:

LAKE LEMAN

PICTURE GALLERY	
MY BEDROOM	

Next to his own bedroom, which received the sun in the afternoon, were two guest rooms, cleaned and prepared for the visitors (together no doubt with all appliances and means to boot) who were to arrive later in the summer.

By the 11th, the house was complete. Pictures had been hung, books had been arranged and order was established. Furthermore, the nightly discourses between the two poets could resume without effort, especially now that the weather obliged both men to remain most of the day in their respective houses. The initial nervousness between Shelley and Byron was over, and now that they had exhausted all reminiscences, anecdotes and nostalgia, their dialogues had become more personal and, consequently, more passionate. On Byron's part, the lake, the mountains, the neighbouring town meant only one thing to him, and that was the image of *the self-torturing sophist, wild Rousseau, the apostle of affliction.* The memory of the man was everywhere. For Shelley, these very things only increased his enthusiasm for another writer, far different in temperament from the Genevese, and yet strangely similar in his philosophy, pantheistic and Romantic, and to whom Byron succumbed reluctantly. 'Shelley,' he later told Medwin, 'when in Switzerland, used to doze me with Wordsworth physic even to nausea.' But such physic, nauseous as it may have been, soon captivated Byron's soul and his poetry, reluctant though he was to admit it:

> When Elements to Elements conform
> And dust is as it should be, shall I not
> Feel all I see less dazzling but more warm?
> The bodiless thought? the Spirit of each spot?
> Of which, even now, I share at times the immortal lot?
> Are not the mountains, waves and skies, a part
> Of me and of my Soul, as I of them?
> Is not the love of these deep in my heart
> With a pure passion?*

But despite such temporary curtsies to the lake poet, pantheism was not really for him. If any Spirit moved in any spot, it was more often a real spirit, flesh and blood, and more particularly it was the feminine re-incarnation of Rousseau's Julie. It was she, not Pan, who walked the wooded glades beside the lake, or who was seen by the waterfall, or glimpsed in the gardens, eyes lowered, pale hands together. *La Nouvelle Héloïse* had become Byron's bible, and already he was planning a tour around the Leman, book in hand, in her wake. In preparation for this, he even bought a boat. His extravagance, now, knew no bounds.

* * *

'I am drowning, Florence. I am drowning. All day and all night the rain thunders on the roof, flooding the walls and

* *Childe Harold's Pilgrimage*, III. LXXIV–LXXV.

covering my window with tears. They reflect my own, coursing down my face in despair. Unable to leave the villa because of the wretched elements, I am obliged to remain within my room, within myself and if it was not for my play I would be lunaticked. But my restraint is tempered with diligence, and I can say with joy that my Tragedy is almost complete. Soon, my employer will read it to all as he has promised, and I must confess the prospect unnerves me. But I am content in that, at least. It is my only consolation.

'You will have noticed that I am now residing at Cologny, which is much quieter than the hotel and consequently very dull. My room is above my employer's and is very respectable, with a view across the trees towards Geneva. It is there I prefer to spend my evenings, since it is made very clear, of late, that my presence is not encouraged at Diodati. Not by L.B. as you might think, but by another who has become a frequent visitor at night. *She* resents me. I, her. It is a mutual disaffection. I will not divulge on the matter of her visits, but they in no way relate to Mister Shelley's, who is at present thrust upon us, God forbid! I have reserved my encounters, Florence, with this 'quibbling quartet' only to Mrs S., whom I continue to tutor in Italian each morning. She is very adept and speaks well.

'Yesterday, I was compelled to join a circulating library, as I have nothing to read except L.B.'s, and borrowed three books in Italian which are painfully tedious but very religious. Consequently, I recommended them to Mister S.!

'Last evening, I visited Madame Odier as it was Wednesday, and found no one. You can imagine my dismay. However, while waiting; I wandered idly throughout the house and encountered young Mademoiselle Odier in the withdrawing room. She was alone. May I say, Florence, that she is exquisite and is reminiscent of that painting by

Mister Romney we saw in London the day Gilbert was ill. Her nose is fine (which is very rare for the Swiss) and she has none of the bovine humour so common to the race. Her hair is fair, as I have said, and she has a fine bosom, very white, and a pretty ear. As I approached, she rose and reddened delightfully, but alas it was not from love for me, but from guilt as she had been clandestinely waving to a gentleman in the street, no doubt her lover. I faked blindness and asked her to play the piano for me. Which she did. 'Ranz des Vaches', *encore*. Twice, with great emotion. Throughout the whole performance, I kept my attention on her young bosom which glowed joyously as the music became more warlike. Such observation, Florence, was naturally seen with the eye of the physician, not of your friend Polidori. People then arrived. Too bad. Too bad.

'Extraordinary thing, Florence. During the dancing, I noticed the ladies all waltzed except of course the English. They, poor wretches, frown and mutter "jib-jib" as if we were all dancing naked at the Hellfire, one against the other, ladies included! Their pomposity stifles me. However, more stifling still is the unusual method of dancing procedure. *Politesse* and decorum are thrown to the Swiss air and one asks without introduction, without formality. Unfortunately, the girls refuse those they dislike, pulling faces and sulking, so that one is left standing over them like a flunkey, obliged to retreat. None as pretty as Miss O., but I can gain nothing there. I did however dance till midnight, since the waltz is very pleasant though confabbing during it is *de rigueur*. Having stayed so late, I was of course locked in and had to sleep in Geneva at the Balance. Expensive.

'From my window, I can see Miss Clairmont departing across the garden. She looks rather cross. Earlier this morning, being above my employer's room, and they not realizing I had returned, I heard Miss C. screaming and shouting in anger, but couldn't make out the sense, though I listened hard. However, she sings well enough.

'Tonight, I am going to a ball at an English lady's. L.B., who knows such things, tells me that because I am born under the sign of Virgo (he being Aquarius), tonight will be very lucky *pour l'amour*. On verra, Florence. On verra.

P.

'Life is lonely, Florence. Isn't it at times? Life is *very* lonely.'

* * *

It was without doubt the worst storm yet, appearing rapidly without warning into a sky that, a few minutes before, seemed almost lethargic and quiet and deceptively complacent. It appeared suddenly from the east, filling the lake with dazzling light as the lightning ricocheted across the mountains, bouncing over the immense expanse of water from Salève and Jura to the Alps of Savoy. For a brief moment there was darkness, the eyes blinded, groping in the night; then a further crash of thunder echoing in the hollows of the hills and the light reappeared, brighter still, and the rain fell. In minutes, streams were flooded, boats were desperately pulled higher up the shore and the Rhône became a torrent. At Diodati, servants hurried on to the balcony to collect chairs and retrieve forgotten books, and shutters were closed. It was the sixth day of rain and there seemed no end to it.

In the salon, Shelley and Byron were alone. It was a warm, comfortable room on such a night, lit sparingly except around the hearth where a large fire blazed, casting deep shadows around the walls. On the floor a large dog slept, stomach up, head on an angle, at the feet of its owner who sat now in his favoured chair to the right of the mantel. Opposite him, Shelley squatted on a stool, gazing into the fire, his head resting on the knees of his nankeen trousers. Both Mary and Claire remained below in Maison Chappuis, reading till the early hours until Shelley returned and Claire left, hurrying up the slope across the lawn to rejoin her lover. On this evening, Polidori was also absent, having departed earlier, before the storm, to attend a ball at Mrs Slaney's in Geneva. 'I'm going to a ball in Geneva,' he had said, and left. His departure was not regretted.

'I have been thinking of an odd circumstance,' Byron said pensively. The younger man turned his head. 'My daughter, my wife, my half-sister, my mother, my sister's mother and myself, are or were all *only* children. My sister's mother, Lady Conyers, had only my half-sister by that second marriage—herself too an only child—and my father had only me—an only child—by his second marriage, with my mother an only child too. Such a complication of only children, all tending to one family, is singular enough, and looks like fatality almost. But I feel that the fiercest animals have the rarest numbers in their litters—lions, tigers and even elephants which are mild in comparison.'

'Do you then consider yourself an elephant or a tiger?' Shelley asked, smiling.

'Oh, I am a lamb. A mere lamb. Nothing more.'

Outside, the rain seemed to have turned to hail, for it rattled on the shutters and on the stone of the balcony and sent up sparks from the fire. For a moment, the two men were subdued. It was not past midnight.

'What of your daughter?' Shelley asked cautiously. 'Do you miss her?'

'In all honesty, I ought to say I do not. I have never been fond of children, least of all my own.'

'Even if you had an heir?'

'An heir to what? When I die I will leave nothing to inherit—except perhaps my ill-fame. Besides, what right have I to inflict a woman like *her* on anyone? We should at least be able to choose our mothers, since they spend more time with us, and are often more intimate than our wives.'

The younger man was silent.

'But *you* have a fine son, Shelley,' Byron added, studying his companion. 'He'll grow up well—that is, if Polidori manages to keep well away.'

'Do you think him a poor doctor, then?'

'On the contrary, I would recommend his medical talents to anyone. Anyone. Look at me. He has done me a world of good, for each time he is out of my sight I feel a hundred times better than I ever did.'

At that moment, there was a knock on the door and the valet Fletcher entered. 'My lord?'

'What is it, Fletcher?'

'My lord, there is a gentleman from the police to see you. It's about the doctor, my lord.'

'Polidori?'

'Yes, my lord. He has been arrested.'

The circumstances of the case were confused but predictable. Returning from Mrs Slaney's ball (beautiful wife, jealous husband, early exit), Polidori had decided to walk home and soon found himself in the midst of the storm. Soaked to the skin, he had refrained from sheltering under the trees for fear of lightning, and had plunged ahead on a different route in order to avoid the woods. Consequently, in no time he was lost. Confused, wet and miserable, he had attempted to retrace his steps and seek out the house of Doctor Gardner with the intention of waiting there till the rain ceased. Unfortunately, the house he entered in the darkness was not Gardner's but that of an irate and slumbering (dogs in the scullery) prefect of the police, who immediately summoned his inferiors. The hysterical pleadings of the accused were of little avail until he mentioned the name of his illustrious employer. Pistols were lowered, dogs were kennelled and an envoy was sent post-haste to the Villa Diodati.

'Man is born free,' said Byron wearily, handing the required release to his valet, 'but Polidori, he is everywhere in chains.'

* * *

The next day (the 14th), a curious practice was unearthed from across the lake. Dismayed that he had been cheated by the departure of his most notorious resident, Jacques Dejean, the hotelier of the Angleterre, had discovered that his inn and Diodati were, in fact, in direct line to each other across the lake. He had also realized that on a clear day he could see without too much effort straight to Byron's residence, if he stood on his highest balcony, and that such a unique discovery should not be neglected. Accordingly, he erected a powerful telescope, its lens directed on to the sixth Lord Byron's window, and allowed his guests to view (for a small charge) the mysterious occurrences in the house across the water. There was, of course, no shortage of clients, as men and women jostled to peer at the activities of the Villa Diodati, and interpreted the sheets that hung out to dry as petticoats ripped from the innumerable mistresses who no doubt scampered bare-bottomed within the very walls before them. Such was the fanciful reputation Byron was acquiring by those he shunned that he had now become a commercial attraction, the subject of obscene jokes and sniggered anecdotes. *I never led so moral a life as during my residence in that country,* Byron retorted later, *but I gained no credit for it. There is no story so absurd that they did not invent at my cost. I was watched by glasses on the opposite shore of the lake, and by glasses too that must have had very distorted optics.*

Distorted they may have been, but many of the voyeurs

went even further and attempted to sneak into the very gardens of the villa, so that he had to put dogs on the loose and guard the door. If they were thwarted by that, they continued to follow him as he sailed or swam, and sometimes young girls, stimulated by his reputation, waylaid him in his carriage, offering all. The more he shunned them, the more he was pursued, and the more implausible the anecdotes, the more they were believed. *I was accused*, Byron sighed, *of corrupting all the grisettes in the Rue Basse. I believe that they looked upon me as a man-monster, worse than the piqueur*.

If he was worse than the *piqueur*, it would only have been Claire who told him so, for already she was becoming disenchanted by the affair. Her lover was obviously growing tired of her, though he had not yet said as much, but had indicated so. He did not know yet, however, that his mistress was pregnant, for Claire feared, understandably, that such a revelation might sever him from her for ever. So for the moment, she remained silent, and for that he was never to forgive her. But in the month of June, ignorant of the true state of her health, he kept her in his bed, and did so as discreetly as possible. In fact so discreetly that none outside the menage ever knew of the affair, and one notable Englishman, desperate for a snatch of gossip for his club, assumed that his mistress was another. His assumption was farcical, to say the least. *Among more than sixty English travellers here, there is Lord Byron, who is cut by everybody. They tell a strange story of his at Dejean's Inn. He is now living at a villa on the Savoy side of the lake with that woman who it seems proves to be a* Mrs Shelley, *wife to the man who keeps the Mount Coffee-House.**

But as with the previous and more disturbing scandal concerning himself and his sister Augusta, Byron made no attempt either to confirm or deny the slanders around him.

* Lord Glenbervie, Diary, July 3rd, 1816.

Instead he ignored them and concentrated on his poetry, his Spartan diet and his daily routine, going to bed at three in the morning (two pistols and a dagger by his side) and rising the next afternoon at two. Perhaps in this image, Claire, for once, has a grain of truth in her caricatures: *Evening — candles just lighted, all dark without the windows (a cup of green tea on the table) and trees agitated much by wind beating against the panes, also thunder and lightning. He says 'God bless me, suppose there should be a God — it is as well to stand in his good graces. I'll say my prayers tonight, and write to Murray to put in a touch concerning the blowing of the last Trump.' Pistols are on the table, also daggers — bullets — Turkish scymitars ...* *

At five, after sailing on the lake, Byron dined alone, eating vegetables only, since, like Shelley he never touched meat. In the evening — green tea and conversation by the salon fire, sometimes with Mary (whom he had grown to like) quietly listening in the corner. Now and again, but very rarely, there was a guest for supper, as on this day, when Pellegrino Rossi, *shrewd, quick, manly-minded fellow*, arrived to dine. He was a good-natured man, two years older than Byron, and as well known in his own country. His fellow Italian, Polidori, liked and admired him enormously and was consequently delighted at his arrival since he himself, though freed from the previous day's arrest, was obliged to remain within the walls of Diodati that evening as a penance. It was to be a memorable one for all.

Perhaps it was the weather, the claustrophobia of being compelled to remain indoors night after night. Or perhaps it was his sudden regret of renewing a past affair, or his irritation at being observed like a bug under glass. Or perhaps again it was his frustration at having to endure the *tracasseries* of his physician or because something in the

* Claire Clairmont, *Caricatures of Albé*, November 1820.

conversation had reminded him of London and of his own exile. Or perhaps it was just his natural melancholy. But whatever the cause, and there may well have been none, Byron's mood that evening was abnormally strange and vindictive, and his choice of victims unjustifiably heartless.

After dinner, the four men left the dining-room and crossed the hall into the salon, where as usual they were to spend the rest of the evening. The conversation was pleasant and ineffectual, sometimes in Italian, and remained so till Rossi left to return to Geneva. Throughout this, Byron remained subdued and had contributed little to the dialogue, merely listening as Shelley and the older Italian discussed anarchy, the former with passion, the latter with compassion. At Rossi's departure, they were joined by Mary and Claire, and brandy and tea were served. It had stopped raining outside, but the temperature had dropped and the clouds remained.

At about midnight, Byron began to reminisce on his travels in the Middle East, recalling oft-told anecdotes, particularly about Turkey and Albania. It was a favourite topic of conversation for him, and his love of the Albanians was well known to those in the room.* They listened, therefore, with interest but without comment.

'There is no doubt that they are brave, braver perhaps than the Greeks, but they are also cruel. It is difficult for an Englishman to accept that trait in their character, I know, but it is part of them. Their attitude towards women, who are very handsome, astounded me at first. They are treated like slaves, *beaten*, and are, in short, complete beasts of burden. They plough, dig and sow ... but on reflection perhaps they are better for it. They are certainly

* So well known in fact that Byron had been nicknamed 'Albé' or 'Alba' by Mary Godwin and he was often called that by Claire and the Shelleys. Many believed that this name was derived from Albanian, but a school of thought insists that, in fact, Albé or Alba is a corruption of the initials L.B. The latter, on reflection, is perhaps more likely.

more passionate. Would you not say, Shelley, that the Englishwoman is spoilt and would do well to be beaten now and again?'

Shelley smiled but didn't reply, glancing across at Mary and then away. By the window, Claire didn't move but stared fixedly at the fire.

'Would you not advocate that treatment?' Byron continued, standing up and surveying the room. 'Let them carry wood and repair the highway like the Albanian mistress. But then it is no great hardship in such a delightful climate. Not like this. Rain. Cold. Rain ... There, Shelley, I bathed in the sea in November and returned to a room where there was not only no fire, there was no *fireplace* either. Such is the predictable heat of winter. Ah ... But the women are beautiful. Did I say that? I say it again. I will perhaps see none as handsome as they. Or as selfless. Don't you think the English mademoiselle is a selfish creature? The bitches I have known in England!'

The room was now quiet, except for the wind, a clock in the corner and the snoring of the dog (Mutz) by the fire. Byron had removed his coat and was leaning against the white marble mantel, dressed in an open-necked cream shirt tucked into olive-green trousers. A scarf was knotted around his neck. His face was paler than usual, his hair was longer and had begun in the past year to turn grey. Flecks could be seen. On his right, sitting in a highbacked chair, Polidori watched Claire's face out of the corner of his eye as his employer continued. The voice was soft but incisive.

'I had a mistress while I was in Constantinople. Did I ever tell you that?'

Silence.

'You'll find it very amusing. I had this mistress, a Turkish girl, who was no more than sixteen, but very handsome. Her skin was the colour of sandal-wood, very smooth. We were lovers within a week and would lie for hours on the open roof of the house under the sky. She and I. Then one day, I discovered that she had been unfaithful to me, that she had another lover. You can imagine my anger — I was then only your age, Shelley, and consequently very melodramatic. I devised a punishment. It was my right, I felt. I devised a punishment for her infidelity. Can you guess what it was, Claire?'

Claire didn't reply, keeping her eyes turned away.

'I sewed her up in a sack and threw her into the Bosphorus. She sank like a stone.'

The faces before him made no reaction, except Polidori who laughed self-consciously, then was silent. From that moment, the stories continued, each more vindictive than the last, and each directed at Claire. Byron talked of Thyrza, the enigmatic heroine of three poems he had written in 1811. *Sweet Thyrza waking as in sleep/Thou art but now a lovely dream.* He told his embarrassed audience how he had seduced sweet Thyrza and had had two children by her. Then, because he refused to marry her, the poor girl had committed suicide and was buried at a crossroads, which was why he could not erect a stone in her memory. *He said*, wrote Claire later, *that he fretted very much about her death, but nothing not even that, would have made him marry her because she was of mean birth.*

Immediately Shelley protested, attempting to laugh aside the stories as fanciful tales designed to shock. Byron laughed, shaking the poet's hand, and then suddenly leant over and kissed his mistress on her cheek, moving a ringlet of hair aside delicately with his hand. It was an unexpected moment, but strangely tender, and the stories were forgotten. Fresh logs were piled on the fire and Fletcher brought in tea.

The evening, however, was not quite over.

'Polly—how are you?' Byron said suddenly, as if noticing the doctor for the first time. 'Rare to see you amongst us lately. We thought you had become too grand. Too grand for us.'

Polidori smiled shyly and scratched his ear.

'Polly here has written a play,' announced Byron, his hand on the Italian's shoulder. 'Haven't you, Polly?'

The doctor, now embarrassed, nodded dumbly, flattered by the sudden attention.

'What is its title?'

'*Cajetan*,' was the reply.

'*Cajetan*?'

'Yes.'

'Polly's play is called *Cajetan*. It is a tragedy I believe.'

All eyes were now on Polidori, and bolstered by the interest he asked the fatal question. 'Would you like to hear it ... ?'

They did. The moment had, at last, arrived. Doors were opened, stairs were scampered up two at a time, and a breathless young man hurried into his bedroom, snatched up a closely-written manuscript and hurried downstairs again into the salon, holding up the papers and exclaiming, 'It isn't quite complete. Not yet. But the foundations are there.' The work was handed to Byron who volunteered to read it aloud, the chairs were brought closer around him, and the author settled himself nervously on the edge of his chair to study the faces of his audience as Act One began. An hour later, he was in tears.

In fairness to the reader, he read well, declaiming the more passionate speeches in a strong, sonorous voice— stopping only now and again to eye the listeners and comment, *Fine stuff! Excellent gravity! Shuddering weight!* But the expectant faces mirrored too easily the quality of the verse and hands were soon raised to hide a muffled laugh. At one point, sick with embarrassment, Shelley was obliged to retire to the darkness of the window, turning his shaking back on the author, handkerchief thrust into mouth.

' *'Tis thus the goiter'd idiot of the Alps*—or is that *gartered* idiot?' asked Byron innocently, and then collapsed into laughter. The tragedy was exposed.

Speechless with humiliation and anger, Polidori could only snatch the papers from the reader's hand and run from the room as Byron declared to the others once more, 'I assure you, when I was in the Drury Lane Committee, much worse things were offered to us.'

But the wound was too deep. When, half an hour later, Mary, worried about her tutor's absence, approached his room, she discovered him still weeping on the bed, the manuscript in pieces in the hearth. His sobs could be heard the length of the gallery. Without saying a word, she closed the door quietly and left, brushing past Byron who waited at the bottom of the stairs, and returned to Maison Chappuis without looking back.

The next morning, a present of a book was delivered anonymously to Polidori's room. There was no note.

* * *

The following afternoon, Polidori was invited by his employer to join him for breakfast on the balcony. The rain had stopped temporarily but the trees and garden were still wet, and the canopy had to be lowered from the wall. It was, on Byron's part, a gesture of friendship, hand extended, which the younger man grudgingly accepted.

'It was unkind of me to behave as I did last night, Polly,' Byron said quietly, glancing at the solemn face across the table. 'But I was in a bitter mood. Believe me, I loathed myself more than you did. If it wasn't for my wretched leg, I would have come up and given you my apologies there and then.'

No answer. Instead, the doctor merely nibbled at a piece of bread and stared glumly out in the direction of the lake.

'Do you forgive me, Polly?'

The reply was muttered and reluctant. 'You had no right to humiliate me like that, my lord.'

'No, I accept that. Then I am forgiven?'

'I gave it to you in good faith. I do not claim to be a writer like —'

'For God's sake, Polly, forgive me or damn me, but let there be an end to it. I have made my gesture.'

Below them they could see a figure walking through the vineyard towards them. It appeared to be a woman holding a parasol, but from that distance the identity was obscure.

'But believe me, Polly, I have read much worse. When I was at Drury Lane, you can't imagine the scenes I had to go through. The authors and the authoresses, the milliners, the wild Irishmen, the people from Brighton, from Blackwall, from Chatham, from Cheltenham, from Dublin, from Dundee, my God, from Hell even. To all of them I had to give a civil answer and a hearing *and* a reading. Much of their offerings were abysmal. *Cajetan* is *Hamlet* by their side. One wretched man, a certain Mister O'Higgins, from Richmond of all places, presented me with an Irish tragedy in which he had tried so diligently to observe the unities that he had chained his protagonist to a pillar throughout most of the play! Oh, Polly, I really am a civil and polite person and *do* hate giving pain when it can be avoided. I used to send the poor authors to Kinnaird when I hadn't the heart for it. So you see, last night was not typical of me. Drink your tea and let us forget it.'

The tea was drunk. On the lawn below them, the approaching figure had emerged from the vineyard and was seen to be Mary Godwin.

'Now there's someone who is a good friend to you,' Byron said, pointing to the garden. 'She speaks often of your patience as a tutor to her.'

Polidori blushed. 'Well ... she is a good pupil and well read, my lord.'

'Well read. Her reading list puts us to shame. Fortunately, despite that, she is not yet a bookworm — that dry-eyed reader.'

As both men glanced down at the subject of their discussion, Mary waved, seeing them.

'Now, Polly,' Byron said in a low voice, 'you who wish to be a gallant ought to jump down this small height and offer your arm.'

The doctor smiled, then agreed, though not realizing that the 'small height' was in fact almost twelve feet from balcony to ground. However, the motion was accepted and he rose from the table and walked to the corner of the terrace, climbed on to the balustrade, hesitated and jumped into the void. Unfortunately, the grass he landed on was wet from the rain and his foot slid, buckled under, and, with a cry of pain, Polidori collapsed and was sent sprawling in agony beneath the very petticoats of the lady he had planned to honour.

Immediately, Byron hurried through the hall and around the house in time to see his physician hobbling grim-faced across the lawn, struggling for a support.

'Don't move, Polidori,' said Byron gently. 'You have sprained your ankle. Take *my* arm now for you are now lamer than I. All we need is Vulcan.'

And so, leaning on his employer, Polidori was half-carried back into the salon where cold water was brought by Fletcher to ease the pain. Then, leaving him on the sofa, Byron went to his own room and brought a pillow to place under the doctor's foot, much to the owner's surprise.

'Well, I did not believe you had so much feeling,'

snapped the injured man as he was made comfortable. Slowly, Byron raised his head and looked coldly at the man on the sofa, then turned and left the salon without a word. The remark was, perhaps, undeserved.

That evening, the thunder returned to Lake Leman. All five members of the circle gathered once again in the darkened drawing-room, but this time the subject of conversation was far different from any other so far discussed. A book had been taken from the shelves and been read merely to pass the time. It was called *Fantasmagoriana, ou Recueil d'Histoires d'apparitions, de spectres, revenans etc.*, translated into French from the original German, and the moment it was read all past quarrels, squabbles, philosophies, polemics were put aside as a new theme took over their thoughts. It was a subject that had fascinated others for centuries and which now, in this ill-lit room battered by rain and storm, was to enthral the occupants for days, even weeks, and was to make one of them instantaneously and surprisingly famous. It was to cause nightmares and hallucinations and much screaming in the night, and yet was to produce one of the most original novels of the century.

The subject, of course, was Ghosts.

[7]

LAUDANUM AND VAMPYRES

It was the age for Gothic horror. Since Walpole had written his *Castle of Otranto* in 1764, countless tales of the supernatural had flooded the bookshops of England, most of them poor imitations of each other, but popular nevertheless. The formula was all much the same—ancient abbey, panelled corridors, virgin on the grass glimpsed by moonlight, screams from the tower, master's turned white. The characters in each story were identifiable with no living creature, but such details were irrelevant, since it was the plot that mattered, no matter how absurd the solution. *I heartily disapprove*, wrote the critic for the *Quarterly Review* (May 1810), *of the mode introduced by Mrs Radcliffe and followed by Mr Murphy and her other imitators, of winding up their story with a solution, by which all incidents appearing to partake of the mystic and marvellous are resolved by very simple and natural causes.*

However, the mystic and marvellous continued in earnest. Besides *The Mysteries of Udolpho*, the novels of Matthew Lewis and Charles Maturin also managed to produce the right amount of horror and sentiment combined to appease the reader. *The Monk, Women, The Milesian Chief* never failed to chill Regency blood, especially that of young ladies in the country who read them behind locked doors, hand on heart.

At Diodati, on the night of the 15th, the stories that were read around the blazing fire were no less horrific, perhaps even more so, for being by Germans, the undisputed masters of the macabre, the sentiment was pared down to the core. *There was the history of the Inconstant Lover*, recalled Mary years later, *who when he thought to clasp the bride to whom he had pledged his vows, found himself in the arms of the pale ghost of her whom he had deserted.* There was also the tragic tale of a sinner whose misdeeds had angered the gods and whose punishment was to give the kiss of death to his own sons when they reached maturity, then to return from the grave each generation and inflict the same doom on his descendants. He would appear from Hades like a giant shadow, filling the night sky, his body covered in chain-mail, and move wretchedly to the room where the sons of his family lay sleeping, kiss their foreheads and then watch in eternal sorrow as the youths *withered before his eyes like flowers snapt upon the stalk*.

As the night moved into the early hours, and the rain continued, the five occupants of the salon found themselves reluctant to leave. Tea had been abandoned for brandy, and they had all huddled closer to the hearth, chairs together. Only Polidori remained in the half-light, compelled to rest on the sofa, his sprained ankle now in bandages (cane at his side), defiantly challenging the existence of ghosts.

'There is only one Ghost, and He is Holy,' he would repeat, glancing over his shoulder, but he could not deny that he was nervous. The gloom, the night, the trees tapping against the window-panes, the panelled stairway, the wind, were all too much like the stories that were being read, and all five listeners were aware of it. Byron, of course, being a superstitious man, believed implicitly in the existence of the supernatural, recalling an experience at Newstead Abbey when he was a child that he had never forgotten.

At dawn, as shutters were opened to allow the welcome light and morning air to enter, *Fantasmagoriana* was finally cast aside, and the guests prepared to return to their beds at last, now that the night was over. As they were about to leave, Byron, obsessed by the mood that had been created, suggested that each of them should write his or her own ghost story during the next few days.

'Let us each take a different theme — whether it be werewolves or sorcery — and write a tale in prose as horrifying and blood-curdling as these. All of us shall do it.'

It was agreed, though Claire finally declined, claiming that her imagination was shallow compared to the others. But to the remainder, it was a stimulating challenge which they intended to accept immediately.

The next day, Polidori himself remained in bed, propped up on pillows and with the counterpane littered with papers, as he attempted his own tale of the macabre. Breakfast and dinner were brought to him on a tray by Fletcher and the fire was lit in the hearth. In the room below, Byron began his own story, but abandoned it constantly since he cared little for prose, finding it a restrictive and pedantic medium. However, a few hundred words were set down, inspired by the Eastern superstition of the vampire, but incorporating other themes, more personal, more Byronic, which to the perceptive reader hinted at darker obsessions in the writer's past.

In the evening, after the inevitable frugal meal, Polidori hobbled downstairs to rejoin his employer and the Shelley party in the salon, and the day's efforts were offered for inspection. Besides Claire, however, there was one other defaulter. Her half-sister, anxious to invent a tale worthy of her illustrious companions, had found her inspiration lacking. Try as she might, no single idea came to her and she had to admit an initial defeat. *I busied myself to think of a story,* Mary wrote, *a story to rival those which had excited us to this task. One that would speak to the mysterious fears of our nature and awaken thrilling horror — one to make the reader dread to look round, to curdle the blood and quicken the beating of the heart. If I did not accomplish these things my ghost story would be unworthy of its name. I thought and wondered—vainly. I felt that blank incapability of invention which is the greatest misery of authorship when dull Nothing replies to our anxious invocations.* That blank incapability of invention was to continue for two more days without release, and was to bring Mary to the edge of despair. Her lover, however, was more fortunate.

'I'm afraid,' Shelley told them, 'that I haven't the mind for fictional horror or even for fiction, since it is the reality of life that inspires me, not the unreality. Also, I must confess, I find the platitudes of prose tiresome, but I have begun at least a tale concerning an early experience in my own life. There is perhaps no ghost to frighten you, but in recalling it there is a spectre that still horrifies me. If I finish it, I will read it.'

He never did finish it and it was never read. His fellow poet, however, was sympathetic.

'Prose is an unnatural manner,' commented Byron. 'It limits the imagery and divorces the writer from his creation. But thinking today of a tale to horrify you, I remembered the superstition in parts of Greece where a man who has committed a heinous crime in life is doomed to vampirise in death, and is compelled to confine his infernal visitations solely to those beings he loved most on earth. Perhaps I was reminded of it by that tale last night of the wretch who killed his sons, but the theme is common in the East and I recall it well. In truth, I wrote of it more naturally before.'*

---

* In *The Giaour*, published in 1813:

> But first, on earth as Vampire sent,
> Thy corse shall from its tomb be rent:
> Then ghastly haunt thy native place,
> And suck the blood of all thy race;
> There from thy daughter, sister, wife,
> At midnight drain the stream of life;
> Yet loathe the banquet which perforce
> Must feed thy livid living corse: ...

Byron then outlined the idea to his listeners, telling a tale of two friends on a journey to Greece who resolved that if one of them should die, the other should pledge never to reveal the incident to anyone. In time, one of the companions did die and the survivor returned to England and discovered to his amazement that his former companion was alive and was a figurehead of society. Silenced by his oath, he watches in trepidation as the re-incarnated friend pursues and makes love to his sister.

The interpretations of the story are infinite, especially if one adopts the reasoning that one of the friends is in reality the other's *alter ego* (evil triumphant over good, incest harbouring guilt), but analysis, pertinent as it may be, has little foundation except idle fancy, since Byron, like Shelley, abandoned the project after only a few hours' work. The subject, perhaps, rather than the medium, had inhibited him.

It was now the turn of the fifth member of the cabal, and the result was a confused story, told by a nervous Polidori, reclining like a fop on the sofa, left leg resting on a silken cushion, left arm along the quilted back. A candle was placed near his elbow, isolating his face, and dark hair that had lately grown longer hung across his forehead. Over a chair to his right lay his claret dress-coat in woollen cloth, padded in the chest and with its revers notched with an M *à la mode*. Its owner now reclined downstage before his audience in a brocade waistcoat in fritillary, starched cravat and shirt, drill pantaloons and a single leather shoe on his right foot. Its companion, the left, snoozed like a puppy on the floor beneath its master. The whole image, dandy on chaise-longue (a study in claret and meadow brown), was well conceived and much appreciated both by spectator and subject. Regrettably, on assuming animation, the pose collapsed like a jigsaw.

'Before I begin, please remember I am a physician, not a scribe.'

The others smiled, mostly in sympathy, recalling the tragic debut of *Cajetan* two days earlier. They were therefore in a tolerant mood and Polidori realized it. His voice was high, the profile turned.

POLIDORI (*boldly*). The heroine of my story is a lady—

CLAIRE (*pertly*). As heroines usually are.

POLIDORI. I mean the protagonist, though I have only random ideas and it is not quite formed. But (*a clearing of the throat*) my heroine is in league with the devil. She is the devil's mistress who is unfaithful to him and returns to earth in mortal shape.

VOICE (*politely*). Why?

POLIDORI. Because she is tired of him.

SHELLEY. Ah. A Christian story.

POLIDORI. Not a Christian story, for her head is turned into a skull.

SHELLEY. Worse. A Catholic story.

MARY (*politely*). Why is her head turned into a skull?

POLIDORI. Her head is turned into a skull because of what she sees through the keyhole.

MARY (*politely*). What keyhole?

POLIDORI. The keyhole in the door.

BYRON. Of course. How foolish of us. The door to the skullery, no doubt.

MARY (*politely*). But what, Signor Polidori, does she see through the keyhole?

POLIDORI. Oh. That I am not sure of yet, but it is something very shocking. I assure you of that.

BYRON. Then it must be the bedroom door. Is it a bedroom door, Polly?

POLIDORI. I don't think so. No. Not a bedroom door. But she sees something horrifying and shocking.

BYRON. And her head is turned into a skull. Tom of Coventry himself suffered less.
(*Pause.*)
MARY (*politely*). Is that all?
POLIDORI. I'm afraid ... yes.
BYRON. *All?*
POLIDORI. All. For the moment ...
BYRON. What happens to her?
POLIDORI. Well, in the end, I thought she could be dispatched to the tomb of the Capulets.
(*Astonishment all round.*)
BYRON. Do you mean — the Veronese Capulets?
POLIDORI. Yes. Those.
BYRON. *Romeo and Juliet's* Capulets?
POLIDORI. Yes. Those ones.
MARY (*politely*). Per ché, signor?

'Well,' said Polidori, 'I'm afraid it isn't very dramatic, but my ankle distracted me. I apologise.'

It was a disappointing start to the exercise. Three stories offered, three abandoned. By midnight, they had all returned to the books. Only Mary retained her enthusiasm for the project, leaving the group early to return to her own room and the blank sheets of paper. When Shelley appeared two hours later he found her still at her desk, not having written a word.

'Have you thought of a story?' he asked and she shook her head. The resolution, however, had been made even if the invention was temporarily lacking. *Everything must have a beginning, to speak in Sanchean phrase; and that beginning must be linked to something that went before. The Hindoos give the world an elephant to support it, but they make the elephant stand upon a tortoise. Invention it must be humbly admitted, does not consist in creating out of the void, but out of chaos; the materials must in the first place, be afforded: it can give form to dark shapeless substances, but cannot bring into being the substance itself. In all matters of discovery and invention, even of those that appertain to the imagination, we are continually reminded of the story of Columbus and his egg. Invention consists in the capacity of seizing the capabilities of a subject, and in the power of moulding and fashioning ideas suggested to it.*

But on the third day since the idea had been suggested, there was no chaos to stir the mind, only frustration. Even the weather was calm during the day so that the two poets were encouraged to go sailing on the lake, and Polidori, despite his ankle, borrowed Byron's carriage and set off for Geneva to attend a ball given by the indomitable Madame Odier in honour of a noble and rather faded Polish Countess.

* * *

'I had to leave. The pain in my ankle was unbearable and I, of all people, know the possible consequences of inflicting my body to such rigours. I attempted to dance (a waltz!!) with one of the Poles of whom there were dozens, but finally had to refrain. I must admit, however, that the sympathy I received was heartwarming, especially as I had always considered the Polish race to be rather cold in their affections. Happily I was mistaken. I rested for a while on a chaise-longue and so allowed myself to study the surroundings. Madame Odier, a dear heart, had dressed the salon in scarlet and white, and was obviously highly nervous of her guests, for she lingered at the door, her face the colour of the bunting, and laughed plaintively (a tripping *hee-hi-hi-hee-hee*) at all and every remark she overheard. Her daughter was *not* present but her absence was not regretted by me, especially in such notable company. Many princesses, as well as the Countess Potocka who is the grand-niece of the late King of Poland,

and was the one who turned the head of Bonaparte himself before he abandoned her for the prettier, and more ambitious, Countess Walewska. Naturally, therefore, no one spoke about Napoleon in her presence, least of all I.

'At nine, I reluctantly returned to Diodati, my ankle an enemy. I avoided the salon since I heard the voices of L.B. and Mister Shelley, and went immediately to my room as painlessly as possible. I knew that below they were all discussing ghosts or whatever, and have no relish for it. I, Florence, am not taken in by the supernatural, unless, of course, it is Divine.

'At twelve o'clock I was about to sleep when there was a knock on the door, and my employer entered. His arrival startled me, not because of the late hour, but because he rarely ascended the stairs to my room on account of his deformity. However, he entered voluntarily and sat on a chair opposite my pillow.

' "We didn't realize you had returned," he said to me in a low voice, and added, "Fletcher tells me however that you have been back three hours or more."

'I told him that that was true and that I had left the soirée on account of my ankle. He was silent for a long time after this and I assumed he had visited me merely to get away from Miss Clairmont whom he had been avoiding of late. But then he asked me politely why I had not joined him and Mister Shelley in the salon. I could not of course give the real reason for my behaviour and consequently said that I had been tired and preferred to retire immediately.

' "Do you not like Shelley?" L.B. then asked.

' "I neither like nor dislike him, my lord," I replied. "He and I are, I believe, of a different mould."

' "But you are both friends of mine," was the answer, "and I would feel offended if there was friction between you."

' "There is none, my lord."
' "Then you will come and join us?"
' "No," I replied as politely as possible, "it is late and my ankle ... "
' "Tomorrow then."
' "As you wish, my lord."
'You see, Florence, how so often I am mystified by my employer's behaviour. Perhaps because unlike Dante or Mister Shelley, my credo is not *Onorate l'altissimo poeta*.
' "As *you* wish," L.B. replied. I was anxious to sleep. "Do you not like the discussions?"
' "I feel out of them, my lord. My contributions are obviously inferior to your own. These ghost stories — I could never write one."
' "Nor I," I was told with great emphasis. "Nor I. But you have a talent for prose and should not abandon it."
' "My story, however—"
' "Take mine. You can take my story of the Vampire. Write that."
'Write that? Write *that*, Florence? Now I knew why L.B. had visited me. He wanted me to write the story — a meagre tale without passion — that he had wrestled with and could not solve. I, of course, declined.
' "If you wish me to be the writer, my lord, then you must be the physician," I replied, echoing words he had said to me weeks before. "Here is my ankle, my lord. Here is my ankle. *Dress it*." '

* * *

The next day, propped against pillows, John Polidori began a short novel based on the macabre adventures of two Englishmen in London and Greece. Its plot was not entirely original, though no credit was granted to the initial creator, but was narrated tolerably well in an unfussy, journalistic style that left little to the reader's imagination, and even less to the writer's. The story was simple, based unashamedly on Byron's account detailed two nights before, and ended happily in tragedy as the reincarnated villain disappears with his companion's sister as bride, and the wretched brother expires without a moan at the stroke of midnight.

Aubrey's weakness increased; the effusion of blood produced symptoms of the near approach of death. He desired his sister's guardians might be called, and when the midnight hour had struck, he related composedly what the reader has perused — he died immediately.

The guardians hastened to protect Miss Aubrey; but when they arrived, it was too late. Lord Ruthven had disappeared, and Aubrey's sister had glutted the thirst of a VAMPYRE!

Without doubt, the book was destined for success. However, on that first day, the initial writing was slow, for though Polidori had the plot itself before him, the characters of the two protagonists eluded him. His knowledge of English society was minimal, and yet he knew that if the tale were to ring true its heroes must be accurately drawn, especially as he intended writing it in the guise of a document rather than a myth. Living models for his characters must therefore be sought, 'since I wanted to give the illusion of truth. I wanted the purchaser to recognize the people I create as personages he might have seen in the drawing-room or at the opera. Only then would he believe my tale, drawing in his breath as he realized that such horror could surround someone he might have seen — or even *know!* — in the safety of a salon. But I needed a model. *There* was the delay.'

The model he sought joined him for tea on the balcony and in the afternoon, the writing began in earnest.

It happened that in the midst of the dissipations attendant upon a London winter, there appeared at the various parties of the leaders of the ton, *a nobleman, more remarkable for his singularities than his rank. He gazed upon the mirth around him, as if he could not participate therein. Apparently, the light laughter of the fair only attracted his attention, that he might by a look quell it, and throw fear into those breasts where thoughtlessness reigned.*

The villain had been found.

In spite of the deadly hue of his face, which never gained a warmer tint, either from the blush of modesty or from the stronger emotion of passion, though its form and outline were beautiful, many of the female hunters after notoriety attempted to win his attentions and gain, at least, some marks of what they might term affection: Lady Mercer, who had been the mockery of every monster shewn in drawing-rooms since her marriage, threw herself in his way, and did all but put on the dress of a mountebank, to attract his notice — though in vain.*

The other protagonist, Aubrey, however, needed no model, though perhaps there is more truth (unconscious though it may be) in Polidori's personal delineation of Aubrey's character than in the more obvious idiosyncracies of Lord Ruthven. Aubrey is *'handsome, frank'* and has *'that high romantic feeling of honour and candour which daily ruins so many milliners' apprentices'*. He is also altruistic, has noble virtues, a fond and frail sister and, like Polidori, is adopted by a notorious lord to accompany him on his travels across Europe. He has also, to the writer's credit, *false notions of his talents and merits* as well as an impulsively vain, and volatile, nature. To the writer's discredit, however, when the book was eventually published in March 1819 under the title *The Vampyre*, it was published anonymously, but with the suggestion that it was written

* An allusion to William Lamb's wife, Lady Caroline Lamb, one of Byron's more notorious mistresses, who reportedly dressed as a page to attract his attention. 'That beautiful pale face is my fate' she had once said of him as well as being, in her own cliché, 'Mad, bad and dangerous to know ... '

by Byron himself. Only after the work was a success, especially in France, did Polidori claim to be the true author, but to his regret his assertion was scorned. The people wanted to believe that it was written by Lord Byron and dismissed the physician as an imposter. Polidori's name, therefore, never appeared on the title page, and his talents as an author, however small, were never recognized.*

If Polidori on his part had begun writing on that day in June with enthusiasm, Mary Godwin had not. Invention still passed her by. The rains had returned to Leman, windows had been closed and the two boats in the small harbour below the house were tied and abandoned. Confined to her room, Mary became increasingly depressed, not only by her own lack of endeavour, but also by that of Shelley, who had not written a word of poetry since leaving England. Perhaps part of the reason was that his awe of Byron (who never stopped writing) had temporarily held his hand, but this dearth of creation had only made him more introverted, and lately his nightmares had returned.

Such nightmares were not new to Shelley, cursed as he was by a restless mind that led at best to insomnia, and at worst to hallucinations. For the former he had been taking laudanum, but this very narcotic taken in large quantities had often led ironically to the latter, especially when, as now, his creative processes were low and depression had

---

* Without doubt Polidori sent the book to the publisher anonymously with the deliberate intention of palming it off as the work of Byron himself. His later attempts therefore, to claim authorship were naturally ridiculed. Byron however did deny any right to the work in a letter to Murray in May 1819: '*I have got your extract and the "Vampyre". I need not say it is not mine. There is a rule to go by: you are my publisher (till we quarrel) and what is not published by you is not written by me.*'

set in.* Under the influence of the drug, he became highly introspective, talking incessantly, his voice high-pitched and melancholy, and this in turn increased his nervousness, distorting his rational mind. On such nights he would often shake with fear at images he created before his mind, even in his waking hours. Tonight, June 18th, was such a night.

In the salon at Diodati he began first to reminisce about his past, and more especially about his wife, Harriet. Though both Byron and Polidori were present, his conversation seemed strangely secretive and bizarre, and yet, to Byron at least, there was more than a ring of truth in the disclosures.

'We had only just been married. Not long. Not long married ... Awesome dampen days in Edinburgh with the rain, and those grey buildings shouldering each other for attention everywhere. Craning. It was a wretched time, I know, and I suppose at first I was glad of Hogg's company. He accompanied us, you see, and in a way I wanted him to be with us. The three of us. Harriet and I and ... And yet I knew Harriet avoided him, refusing to be left alone with him. I am not jealous. I perfectly understand the beauty of Rousseau's sentiment. Yet Harriet is *not* an Heloisa, even if I were a St Preux — but I am not jealous. Not in that way. Not even of Hogg's intentions, for I, of all people, could never discredit a man for that. Oh, Heaven knows that if the possession of Harriet's person or the attainment of her love was all that intervened between Hogg and I ... '

Across the room Polidori looked up, realizing what was being said and gazed steadily at the speaker. Beside him, Byron didn't move but remained facing the fire, head turned away. It was now eleven in the evening.

'I had to leave them both in York,' Shelley continued,

* Certain authorities suggest that Shelley may well have been a laudanum addict.

hunched up on a stool in the half light. His face was paler than usual and partly obscured by his hair, parted in the centre, that hung now almost below his shoulders. 'There was nothing else I could do. I had to return to Sussex or we would have starved, even though Harriet begged me not to leave her with Hogg, even though I knew Hogg's will. He had told me so, *asked me* to allow him to share her love. But I say again, jealousy has no place in my bosom. But Harriet was prejudiced. She was ... prejudiced, and on her opinions of right and wrong alone did the morality of the case depend. I myself would have given Hogg to her, *given*—for would I be so sottish a slave to opinion as to endeavour to monopolize what, if participated in, would give my friend pleasure without diminishing my own? Would I?'

The question was repeated again and Shelley turned quietly around staring up at his listeners, glancing from one to the other, his eyes bluer and more translucent than ever. Neither man replied. There was then silence, and with a moan the speaker looked away, standing up and walking into the darkness of the room to sit alone beneath a portrait on a far wall. Nothing more was said till 11.30, when Mary and her half-sister arrived, wrapped in cloaks against the rain, and Fletcher brought in tea.

By midnight, the subject of ghosts was raised once more, but took a more original turn than before. The shutters of the salon remained ajar so that the three large windows facing the lake were open to the night and the storm and to the thunder that grumbled in the mountains across the water.

> How the lit lake shines, a phosphoric sea,
> And the big rain comes dancing to the earth!
> And now again 'tis black...

Lightning illuminated the room and caused Byron to

recall an incident of a tree being brought to life, vivified by a thunderbolt rather than destroyed.

'It reanimated it,' he added. 'When, before, it was dead, the lightning had given it life. In that bolt there was the power to re-create, even if only a tree.'

'I have also heard, my lord,' interrupted Polidori, 'of the heart muscle being shocked into life, but I have no proof, nor in my experience have I encountered it.'

'But it could happen?' asked Byron.

'Perhaps ... '

'But you said you have heard of it, Polly. Could not a heart be made to beat faster? A heart that was sluggish?'

'If we could find a way to administer the power, yes. Perhaps it could.'

'There,' exclaimed Byron with delight.

'I have also read of the experiments of Doctor Darwin,' continued Polidori, now aware of the attention, 'who preserved a piece of vermicelli in a glass case till by some extraordinary means it began to move with a voluntary motion.'

'Maggots,' remarked Claire with a laugh. 'Just maggots.'

'Not at all,' replied Byron, 'for you under-estimate Darwin if you think he was misled by maggots. Let us hope he is not misled by women either.'

Silence. In the corner of the room, Shelley remained alone, saying nothing and staring out at the night sky. Only Byron stood, leaning against the mantel, with Mary in the chair at his right, seemingly preoccupied. Then suddenly, as if after a long meditation he said quietly, but without frivolity, 'If a tree, why not a corpse?'

'A corpse?' asked Polidori.

'A corpse. Why could not a man bring a corpse to life if he had the power?'

Perhaps a corpse could be reanimated. Galvanism has given

token of such things; perhaps the component parts of a creature might be manufactured, brought together and endued with vital warmth.

The subject suddenly excited the people in the room and once more it seemed they would spend the night sleepless and away from their beds, huddled in the salon before the embers of the fire. But an incident took place, so unexpected to all, that the dialogue was abruptly interrupted before it had barely begun.

For a brief moment the conversation turned to witchcraft and satanism, and Byron, ever the protagonist in such talk, recalled some lines of Coleridge he had read two years before. They were from *Christabel* and described a Hecate as she disrobed till she was naked to the waist. Remembering them with a smile, he recited them to the four listeners before him:

> 'Then drawing in her breath aloud,
> Like one that shuddered, she unbound
> The cincture from beneath her breast:
> Her silken robe, and inner vest
> Dropt to her feet, and full in view,
> Behold! her bosom and half her side—
> Are lean and old and foul of hue — '

Suddenly, Byron was interrupted by a horrendous scream, and from the corner of the room Shelley leapt up, his face as white as death, his eyes transfixed by Mary who had moved towards him, and then with another cry, he ran out of the room clutching a candle in his hand. The action was so startling and so sudden that Shelley was out of the house before the others realized what had happened, and even then did not connect his behaviour with the lines that had been spoken. It seemed as if he had seen an apparition or a spectre, though his gaze had been directed solely upon Mary. Whatever the cause, Byron and Polidori hurried after him as best they could, emerging into the garden to discover that Shelley had disappeared. At first they searched the vineyard, wet with rain, calling out Shelley's name but found no one; then they moved farther down, their clothes soaked, to the beach and the harbour, and finally found the poet in his own house, hunched up against the empty fire, shivering with fear.

Without hesitation, Byron ordered Polidori to fetch some ether, and then put his coat around the trembling figure at the hearth in a vain attempt to comfort him. When the doctor returned, the ether was given and finally Shelley relaxed, though his eyes still stared into space as if the image might reappear.

At first, Byron attempted to comfort the man, asking him repeatedly the cause of the incident, but Shelley seemed reluctant, or too terrified, to reply. It was not till the ether had begun to take effect, and the trembling ceased, that the reason — bizarre as it was — was related.

'While you were reciting that verse,' Shelley said finally, his voice almost a whisper, 'I was staring at Mary. She had approached me and I was staring at her and suddenly I saw her breasts and they were naked. They were naked, but instead of nipples, her breasts had eyes ...'

The story of Shelley's agitation is true, wrote Byron some time later, *but I can't tell what seized him.* Polidori could. Leaving Byron at Maison Chappuis, he hurried back through the rain to Diodati, his ankle forgotten, in time to meet Mary as she waited anxiously in the hallway. Calming her fears he told her Shelley was safe and well and had been looked after.

'Oh, Polidori,' said Mary gratefully, touching his arm, 'I am so glad. It is a blessed relief that you are here.'

Then with a smile, she moved quickly toward the door to the garden.

'Miss Godwin?'

It was Polidori. Warmed by her remark, he had turned and followed her, one hand now resting on the door, barring her way.

'Miss Godwin, I am a doctor and have seen the symptoms before. I am not fooled like the others.'

Mary looked at him, disturbed by his voice. 'What do you mean?'

'I mean, Miss Godwin, that I believe Mister Shelley is addicted to a drug and that the drug is laudanum, a tincture of opium. I also believe that this was not an isolated incident.'

'But you can't be sure?'

'No ... not without a thorough examination, but—'

'*But*, Signor Polidori, you have not had a thorough examination. I know Mister Shelley better than you, but I thank you anyway. I'm sure your advice is well intentioned. Now I must return to him.'

The door however remained barred. 'He talked of his wife tonight, Miss Godwin, before you arrived, and gave the impression that he would not object if—'

'Signor Polidori, I wish to leave. Please open the door.'

Behind them, Claire had appeared from Byron's bedroom, glass in hand, and was watching silently.

'Miss Godwin ... '

Polidori's voice was lowered as he looked at her, then slowly he put his hand on hers. For a moment, Mary was startled by the unexpected intimacy of a man whom she had considered only as a tutor and physician and nothing more. She withdrew her hand.

'Signor Polidori, please be not offended. I like you and respect you and have come to think of you sometimes as a brother. But that is all. Now, please let me pass.'

Gently, but determinedly, she moved past him and opened the door.

'Good night, Signor Polidori.'

And she was gone. '*Mrs S. called me her brother.* She called me her brother, Florence, and that is all. I will avoid her in future. It is not I, not *I*, who seeks love with his sister!'

* * *

It had been the worst of nights for Mary but it was not over yet. It was not till the early hours of the morning that she finally retired to her room, but the events and discussions of the evening had disturbed her and she could not relax. *When I placed my head upon the pillow I did not sleep, nor could I be said to think. My imagination, unbidden, possessed and guided me, gifting the successive images that arose in my mind with a vividness far beyond the usual bounds of reverie.* The earlier talk of reanimation and the rekindling of dead matter spun in her mind until, without realizing it, she herself experienced in her sleep a grotesque nightmare that was so vivid that she felt it was happening within her very room. She saw a manufactured corpse stretched on the floor, a thin figure kneeling beside it, and then she witnessed the corpse stirring, moving, coming to life. *He sleeps; but he is awakened; he opens his eyes: behold the horrid thing stands at his bedside, opening his curtains and looking on him with yellow, watery but speculative eyes.*

Starting up in terror, she was no more comforted when she saw the familiar room, the closed shutters, the dark parquet flooring, the patterned walls, for the vision haunted her still. In vain throughout the night Mary attempted to banish the images from her mind, but they returned constantly, until by dawn she realized at last that there was only one thing she could do. *I have found it! What terrified me will terrify others; and I need only describe the spectre which had haunted my midnight pillow.*

In the morning, therefore, she joyously announced that

she had finally thought of a story, and sat down that very day to set it down in writing.

It was on a dreary night of November that I beheld the accomplishment of my toils. With an anxiety that almost mounted to agony, I collected the instruments of life around me, that I might infuse a spark of being into the lifeless thing that lay at my feet. It was already one in the morning; the rain pattered dismally against the panes, and my candle was nearly burnt out, when, by the glimmer of the half-extinguished light I saw the dull yellow eyes of the creature open; it breathed hard, and a convulsive motion agitated its limbs.

The story, conceived so horrendously by this polite, shy, eighteen-year-old girl, was none other than *Frankenstein*.

[8]

ABELARDS

On June 20th, with the same suddenness that marked their arrival, the storms of Leman departed and left the lake still and blue, blue even without the reflection from the sky, and clear enough so that in parts one could see the shoals of tiny fish, natives of these waters, hovering in their legions more than four, five or six feet below the surface. The air became warm and fragrant, and by midday dozens of small boats had been taken from the harbours, and women returned to the vineyards on the slopes above Vaud. At the Villa Diodati the reappearance of summer was welcomed by all, as windows were opened wide, linen was aired on the lawn, and the residents, rescued at last from the long confinement in the salon, took a chair into the garden to read or write under an apple or a chestnut tree. Tea was picnicked on the grass (Mary appearing through the orchard with William) amidst the smell of cut grass and honeysuckle, and boys were hired to polish the carriages. Shelley's spirits were renewed, Mary's industry was exhaustive, now that she had at last begun her novel, and Byron's melancholy was temporarily eased. Only Polidori regretted the sun, for he was obliged to remain indoors once more, his ankle worse.

The next day, the warm weather continued and seemed destined to last, despite the clouds that still lingered in the north above Jura. Accordingly, Byron, restless and anxious to be away from Claire for a few days at least, realized that the time was now ideal to fulfil his earlier ambition to tour the lake in the wake of Rousseau's heroine. It was an excursion he had planned for some weeks, stimulated by re-reading, as he sailed alone in the water below Cologny, the small books of letters that comprised *Julie, Ou La Nouvelle Héloïse*, written and set in the woods and fields around the very lake beneath him. 'Go to Vevai,' urged Rousseau himself in the *Confessions*, 'visit the land around it, examine the sites, take a tour of the lake, and say if Nature has not created this beautiful country just for a Julie, or for a Claire or for a St Preux.'

It was an invitation Byron was eager not only to accept, but to accept immediately. He had almost completed the third canto of *Childe Harold*, and could conceive no more appropriate place to conclude the lyrical journey, begun at Dover three months before, than in the groves and meadows of Meillerie and Clarens, in the footsteps of Mademoiselle Julie. Moreover, he had long decided to take only Shelley with him (as opposed to Polidori) and realized that now that the doctor was temporarily disabled Byron could be spared the ignominy of explaining why he was not being included on the tour. Polidori, nonetheless, was not appeased.

'It is not my ankle that keeps me here, though to my employer it has suddenly assumed the magnitude of Achilles' heel, with Rousseau as Hector — or should it be Apollo? — running through the woods, arrow poised to shoot. It is a pastoral frieze they have invented for themselves in which I myself am not present; a frieze of olive trees and Arcadian temples, with L.B. as Pan, no doubt, and Mister S., sylvan splendor'd, stark mad at a stream surrounded by a dozen naked Naiads, water-lilies in their hair (Mister S. included) and eyes in their bosoms! I assume, Florence, I am to be dungeoned at Diodati so that I may not upset the barge as Julie herself floats past, Godiva'd in her *bosquet*, with swans at the prow. For God's sake, if L.B. insists on being Jean-Jacques, and Shelley St Preux, why not I as Wolmar? I am not loath to being the demon. It is a role I have often played before, have I not?'

The reaction was inevitable, but Byron was determined. His only companion on the tour would be Shelley, who surprisingly, unlike Polidori, had not read Rousseau's novel, though he knew of it well. An English translation was given to him and the two poets planned to leave the following afternoon, sailing in an English boat Byron had recently had delivered from Bordeaux, and accompanied only by two boatmen and a servant. They envisaged the journey lasting a week, if the fine weather held, and so took the necessary clothes and money as well as a writing-case.

When they finally set sail from the harbour at 2.30 on the 22nd, the lake was calm and the air warm and sunny. It seemed a good omen, and both poets suddenly looked forward to being alone for a few days in romantic communion with *that apostle of affliction,* whose *love was passion's essence.* Their guide was a book and the memory of its author, and that was all that mattered. To the others who were obliged to remain behind, only one did not resent the departure, for she was preoccupied by her own fantasies, far removed from idyllic romance.

June 22. L.B. and Shelley went to Vevey was all Polidori would say, or was ever to say on the matter in his Diary, while Claire said even less. It was not surprising, therefore, that as the open sail-boat moved out of the harbour of Montalegre, there was only Mary, standing on the shore, to wave farewell.

* * *

The story perhaps is a familiar one, except that the new Héloïse has become the emancipated, free-thinking elder sister of the old, freed in part from medieval superstition and bigotry, but nonetheless still a victim of prejudice, Age of Reason or no. The true tragedy, in fact, remains the same, though the details may be more sophisticated and Rousseau's heroine more obsessive in her ideals. The success of the book, however, was unquestionable, especially with women, who saw in Julie a woman they could identify with at last, who used not her body, but her mind, in her combat for self-expression. *Stories were told of fine ladies, dressed for the ball, who took the book up for half-an-hour until the time should come for starting; who read until midnight, and when informed that the carriage waited answered not a word, and when reminded by-and-by that it was two o'clock still read on, and then at four, having ordered the horses to be taken out of the carriage, went to bed, and passed the night in reading.** But the plot, apart from the philosophy, was hypnotic enough in itself to induce insomnia.

Narrated through a series of letters, it tells the story of the young tutor, St Preux, and his love for his fair-haired pupil, Julie. The affair is consummated in secret, and then discovered by the girl's father, and the tutor, in remorse, is compelled to flee the country. Tragedy follows tragedy as the unhappy girl's mother dies, the father sinks into penury and Julie marries a man (Wolmar) much older than herself, who returns her loyalty by imposing his own intellectual bigotry on her. Inevitably, the exiled lover hears of the marriage, contemplates suicide, but forgoes the action in preference for (bizarre choice) a place on board Admiral Anson's celebrated ship as it sets out to encircle the globe.

Years pass and St Preux is still at sea — at this point, one reader at least, no doubt less Romantic than Byron, laughed and then hurled the book out of the window†—

* Morley, *Rousseau and the New Heloisa* (1873).
† Voltaire.

but finally returning to Europe, he is invited, to his surprise, by Wolmar to pay him and his wife a visit. Confident of his relationship with Julie, Wolmar leaves her and her former lover together, and even plans to hire St Preux as a tutor to his children, born of an unloving but obviously not uncharitable wife. St Preux is naturally over-joyed, but his delight is premature. Julie has taken to God, unlike her husband, and unlike also, it appears, her ex-lover. *I fear*, she writes to him, *that you do not gain all you might from religion in the conduct of your life, and that philosophic pride disdains the simplicity of the christian. You believe prayers to be of scanty service. That is not, you know, the doctrine of Saint Paul, nor what our church professes. We are free, it is true, but we are ignorant, feeble, prone to ill. And whence should light and force come, if not from him who is their very well-spring? Let us be humble, to be sage; let us see weakness, and we shall be strong.*

St Paul's doctrine, however, was not St Preux's, no matter how much he was chastised. Julie had obviously cast aside personal love in favour of the sanctity of marriage, finding mystical solitude and peace only in her own Elysium she had created out of Nature. Moreover, her love now was for all mankind. Philanthropy had replaced passion, and the wretched St Preux—who at one point is even encouraged by Julie to marry her cousin—can only remember the past and the love that was, since the woman he now knows has become a priggish and rather tragic stranger. 'The book has everything,' wrote one contemporary critic, 'except common sense.' Perhaps he was right, but like St Preux, the readers of the novel revered Julie as the eternal female creation of the age, even though she herself was the very person who sought to destroy that illusion. Byron, himself, was one of the enchanted, together with his new-found disciple. *I read Julie all day*, wrote Shelley, *an overflowing, as it now seems, surrounded by the scenes which it has so wonderfully peopled, of sublimest genius and more than human sensibility.*

If Byron, however, was momentarily bewitched by the echoes of the Swiss Romantic's creation about him, he was not, like Narcissus, so immersed as to confuse his own image with that of Rousseau's. 'I can't see the point of resemblance: he wrote prose, I verse: he was of the people, I of the Aristocracy: he was a philosopher, I am none: he published his first work at forty, I mine at eighteen: he married his housekeeper, I could not keep house with my wife: he thought all the world in a plot against *him*, my little world seems to think *me* in a plot against it, if I may judge by their abuse in print and coterie ... I don't say this out of pique, for Rousseau was a great man, and the thing if true were flattering enough; but I have no idea of being pleased with a chimera.'*
Nevertheless, it was Rousseau, not the chimera, that guided his boat on that first afternoon of the tour as they set sail and headed east along the shore of the lake towards Evian.

Leaving Cologny and sailing due north-east along the southern side of the lake, the land appears wild and uninhabitable, composed in the main of deep woods that descend the slopes almost to the beach. At some points trees are actually waist high in the water, and no houses can be seen, not even a rich man's villa, for carriage roads have passed this area by, preferring to cut across inland in a direct route for Thonon and the main route to the Rhône. The shore here (shingle, rocks) merges into the lake in the form of a promontory, perhaps ten miles from point to point, forming the only major irregularity in the outline of the lake, so that from the air the expanse of

* Byron, *Detached Thoughts*, October 15th, 1821.

water takes on the form of a feather, with quill tip set in Geneva. There is no town, not even a village for twelve miles east of Diodati, so that boatmen have to row for three hours before landing for the first time at the fishing town of Hermance. Here, Byron and Shelley disembarked to stretch their legs and to tour the only interesting feature of the spot—a ruined tower built, so legend had it, by Julius Caesar himself.

The travellers were impressed but impatient to move, since their goal was the area at the east of the Leman, twenty-five miles away and two days' sailing. However, the journey was pleasant, the weather was fine and they could both relax at the stern of the boat, with Shelley (straw hat, cotton shirt) sitting at the tiller, and his companion, legs across a bench, his back to the sun, reading out loud from the book in his hand.

By sunset, they had reached Nernier, a lakeside hamlet in russet and white built on the toe of the promontory, and inhabited, as Shelley observed, by deformed children. He saw them as he was walking along the shore, enthralled by the beauty of the mists, purple and grey, that clung to the rocks and to the craggy islands scattered along the dark mass of the water. The children were playing a game of nine-pins and it was only as the two poets approached closer that they noticed that all the players *appeared in an extraordinary way deformed and diseased. Most of them were crooked and with enlarged throats.** The reason for their appearance was not discovered, but Byron, moved by the gentleness of the creatures, as if he were Gulliver in a mythical land, attempted to talk to the boys and even gave them some money. The coin was accepted in silence but with a grateful smile, and the child returned to the game. *All this might scarcely be; but the imagination surely could not forbear to breathe into the most inanimate forms some likeness*

* Shelley, letter to Thomas Love Peacock, July 12th, 1816.

of its own visions, on such a serene and glowing evening, in this remote and romantic village, beside the calm lake that bore us hither.*

The first night was spent in a gloomy inn set on the shore, fading white in the darkness, and inhabited by lizards.

'It's five years since I slept in a bed like this, in a room such as this,' remarked Byron more with nostalgia than enthusiasm. 'It reminds me of Greece.'

Shelley was unimpressed and retired to his own room to read, and then fell asleep *with no unpleasant sensations, thinking of our journey tomorrow and of the pleasure of recounting the little adventures of it when we return.*

* * *

'They are gone. I am alone in Diodati like a mutineer who has taken over the ship and found himself abandoned not only by the crew but also by the elements; abandoned like the Mariner. The first evening is unnaturally quiet and no fire burns now in the salon. I wander the rooms and gardens and realize, despite myself, that I miss L.B.'s presence, if only to talk to someone. In despair, I visited Geneva, but even Rossi avoided me, Madame Odier was absent and I was left to share tea with the women at Chappuis. I am lonely and want to sleep, but my ankle pains and keeps me awake, and insects appear at the window. Tomorrow I must find some solace, even if it is only in the Rue Basse. Solitude, Florence, is an awesome spectre when night descends and the candle dies.'

* * *

The next day, the landscape suddenly changed as if aware

* Shelley, letter to Thomas Love Peacock, July 12th, 1816.

that it was heralding the entrance to Rousseau's territory. Passing Yvoire, the voyagers could see groves of walnut and chestnut trees lapping the water on the starboard side, and beyond them dense expanses of pine forests scattered along the slopes of the mountains of Savoy, where the summits were so high that they were bright with snow despite the heat and the azure of the sky. Birds were seen in their thousands, nesting along the rocks or hovering over the boat like sea-gulls, though they were smaller in size and were marked in purple along the length of their backs from neck to tail.* The weather, however, was restless, and to the dismay of the travellers, rain began to fall by the afternoon, and as they approached Evian on the Savoy coast, thunder was heard and they seemed to be pursued by a black cloud that hung over the boat, cutting out the light. For a while, their spirits dropped and were barely eased by their arrival at the Savoy town, for both men had failed to realize that they were now on foreign soil. *I am on shore for the night,* wrote Byron that evening to Hobhouse, *and have just had a row with the Syndic of this town, who wanted my passports, which I left at Diodati, not thinking they could be wanted, except in grand route.* However, Shelley's presence of mind saved the day.

'Do you not realize who my companion is?' he asked the Syndic as defiantly as possible. 'This is George Gordon, the sixth Lord Byron.' And then adding as if it were his trump card, 'He is an Englishman. Like myself.'

Authority immediately bowed to rank, apologies were extended all round, especially to the sixth Lord Byron, who was by now shouting very loudly in English, and threatening to speak to his Cagliari Majesty himself whom he had once met at the opera. His temper however was eased as both he and Shelley were offered the best inn in the town, and the choice of the finest Savoy cuisine. It was

* They are in fact besolets, an inedible bird of passage native to the lake.

a small victory but Byron was delighted. Moreover, he knew that the next day would find them both back in Switzerland and in Meillerie at last.

At first, the wind was regretted. It seemed all too clear that the few days of sun did not prophesy a fine summer, for clouds were in the sky the next morning and the surface of the lake was troubled, so that coats had to be put on and water bailed. However, any depression was immediately erased as soon as the two poets set foot on the shore of Meillerie. Here finally was Rousseau's Arcadia, and here finally were the very stones and lanes where Julie walked and where her lover inscribed her name upon a rock before the tragedies had begun. The two men were not disappointed. Even without the creation of the book, the creation of Meillerie would have inspired even the most insensitive passer-by. *He (Rousseau) has added to the interest of his work by their adoption; he has shown his sense of their beauty by the selection; but they have done that for him which no human being could do for them.*

It was magical ground, where the two men could dine on honey, and wander through the groves of pine and chestnut, and through forests heavy with the scent of thyme and filled with flowers. 'In the midst,' writes St Preux, 'of these noble and superb objects, the little spot where we were, displayed all the charms of an agreeable and rural retreat; small floods of water filtered through the rocks and flowed along the verdure in crystal streams. Some wild fruit-trees leaned their heads over ours; the cool and moist earth was covered with grass and flowers. Comparing this agreeable retreat with the objects which surrounded us, designed as an asylum for two lovers, who alone have escaped the general wreck of nature ... '

It was also inspired ground, for not only did Byron

continue the stanzas of his poem, but Shelley, for so long silent, began at last to conceive a poem that was later to be his 'Hymn To Intellectual Beauty'. However, though both men were happily aware of the influence of *La Nouvelle Héloïse* as they walked the ground of Meillerie, an incident was to occur that day that only in retrospect could be seen to relate to the fictional events they knew so well. It was an incident neither man would have wished to happen and that was almost to cost one of the poets his life.

The lake, at first, seemed calm, and though the small boat was overloaded, there seemed no chance of danger since no storms were forecast and the boatmen sailed close to the bank, sheltered by trees. However, as had often been demonstrated, the weather in the area was unpredictable, and such a lake, vast as it was and set within high mountains, took on the properties of a sea, prone to changes in current and sudden squalls that appeared without warning and with great force, often leading to a capsized boat and reports of drowning. The perils were well known, and visitors, forewarned of the dangers, entrusted themselves only to the most skilled of boatmen who were used to emergencies, though such a crew was naturally very expensive and in great demand. Whether Byron was deceived by the talents of his own sailors, or whether he had deliberately hired men who were less experienced in order to save money, is an open question, but when the incident happened, it was the boatmen who panicked and not the passengers.

They had been sailing for only half an hour when the wind arrived, coming from the farther corner of the Leman and increasing in violence all the way, so that when it reached the boat the waves began to resemble an Atlantic tide and the surface of the water was white with foam. Immediately, the boat was spun round and with such strength that the rudder was smashed and all control vanished as the craft began to keel over. The initial reaction for any sailor in such a situation is to lower the sails without delay in order to cut down the force of the wind and decrease the speed of the boat. However, one of the boatmen, *a dreadfully stupid fellow, persisted in holding the sail at a time when the boat was on the point of being driven under water by the hurricane.* The boat was now filling fast, and the crew realized their error too late, for it seemed inevitable that they would all be capsized and have to swim for the shore, one hundred yards away. Unfortunately, Shelley had never learnt to swim, though strangely this handicap seemed not to trouble him at all. For almost as if he wanted to drown, he remained calm, folding his arms and waiting patiently as the boat began to sink beneath the waves.

Byron had now stripped off his coat, and realizing the danger, called out to Shelley not to struggle and that he would save him. His companion, however, already soaked to the skin and half in water, called back to him, his voice steady and unconcerned that *he had no notion of being saved, and that I would have enough to do to save myself, and begged not to trouble me.* The sentiment was noble and yet oddly sinister as the boat began to approach the rocks and Shelley, arms folded, his face composed, awaited the inevitable.

The inevitable, however, did not arrive for miraculously the boat righted itself, the wind subsided and with effort the craft was brought into the near-by harbour.* It had

---

* As a footnote to the incident, Byron recalled later its similarity to an occasion in *La Nouvelle Héloïse*: I had the fortune (good or evil as it might be) to sail from Meillerie to St Gingo during a storm which added to the magnificence of all around, although occasionally accompanied by danger to the boat, which was small and overloaded. It was over this very part of the lake that Rousseau has driven the boat of St Preux and Madame Wolmar to Meillerie for shelter during a tempest.

The relevant passage is thus: *The waves soon began to grow dreadful; we endeavoured to make for the coast of Savoy and tried to land at the village of*

been a narrow escape and yet to the younger poet, so near to the death that was to come to him six years later, almost to the week, his feelings on stepping on to dry land were not of relief, but of despair. *I knew that my companion would have attempted to save me and I was overcome with humiliation, when I thought that his life might have been risked to preserve mine.* Byron himself, however, reported later that he never once feared for his own life but only for Shelley's, whose coolness and courage before danger filled him with admiration. Unquestionably, the two poets now felt closer than ever in spirit as they stepped on to the jetty of St Gingolph to be praised and congratulated by the villagers who had watched everything and had feared the worst.

That evening, as if nothing had happened, Byron went to his room to write, and Percy Shelley, after a casual promenade around the town, retired with an extra candle, to remain awake half the night, preoccupied by a book.

* * *

It appears fragile and elusive, neither part of the lake nor

Meillerie, which was over-against us, and the only place almost where the shore affords a convenient landing. But the wind changing, and blowing stronger, rendered the endeavours of the watermen ineffectual and discovered to us a range of steep rocks somewhat lower, where there was no shelter.

We all tugged at our oars; and at that instant, I had the mortification to perceive Julie grow sick and see her weak and fainting at the bottom of the boat. Happily she had been used to the water and her sickness was not of long duration. In the meantime, our efforts increased with our danger; the heat of the sun, the fatigue and profuse sweating, took away our breaths, and made us excessively faint. Then summoning all her courage, Julie revived our spirits by her compassionate kindness; she wiped the sweat from off our faces; and mixing some wine and water, for fear of intoxication, she presented it alternatively to those who were most exhausted.

(*La Nouvelle Héloïse*, Letter CXXXVI 'To Lord B———'.)

of the land, its origins clouded in mystery as if it had appeared overnight to illustrate an obscure fairy tale long since forgotten. Certainly kings have lived at Chillon in the twelfth century, and others have died there in the eleventh, but before then there is only speculation, mixed with legend and a little truth, to justify that the castle had any factual beginning at all.

In the Middle Ages it was the home of Peter of Savoy; that same Peter of Savoy who, as Earl of Richmond, would be seen on all fours in the English country houses playing a guessing game called 'What's this I'm carrying on my back?' with the ladies of the queen. When vertical, Peter was reported to have re-designed the building into its present amalgam of sepia tiles and covered walks, with frilled turrets placed around the mass like ruffles on a leg of lamb. Set firmly on a rock of granite, moored to the land by a roofed wooden bridge, it is constructed in the shape of an eye, fringed on the surface with sumptuous chambers and halls that are linked to each other by shaded courtyards where stone fountains stand on cobbles beneath cherry trees and carved balconies. During its active life, when the sun was high, birds nested in the trees within the walls, spangled banners hung from windows, and chatelaines invited musicians from Vevey to entertain their guests beneath the panelled ceiling of the Grand Hall. At such times, the castle seemed to sustain its illusion of romance; a stage-set designed by a dreaming child to be peopled with princesses and dukes in silks from Savoy, where the sounds were not of war (though battles were fought) but of idle gaiety. Guests and their wives journeyed from distant châteaux to lodge in painted rooms above the waters of the Leman and to dine in halls striped pink-and-white or blue-and-beige. The colours are still there— bright, paint-box hues that sparkle still as one wanders through the now-empty salons, the lake always on one's left, silent and clear in the summer months, the place where Julie and her child were to lose their lives. Little wonder that poets and visionaries have flocked to such a place, and yet, tragically, the image is deceptive. Without doubt, many courtiers did live in the sunlit rooms above the waters, but many more died in darkness in the granite dungeons below. For Chillon was built as a prison, and eight hundred years later, it was a prison still. *I never saw*, wrote Shelley, *a monument more terrible of that cold and inhuman tyranny, which it has been the delight of man to exercise over man.* His horror was justifiable, though only Byron was inspired to put it into verse.

The two poets arrived at the castle on the fourth day of their tour, and were accompanied from the jetty across the wooden bridge by a gendarme, who was to act as a guide. They were taken, like Rousseau before them, through the courtyards under stone arches and past ancient stables to the Grand Hall of the High Bailiff (wooden pillars, fluted ceilings, stone seats by the window), and then through innumerable ante-chambers and bedrooms, some no larger than a dray, where balconies hung over the lake, clinging to the steep walls like limpets. Then up through the Knights' Hall, decorated with escutcheons, or along patrol galleries, narrow enough perhaps for only one man in full armour, into more bed-chambers, each more decorative than the last, stopping only to examine a pulpit in the chapel (*Romainmôtier ambo*) or a carving in the court. Byron himself was enchanted, plaguing the guide with innumerable questions, despite the grudging reluctance of his companion. Finally, Shelley abandoned the journey altogether, exhausted and unimpressed, and retired to a courtyard to sit alone beneath a tree, his pale grey coat folded beside him. He could be seen by the others as they walked above him, glimpsed from shuttered windows or from the highest parapet, seemingly suspended from above, as the castle was spread out beneath them — a jumble of tiles and turrets and watchtowers set beneath obelisks like baroque bird-houses.

At noon, Byron returned to the small square where Shelley waited, half asleep, and told him they were now to see the dungeons. Grudgingly, Shelley agreed and the two men followed the gendarme down darkened steps into the very rock itself. Slowly, they were led by torchlight through stone corridors carved roughly out of the granite and illuminated only by narrow windows on the western wall, set a few feet above the water. They emerged to find themselves in the arsenal, and then on through heavy doors into a narrow cell where a beam was embedded in the rock, acting as a gibbet, where prisoners were hanged by night. The cell led into a large room, its roof supported by seven pillars with fluted capitals so that it resembled a cloister but was in fact known as Bonivard's prison.*
Here there was a story to tell, and Byron listened enthralled.

Relying more on fancy than fact, the gendarme told his audience how François Bonivard, a Genevese prior and patriot, had been captured by the Duke of Savoy in 1530 and imprisoned in the very dungeon where they now stood, chained to the fifth pillar with his two brothers, who dutifully died and were buried as the lake flooded the floor and rats appeared. Such a history, told in the damp prison itself smelling of keys, was moving indeed, especially as the fifth pillar was touched, the steel rings were studied and legend was embellished. Already Byron was eager to set the melodrama down on paper, undismayed by

---

* *They had cut cellars and kitchens into the rock below the level of the water, which when required could be let in by means of taps. It was here that they imprisoned for six years François Bonivard, the prior of St Victor's, that man of rare worth and unshakeable rectitude and firmness, who though a Savoyard and a priest loved liberty and toleration.* (Rousseau).

Shelley's apathy and possible scepticism,* and so remained behind to learn more (and also to carve his name on another pillar), while his companion, anxious to quit the oppressive atmosphere, hurried out into the sunlight once more to wait on the jetty, hat on head, and to continue reading the final part of the romance that had inspired the visit.

When the poets finally set sail again, on a turbulent tide, it was to Clarens, *sweet Clarens birthplace of deep Love*, where they walked as if on holy ground. Here was the Elysium that Julie had created for herself, a natural Utopia on the edge of the lake beneath her house. Here, more than at any other spot, was where Julie had wandered alone, her hair hanging loose, to be at peace with her God or Nature, and where she and her lover first kissed in the long grass of the orchard many summers before.

When St Preux was exiled, it became an enclosed Eden, a sanctuary to Julie's thoughts, tended only by her as if out of Nature she could create the love that had been taken away. Flowers were planted in their thousands, intermingled with fragrant herbs such as wild thyme and balm and sweet marjoram. The branches of trees were bent so that they hung to the ground as if weeping, and in their turn created small bowers and arches entwined with roses and honeysuckle; these same trees were themselves then interspersed with small plantations of lilac and syringa or broom, so that the flowers took on the aspect of exotic

---

* And justifiable scepticism at that, since the true facts of Bonivard's life were a little less romantic. Known to be a rather inconstant believer, especially when his neck was at stake, and to prefer to praise the breasts of his mistresses rather than the hearts of the loyalists, he was imprisoned for six years in a cell that was never below water and where any severe hardships were announced solely by him in his own memoir written on release. He died rich, fat and happy in his own bed, thirty-five years after leaving Chillon.

weeds and no grass could be seen. The only paths were neither straight nor uniform, but wound naturally through thickets and groves, often turning back on themselves in a pirouette to run under branches where garlands were scattered overhead and where the paths were formed only of the softest moss so that Julie could walk barefooted, as she did at night when the children were asleep and the moon was high. *Here, who hath loved not,* wrote Byron, *here would learn that love and make his heart a spirit.* And yet when the two men arrived at the Elysium, they discovered to their grief that most of it had been razed to the ground by a handful of monks and had been fashioned into a rather polite vineyard.

This *bosquet de Julie* had first been indicated to Byron by the landlady of their inn, pointing through an open window to the trees beyond. Without hesitating for a moment, the two poets hurried out into the garden and began to walk in the direction of the Elysium. It was a warm evening, with the sound of cicadas in the air and the voices of the haymakers under the trees. However, on reaching their goal, only the vineyard was to be seen. No flowers, no orchards, no Eden; only a pile of stones to mark the place where a little chapel had once stood.

'It was pulled down by the monks of St Bernard,' they were told. 'They own the land.'

'They *own* the land?' snapped Byron, overcome with rage. 'They own the land! Is it not God's land, not theirs? It is not even St Bernard's.'

'Why did they pull it down?' inquired Shelley. 'Was it to build a church?'

'No. Not a church.'

'A shrine then?'

'No. A vineyard,' was the reply. 'Wine for the monastery.'

'For *wine?*' exclaimed Byron, incredulous. 'The prior of

St Bernard has cut down a paradise for the sake of a cask of wine?'

I knew before, Shelley lamented later, *that if avarice could harden the hearts of men, a system of prescriptive religion has an influence far more inimical to natural sensibility.*

It was a tragic disappointment, and yet, despite it all, the beauty of Clarens and the woods about it, coupled with the memory of its dead heroine, moved Shelley uncontrollably to the verge of tears. Even as the light faded, and slowly the trees and the hills and the shore were swallowed up by the darkness, the poignancy of the mood remained, silencing both men into pensive meditation.

Later, as they both stood on the shore of the lake, lit only by moonlight, with the sounds of the night and the tide behind them and with Clarens before them, Byron spoke the first words for perhaps an hour. 'Thank God,' he said, almost to himself, his voice quiet and low, 'thank God, Polidori is not here.'

* * *

Polidori thanked God he was not there too, for, as if in answer to his prayer, he had, once again, fallen in love. Mademoiselle Odier was forgotten, and into his life appeared another, no less beautiful, who not only smiled at him but also held his hand long after the dance was over. 'I deserve to be in love, but not with her,' he said later, 'for if she does not love me, why should her day be clouded by my constant avowals? I, of all people, should allow her to be free and that is the absurd tragedy of it.' Fortunately, at first, such was not the case.

He met her on a Friday, after three days of storms when he had been compelled to remain at Maison Chappuis in the company of Claire, who spoke little except to pester him about his employer's intentions. Without doubt, she was aware that the affair, however intense, was ending, and that Byron cared little for her. He had refused to see her during the day and had talked little to her in the evening. No presents were exchanged, no billets-doux and only a single verse testified that he had ever recognized her existence as a lover at all.*

'Even a mistress is paid,' she told Polidori one evening, having underestimated the wine, 'but at times I am not even that. I do not ask for his love, for I know he has none to give, but I demand his affection. His attention too. Does he never talk about me? Not even a word?'

But her listener was not prepared to be her ally, for it was too late. She had rebuffed him before and Polidori had a long memory.

'I am employed as a physician,' he replied, 'and a physician is trained to be discreet. Whatever my Lord Byron confides to me — and he confides much — I keep it to myself.'

'Then I hope you are a good physician, Doctor,' snapped Claire, 'for you are a poor friend.'

'To you, perhaps. But then I know more about you than anyone else, do I not?'

'More about me, Doctor? Not that I recall.'

Polidori stood up, a dramatic gesture, and walked to the door, stopping only to look at the girl at the table and reply, 'I *am* a good physician, Miss Clairmont. You may be sure of that, for you see, I have been observing you of late. You faint and say it is the heat. You are tired at noon and complain of insomnia. You hesitate in the vineyard on your walk up the hill and mention an insignificant ache.

---

* The lyric to Claire, written in March after their first meeting, beginning:

>There be none of Beauty's daughters
>With a magic like thee;
>And like magic on the waters
>Is thy sweet voice to me ...

You eat too much of one and nothing of another, then suddenly you do not eat at all. You, in short, behave unpredictably. To the others you are over-tired or worried or bilious or demanding of attention. But to me ... '

He paused and then opened the door. Behind him, Claire was silent, her face white.

'You are speculating, Doctor,' she said finally.

'Perhaps, Miss Clairmont. Perhaps. But such a condition — and I will not enlarge on that — cannot be hidden for long. It is not like toothache or the cramp that can be endured in secret until cured. It is not like that. Such a condition makes its presence known all too soon. Goodnight, Miss Clairmont.'

And with that, Polidori left Chappuis and hurried to the stables of Diodati to prepare the carriage. He could endure Cologny no longer and was eager to visit Geneva, even for the night. Within minutes, the horses were ready and he boarded the coach to depart, after perfuming his hair and changing his cravat. However, as the gates were being opened he heard his name being called, and leaning out of the window saw the distraught figure of Claire hurrying towards him.

'Doctor Polidori,' the voice out of breath, 'please wait.'

Polidori sighed, gestured to the driver, and the carriage stopped in the driveway to allow Claire to reach it. As she ran, a dog followed her at her heels, barking loudly, so that lights began to go on in the house.

'What do you want, Miss Clairmont? I am expected in Geneva.'

Glancing round and lowering her voice, his pursuer moved close to the window, her hair in disarray, and leant towards him. She was indeed quite an attractive woman, though too heavy for the doctor's taste, but she had fine eyes and a good mouth. Her ancestry, he believed, was Swiss.

'Doctor Polidori, I beg you,' she said anxiously, gripping his arm, 'will you say nothing to Byron about ... about our conversation?'

'Our conversation?' asked Polidori blandly, moving his arm away and casually adjusting his waistcoat.

'I beg you, Polidori, I will be eternally grateful.'

There was a silence and the occupant in the coach turned his head slowly and looked down at Claire, staring into her eyes and at her scarlet dress, that revealed her shoulders despite the cold wind. For a long moment he didn't reply, savouring the situation, then casually taking one of Byron's cigars from a box behind his head, he lit it and turned away, showing his profile.

'I don't think you can do anything I would be grateful for, Miss Clairmont,' he replied, his voice unnaturally steady and cold. 'Not a thing. May I recall you once asked Lord Byron to "get rid of me". I think those were the words. You also said that I should be sent to find a ladylove of my own, in order to be out of your sight. Well, Miss Clairmont, I am going to do just that. Good night, Miss Clairmont.'

The window was slammed shut, the driver was signalled, and Polidori in Byron's carriage, smoking Byron's cigars and wearing Byron's greatcoat, turned his back on Claire and allowed himself to be driven out of the gates of Diodati and on to the road to Geneva.

[9]

VENUS TO POLIDORI

THE restaurant was large and yet intimate, since the designer had carefully placed the candelabra high enough to illuminate the food and yet not so high that women avoided the place for fear of being seen at a disadvantage. The waiters were Italian, the cuisine French and the clientele international, and consequently La Poêle was an unqualified success. Its reputation spread farther than Geneva and attracted customers of all ranks and professions who tipped handsomely, ate silently and called each other by their first name, with the obvious exception of magistrates, clerics and Englishmen. Moreover, no one was ever rude to the wine-waiter, unsympathetic to the chef, and the owner (Marcel) was acclaimed the perfect patron since he never appeared, teeth revealed, to embarrass his customers. The décor was superb and tasteful and was enhanced nightly by the appearance in the main salon of some of the most beautiful women in the canton, who came unaccompanied either by husband or uncle, and who sat, eyes lowered, bosom powdered, at the most advantageous tables within earshot of the rich, the handsome and the titled. Polidori was overjoyed, sitting as he now was in the company of Rossi and a Monsieur Saladin, with his back to the wall and his eyes focused on an opposite table graced by three of the most exquisite ladies he had ever seen.

'Actresses,' whispered Rossi in his ear, as if the word was the key to paradise. 'Actresses.'

His companion nodded enthusiastically, helped himself to more wine and assumed a pose of studied nonchalance, eyes narrowed under his dark eyebrows, as he observed the youngest and prettiest of the trio over the rim of his glass.

She was perhaps seventeen years of age, and wore her fair hair pulled back from a broad forehead and tied into ringlets that hung pleasantly on each side of a narrow face. The eyes were not over-large, but very clear, though it was the mouth (wide, full, a pouting upper lip) that turned the head and attracted Polidori's attention. In repose, the mouth seemed to curve downwards at the corners, not in disdain, but as if it contained a marshmallow or a small fruit which the owner was reluctant to swallow. But that expression was rare, for the girl seemed to be constantly laughing, and then the mouth was wide, almost unnaturally so, the lips parting to reveal teeth that were exceptionally white and even. A long neck, smooth shoulders decorated by a necklace that rested its single emerald in the vale between the girl's breasts, matching in colour, though the tone was lighter, the wearer's satin dress. The girl's companions, surprisingly, also wore green, though their gowns were fussy, more extrovert, and were over-decorated with brooches and bows, as if to demonstrate that they, in fact, were older and more experienced. But it was the central girl that Polidori saw, and her only, and to his delight she acknowledged his gaze and smiled back without colouring.

'Who is she?' he asked a neighbour to his right who had invited them all to dine. 'I must meet her.'

'I have no idea,' the host replied, 'but I do know her friend on the right.'

'Don't we all?' added another guest, Le Tourneur, overhearing and nudging Polidori. 'We have all seen Mylene naked.'

Polidori's eyes widened and he stared at the subject of conversation—a red-haired girl with an upturned nose and a skin as white as note-paper.

'Naked?' asked Polidori, anticipating the image in his mind. 'Where? How?'

The host, Poirier, laughed and whispered, 'At Brerier's. She is Dido to Aeneas on Thursdays. Or Circe to Odysseus on Wednesdays. Or Venus to us all on Mondays. No matter, her costume is a diadem and nothing more. Fuseli painted her, I am told, as Leda, so you see she is well versed in the classics, as well as having the finest buttocks I have ever seen. You will see them tonight if you wish. Just stay with us.'

'And the other? The girl in the centre?'

'I have never seen her before. But if she is your fancy, I will introduce you later.'

To Polidori, the prospect was unbelievable. At last he felt relaxed, aided by the wine, after the endless weeks of lackeying to the tantrums of others. Immediately, Diodati was forgotten and he was mercifully relieved that he had not insisted on accompanying Byron around the lake. 'I could not care a fig, even if they had found the Elysium they sought,' he wrote to Florence later, 'for my Héloïse was sitting opposite me, a primavera in green and yellow, and breathing and laughing like no fictional heroine could ever do. Suddenly I found L.B.'s quest to be rather sad; that such a man should prefer the ghost of a myth to the enchanting vision of flesh and blood that smiled at me now. I could only pray that my own Elysium would be hers, though I did not yet know her name.'

It was, in fact, Janine d'Alvers, and she had never appeared naked in public, not even with a diadem. She was introduced to Polidori at Brerier's two hours later, a place that was much more respectable than the doctor had anticipated. It was situated in the Rue Merceau, a modestly bourgeois quarter, and was the baroque mansion of one of Geneva's more successful bankers whose popularity outside the world of finance was based on his ability to present the finest and most exclusive soirées in the town. It was here Mylene cast off her clothes to appear (usually upon a shell or emerging from a font) as the central and most appealing segment of an elaborate tableau designed to illustrate the more imaginative episodes of Greek mythology. It was unquestionably the high point of the evening, and on this particular night, the theme was a popular and highly requested one.

Daphne Pursued by Apollo and her Metamorphosis into a Laurel, read the programme note, *with Mlle Mylene Brie and Jules Courceau and Others.*

The *Others* appeared first as the curtain rose to reveal a painted backdrop of sky and leaves, upstaged by silken trees that hung from the ceiling, and a gauze of sunlight. Marble statues of fauns and centaurs were placed in a semi-circle to form a mythological garden, and real butterflies flew in glass spheres suspended from jewelled branches. As music played, four men and four women appeared, wearing masks to indicate that they were a deer or a hare or a unicorn, and performed a slow dance around a statue before assuming a rather awkward pose on both sides of the stage. All of the performers were bare to the waist, but decency had covered their thighs with draperies that hung to the floor and were spangled with jewels. The women, who were all young and rather overweight, wore rubies on their toes and around their necks and each carried a musical instrument which they mimed to a hidden orchestra.

After a suitable pause, the mood changed and Polidori, noting the restlessness in the audience, realized that the entrance of Mylene was imminent. He was not disappointed. She appeared, as if by magic, from the air, swathed in a cloak of flame, and then proceeded quite calmly to perform a flat-footed dance in a vague parody of classical ballet. The movements were absurd and naive, but the sheer charm of the performer won the spectators over, especially as slowly the cloak descended to the ground to reveal the dancer totally naked to the world. The applause was spontaneous as Mylene, fully aware of her talents, like the notorious Miss Chudleigh before her, pirouetted around the stage, exhibiting a tall slim body, perfectly proportioned, and blessed, as Polidori agreed, by the most delectable bottom. It was this last feature that remained exposed to the audience as Mylene froze and the masque was compelled to act out the tired formalities of the myth. Apollo enters, Daphne runs, Apollo pursues, Daphne panics (hand to cheek, mouth agape, bosom throbbing), and then is turned into the laurel tree as leaves fall from above and cling to her body like magnets and the curtain drops.

It was an epic performance and the guests were in raptures. Polidori, however, was impatient to find the girl he had seen at La Poêle. It was, in fact, Saladin who introduced them, fifteen minutes later, as the party assembled in the garden where a marquee had been erected for fear of rain. It had served earlier as a dressing-room for the performers and Mylene Brie, now clothed, was holding court there.

'Mademoiselle d'Alvers,' said Saladin, leading a nervous Polidori across the enclosed lawn, 'may I present Doctor John Polidori. Doctor Polidori — Mademoiselle Janine d'Alvers.'

It was achieved. The head was raised, the hair falling away from her face, the eyes were narrowed and then with a sudden smile, Janine acknowledged Polidori's bow and they were tactfully left alone. Around them, the guests drank champagne or flirted with the masque performers, except for a group of French hussars who stood at the far side of the tent, dressed in blue and gold, their braided hats under their arms. For a moment, nothing was said between the new acquaintances except for a shy comment on the party and the weather. Finally, Polidori felt it was time to be more direct.

'You live in Geneva, mademoiselle?' he asked, studying the girl's face. She was shorter than he had expected (*five feet two from crown to ground*) and rather frail, and appeared surprisingly nervous.

'No ... I am rarely here,' was the reply, her voice soft and blurred only by the slightest accent. 'I live at Genthoud near the Countess Breuss. Do you know her, monsieur?'

'No, I do not. Should I?'

'I think perhaps you would like her. We have many fine evenings there, performing in plays which the Countess writes herself.'

'I do hope they are not like *Daphne and Apollo*,' commented Polidori with a smile, and was amused to see his companion blush and shake her head.

'No, monsieur, nothing like that ... '

She then suddenly became very distraught avoiding his eye and appeared to glance anxiously across the grass towards the entrance to the marquee. Following her gaze, Polidori saw that they were being observed very intently by the hussars.

'Do you know them, mademoiselle?' he asked casually, but she replied by moving away from him, hand to throat, saying quickly, 'Excuse me, monsieur, I must leave.'

Across the tent, three of the hussars had set their drinks down and were walking slowly, shoulder to shoulder, towards them. Unsure of the situation, Polidori moved forward and impetuously took Janine's arm.

'Mademoiselle, I wish to call on you. I am at the Villa Diodati and can visit you any day.'

'That is impossible,' was the breathless reply as the approaching officers reached them and stood silently staring at Polidori, their hands resting on the hilts of their swords, their faces expressionless. Polidori glanced at them, sensing the hostility, but did not retreat.

'Mademoiselle d'Alvers est avec nous, monsieur. Bonne nuit.'

And without waiting for a reaction, the three hussars turned away, Mademoiselle d'Alvers between them, and began to return to the table in the corner. Stunned that he should be so unexpectedly barred from someone he had already fallen in love with, Polidori, casting etiquette to the winds, seized the short cloak of the nearest hussar and spun him round. Immediately the guests who had been watching the events were silent and stared unashamedly. The hussars, however, were a poor spectacle.

'Laissez-moi, monsieur,' said the nearest officer, his face crimson. Polidori's bravado, however, was undiminished.

'I wish to speak to Mademoiselle d'Alvers and you are in my way, sir,' he replied, his voice steady.

The gauntlet was thrown down, but fortunately for Polidori it was not picked up. 'He was now prepared for another Waterloo, Florence, believing me to be English. It was the first time I had encountered such hatred and I must confess I was not at ease. I could see Mademoiselle d'Alvers being drawn from my sight, and I realized that I might not see her again. I had to act immediately, but how could I without incurring the wrath of this arrogant Frenchman who seemed to be determined to run me through? I am not a man of slow temper as you well know, but tonight I was calm. "You are in my way, sir." I repeated and pushed past him, my heart in my mouth, and was astonished to discover that I was not laid low from behind. Instead I reached the lady who so inadvertently caused this minor *éclat*, and took her hand. "I understand there is dancing in the house," I said. "Would you join me, mademoiselle, for a waltz?" It was a reckless gesture, but rationality is rarely the bedfellow of love.'

Reckless or not, the gesture was a success. Whether the hussars feared that their opponent would go so far as to involve himself in a duel, which they realized they would be forced to decline, or whether common sense alone won the day, they retreated without further comment, and so unexpectedly that Polidori for a moment suspected a trap. But, as he led his conquest out of the marquee towards the lights of the house, no officer followed, and as Mademoiselle d'Alvers's grip tightened in his without resistance, he knew he had won. Five minutes later, they were face to face on the dance floor, the orchestra behind them, and Polidori found himself blissfully in love. All that was said on the matter was that Jugon, one of the hussars, had pursued his partner across France and had repeatedly made his intentions clear. For the moment, however, he was forgotten as the waltz began *and my Daphne remained, sans feuilles, before me.*

'The next morning, I returned to Diodati a far happier man. We had danced and talked all night and I had learnt everything about her, but nothing more enchanting than that she wished to see me again. Janine d'Alvers. Even as I write her name, my heart races. *Janine d'Alvers.* I will engrave it everywhere.'

* * *

That same night, forty miles away across the lake, Byron and Shelley were lodged in a hotel in Ouchy, set on the shore below Lausanne. They had arrived there in the inevitable storm, and had been compelled to remain at the Hôtel de l'Ancre* for two nights till the waves receded. It

* Now the Hôtel d'Angleterre.

was a three-storey building with a high pointed roof; a solid structure decorated by circular windows set in the tiles. The main entrance was on the first floor, approached on both sides by steps set against the wall, leading into a large hall where a circular oaken staircase ascended to the rooms above. Lombardy poplars framed the building, chestnuts and oaks spread out behind, and the Leman lapped within a few feet below. It was an attractive hotel and Byron rarely left it, preferring to remain in his room at the eastern corner of the second floor, looking out on to the lake, and writing till the early hours. The poem was *The Prisoner of Chillon*, and by the time he had left his room after two days it was finished.

Perhaps his diligence in writing the poem without a break was due not only to the inspiration of Bonivard's story, but also because he was finally tiring of Shelley's company and preferred to be alone. There had been no quarrel to speak of, and no major difference of opinion, but merely the return of Byron's restlessness and despondency, now that the tour was drawing to a close and the prospect of returning to Diodati, to Polidori and Claire was imminent. Perhaps he welcomed the storm and was glad of the opportunity to finish *Childe Harold* and the second poem before he was thrown once more into the midst of a society he felt little sympathy for. Indeed, even Rousseau was overstaying his welcome, for Byron's amourette with Julie seemed to be over. She remained alive only in Shelley's heart now, as he found himself dining alone on the terrace of the hotel while Byron wrote in the room above. There was, however, one visit on the agenda which the poets shared (though their reactions to it were predictably different) and that was to the home of Edward Gibbon half a mile away.

They chose June 27th to visit the house in Lausanne, the anniversary of Gibbon's completion of his *Decline and*

Fall of the Roman Empire, and walked together through the overgrown garden where weeds now grew on the lawns on which the historian had himself walked and rested thirty years before. They were shown the summer-house where he had worked, and gazed at it in regret as it was now in ruins, having been neglected by the custodians. It was a further demonstration to them of the insensitivity of the Swiss towards beauty and art, but Byron, as if to make at least one gesture in remembrance of the dead writer, gathered some rose leaves and a sprig of acacia in recollection of Gibbon's final tribute to his work.* Shelley, however, who unlike his companion was never in the habit of collecting souvenirs, refrained from touching anything, *fearing to outrage the greater and more sacred name of Rousseau; the contemplation of whose imperishable creations had left no vacancy in my heart for mortal things.*

On June 29th, the weather cleared and the boat was ready to sail. In two days they would be at the shores of Cologny and the routine of Diodati would begin once more. The tour would become a memory and Rousseau, as if exorcized from their soul, would have no more influence over either of them. *It is singular*, wrote Byron, *how soon we lose the impression of what ceases to be constantly before us. A year impairs, a lustre obliterates. There is little distinct left without an effort of memory; then indeed the lights are rekindled for a moment; but who can be sure that imagination is not the torch-bearer?*

At the villa, the green-tea discourse would no doubt be resumed, and so would the whole, inevitable monotony of it all. The quarrels, the frustrations, the solitary walks along the shore, and the rare moments of peace, writing

* *It was on the day, or rather the night, of the 27th of June 1787, between the hours of eleven and twelve, that I wrote the last lines of the last page, in a summer-house in my garden. After laying down my pen I took several turns in a berceau, or covered walk of Acacias, which commands a prospect of the country, the lake, and the mountains.* (Gibbon, in his Autobiography.)

alone on the lake. He would return to the gawpers who pestered him at the gate, the bitter unexpected memories from England, the absence of friends, and the companionship of an insensitive physician, a possessive mistress and a humourless visionary. Such a prospect, inevitably, depressed him more than ever and he resolved, as he crossed the lake back to Cologny, to break away from his confinement and move once more into society, if only to ease the ennui. Familiar faces had already arrived at Geneva, he had received invitations to dine, and Madame de Staël herself had recently returned to Coppet across the water. He would visit them all, if only once, in the hope that he would find some distraction away from the claustrophobia of a single salon at Diodati. His Calvinist background may well have predestined him to be damned, but not yet, not in Switzerland at the age of twenty-eight, now that it was July and the summer halfway over.

[10]

LAMENT

THE suicide note was badly constructed but carried a certain charm. 'My life has nothing to offer the happiness of this world, except by taking leave of it,' it began, the words clear and legible as if in copperplate. 'I am a wretched creature, an amusement to others and a tragedy to myself. I wish nothing more of life's blessings, not even a tear, for I depart from it without sorrow and without regret, conscious only that such an act is despicable in the eyes of Him who has deserted me. And yet how can it be more despicable than life itself. I am, I was, and I pray I will be.'

The sentiment is now maudlin but forgivable, though one is surprised at the sudden allusion to agnosticism. A few more sentences in like manner follow — 'I ask forgiveness of the God who may observe me now. I cannot believe He can allow me to live as I have, in such unhappiness' and suchlike — and then the tone of the letter takes on a poetic imagery which is perhaps quite moving under the circumstances. 'Her face' (one assumes it is the face of a mistress) 'appears before me like a recurring dream, and she alone, so recently encountered, darkens the page with tears as I recall the only night I was truly happy. I see her eyes, wide and clear, looking into me and yet turning away and am left only with the rain on the window and the cold embers in the hearth. If I have achieved anything in my twenty years, it is to realize that I am a mere grub to mankind, vulnerable and unseen, to be walked on by a casual passer-by, my cries unheard in the void. Oh God, guide my hand. Lift the glass to my lips. Transport my soul.' Words are crossed out now, obliterated to the eye—one can discern a name that looks like *Jeanne* but could perhaps be *Genève*— and then a further sentence and then nothing more.

There is no signature, as if the letter is unfinished, either out of faintheartedness or because the writer is dissatisfied with his last epistle. On another page, the note begins again, but only a single line: *I write this not to be remembered but to be forgotten.* A blank page, a quotation from Alfieri, another page, the writing now illegible. On a further page, one discovers a doodle (a woman's face, not without style) but this may well be an earlier effort, drawn on a more optimistic moment. Now a woman's name written over and over again in a single column, assuming in its fifth appearance the surname of another. Thus:

Janine d'Alvers
Janine d'Alvers
Janine d'Alvers
Janine d'Alvers
Janine Polidori

Near by, a bundle of letters, seemingly written daily and yet never sent, detailing the writer's agonies and experiences without inhibition. A Diary, too, recounting a journey from Dover to Geneva and now thrown into a corner. Above the Journal, the feet of the diarist, and above them, the diarist himself, combing his hair prior, one assumes, to the act. Footsteps can be heard on the stairs.

The circumstances, understandably, are confused. A series of incidents, none on the surface tantamount to disaster in a rational mind, but having perhaps an incentive. One begins with a song, sung rather well in a high soprano by a girl with dark hair, who waits nervously and yet like a Lorelei in the salon of a villa. Below, a boat has arrived and she sees one of its passengers making his way slowly up a path, bordered by yew hedges, towards the house. He is followed by two servants carrying luggage and walking deliberately slowly as if conscious of the effort of their employer who has to use a stick to ascend the slope. The man, Byron, reaches the garden below the balcony of the salon, and the singing stops. A face appears at the window. He looks up, having recognized the voice, then walks away without entering the house, and rests on the lawn for a moment before descending once more to the smaller house below the vineyard. Half way down Claire appears in a new dress, running from the villa and calling his name. A conversation then takes place in which tempers rise and then the first key line that overtures the suicide note four hours later is heard.

'I want you to get rid of Polidori,' Claire said suddenly as Byron began to walk away. 'I want you to get him away from Diodati.'

Immediately, Byron spun round and glared at her. 'You want me to get rid of him? *You* do? Why?'

'Because he is offensive to me.'

'Offensive to you? I am also offensive to you, am I not? Do you wish to get rid of me too?'

'No—'

'Don't tell me he has attempted to seduce you? Does that inflame your sensibilities?'

'He is offensive to me.'

'Offensive for *what*? My God, woman, am I to stand in the garden like a fountain listening to this? Bring the doctor here and let us ask him for ourselves. He *is* still here is he not?'

'I don't know,' replied Claire nervously, 'I don't know. He is in love and may well be anywhere—'

Byron had moved away and was about four yards down the slope when he stopped as if struck by a bolt and turned slowly round.

'What did you say? Polly is in love?'
'Yes—'

A sudden yell of laughter. An incredulous giggle. 'With whom? Where? Polly in love? Not with you—no, heaven forbid that. In love?' A flurry of questions. 'Where is he? Is he here? Where?'

He was, in fact, at Maison Chappuis, reading in Italian to Mary Godwin, who sat minding her child by the window. A fire had been lit in the hearth to welcome Shelley's return and tea had been made. However, not wishing to disturb the lesson, Shelley had retired to his room on the first floor leaving tutor and pupil alone. Both expected to see Byron before nightfall, probably after dinner, and so were surprised when the door suddenly burst open and he appeared, grinning like a schoolboy, and seized the startled doctor's hand, shrieking enthusiastically, before collapsing into a chair in laughter. Before him, the occupants of the room could only gape in amazement, and so encouraged his hysteria until he had to leave the room, unable to keep a straight face, before returning. *He was in the highest and most boyish of spirits, rubbing his hands as he walked about the room, and in that utter incapacity of retention which was one of his foibles, making jesting allusions to the secret he had just heard.**

At first, his curiosity appeared to be genuinely sympathetic and Polidori, embarrassed but pleased by the attention, responded coyly.

'Who is she, Polly? Tell me—I must know.'
'You ... don't know her, my lord—'
'But I must. Where did you meet her? I want to hear all.'
'In Geneva.'
'In Geneva. Where?'
'Well ... '
'Not in the Rue Basse? Not a *grisette*?'

* Thomas Moore, *Life, Letters and Journals of Lord Byron* (1838).

'Oh no, my lord.'
'Then where?'
'At Brerier's —'
'Brerier's? I am a week away and you are at Brerier's? Is she one of the Venuses I have heard so much about?'
'No, my lord.'
'She *is* a Venus, is she not?'
'She is not my lord.'
'*Pray God she is not.* At least not the Venus my employer had in mind. If I say I was stunned by the callousness of the questioning, I would not be exaggerating. Stunned and puzzled that I could be humiliated like this and especially as only Miss Clairmont — oh, why could I not contain my secret within myself? — knew of my passion. It was she who had told L.B., of that I was certain, and for that I could never forgive her. To be subjected to such cruelty from a man who claims to be a poet, an observer of humanity, was more than I could bear. I refused to retreat and submit to his attack and so challenged him. "I have never met with a person so unfeeling" I told him, controlling my tears before all. His reply was not untypical, delivered with all the bitterness and vanity of one who fears all women — and distrusts all men. *Call* me *cold-hearted* — me *insensible,* he shouted, his face black with fury. *You might as well say that glass is not brittle, which has been cast down a precipice and lies dashed to pieces at the foot!* At least, L.B., glass does not disguise its contents or hide the nature of its properties. If one mistakes poison for honey, it is not the fault of the glass.'

Nor indeed could Polidori be condemned if he, not being the most placid of men, seized a brass poker that stood within reach and in an embittered attempt to protect, not his own name, but that of a woman he hardly knew, hit out with the weapon and struck his inquisitor on the knee, bringing him to the ground in agony. Immediately, the room was silent (Mary having already retreated to a corner, babe in arms) as Shelley, attracted by the noise, and Polidori looked down at the huddled figure who soundlessly clutched his leg, his face paler than ever. Then slowly, refusing assistance from his fellow poet, he stood up and turned towards his assailant, who still clutched the poker in defiance and was seemingly prepared to strike again if provoked. Byron however was in no mood for further frivolity.

'Be so kind, Polidori,' he said finally, his voice steady and emphatic, 'be so kind another time to take more care, for you hurt me very much.'

'I am glad of it,' was the unflinching reply. 'I am glad to see you can suffer pain.'

Then, throwing the poker dramatically into the hearth, Polidori made for the door. However, halfway across the room, he was seized by his employer, a far stronger man, and spun around. 'Let me advise you, Polidori,' Byron said calmly, his face inches away from the other man's, 'when you, another time, hurt anyone, do not express your satisfaction. People don't like to be told that those who give them pain are glad of it, and they cannot always command their anger. It was with some difficulty that I refrained from striking you down on this very spot, and but for Miss Godwin's presence, I should probably have done some such rash thing. Now leave me before my temper returns.'

Polidori was released, and seeing no sympathy from anyone, turned and ran out of the room, having burst into tears. One hour later, he did not appear for dinner.

At seven o'clock, Byron was informed that there was no reply when Fletcher had knocked on Polidori's door to inquire if the doctor was hungry. He knew that he was in the room, since he had seen him go there three hours earlier.

I am a wretched creature, an amusement to others and a tragedy to myself. I wish nothing more of life's blessings, not even a tear, for I depart from it without sorrow and without regret ...

The footsteps drew nearer and were replaced by a banging on the door.

'Polly! Are you in there?'

The voice is loud and anxious. More banging, more footsteps, and the door is forced. It breaks easily and Byron enters to discover his physician hunched up on the bed, a pen in his hand, an arm hiding his face. On his bedside table stands a glass containing poison. It is filled to the brim and has not been touched. Realizing the situation, Byron orders the servants to leave, then picks up the tumbler and throws it out of the window. On the bed, Polidori doesn't move, though he is far from dead.

'Polly,' says Byron gently, 'why do you allow me to bring you to this?'

In despair, he sees the papers on the desk, the letters tied in a bundle. The Diary lying in the corner, up-ended like a tent.

'Take my hand, Polly. Let us shake on this, and forgive me.'

Polidori still does not move, but Byron nonetheless seizes his hand and shakes it, then after studying the figure on the bed, unable to see the face, turns away and returns to the door.

'Fletcher will make you a dinner. In the salon. A fire has been lit and it is warm. Tonight, Polly, I am alone. I have had my share of the Shelleys and shall keep them away. There is only you and I.'

There was no reply, no reaction of any kind until Byron had quietly left the room and returned to the floor below. An hour later, Polidori still hadn't moved though he was now in darkness. At nine o'clock, however, he fell asleep and would have slept till noon if he hadn't woken in the early hours to find that the window was still wide open and that he was shivering with cold.

* * *

Claire was now in despair. Everything she had planned in Byron's absence had shattered into pieces and ironically she had succeeded in achieving only the opposite of what she had intended. Polidori had not been sent away, but had been reinstated even closer in Byron's menage — *the underdog in preference to the bitch* — while Claire had been cold-shouldered out of the bedroom. So far the doctor had not announced Claire's pregnancy to the world, for reasons of his own, though perhaps he realized that as long as he kept the condition secret he retained some control over Claire's influence against him. He need not have worried, for Claire no longer had any influence over anyone.

It was a confused maze of emotions and intrigue, the plot for an operetta, and Byron was sick of it. Playing the conjuror was not for him. *L.B. and I are now equal again,* Polidori could write the following day, but it was a meagre achievement. The L.B. he was equal to was a poor substitute for the Lord Byron who so recently thumbed his nose at London society and quit England defiantly for ever. The poet who lodged at Diodati in early July had no such pride and, like all men who stoop to self-pity, he was extremely vulnerable, protecting a scratch with a sword. Claire was only one of his victims. *Lord Byron,* wrote Shelley not long after, *is an exceedingly interesting person and as such it is to be regretted that he is a slave to the vilest and most vulgar prejudices, and as mad as the winds.* Vile and vulgar he may have been, but he was not deceived by his madness. To Byron there was a cause, though he would not announce it openly, but which he hinted at shyly, as if anxious to attract some sympathy, some relief, for the pain, no matter from what source.

'Do you think I am a terrible person?' he had said to Claire one day. His mistress, though barred from the bedroom, had not been excluded from the study, having volunteered to copy his poetry (*Childe Harold*, *Prisoner of Chillon*) into a presentable state for publication. She had been accepted in this task, since it was an arduous one and needed to be completed as soon as possible. An amanuensis, after all, could be fired if unsatisfactory, and demanding only money as payment was far cheaper than a mistress, and much quieter. 'Do you think, in truth, that I am a terrible person?'

'No, I won't believe that,' Claire replied as tactfully as possible, puzzled by the questioning.

Immediately, Byron left the room and returned with a number of letters and spread them out on the table. At first glance the letters seemed mundane enough, and were apparently written by the same person — the writing being fine and legible and probably feminine.

'They were written to me by my sister, Augusta,' Byron told her casually, studying Claire's face for any reaction. And then picking up one or two, he thrust them into her hand and told her to read them if she wished. Intrigued, and yet aware of the scandal that had precipitated the exile, she was apprehensive at the reason for this disclosure, if there was to be one. Nevertheless she began to read, conscious of Byron's nervousness as he paced up and down avoiding her gaze. The letters however afforded no confirmation of any incestuous affair, not because they denied it, but because they were written in code. *The beginning was ordinary enough — common news of their friends, her health, and then came along spaces written in* *cyphers which he said only he and she had the key of—and unintelligible to all other people.**

For a moment, Claire felt uneasy, as if she had been admitted to a clandestine ceremony, an Eleusinian mystery, but at the last moment had been refused entry and had been obliged to remain outside, peering through the glass. Fearful of Byron's mood, she therefore refrained from asking the meaning of the code words, and the letters were gathered together again like playing cards, stacked into a pile and counted. Suddenly, Byron let out a cry and began to shout, accusing Claire of stealing one of the pages. Terrified, she backed away declaring her innocence and begged her accuser to count the letters again. Reluctantly, Byron did so, the missing page was found and still agitated, he apologized, seized the letters and hurried out of the room.

What the meaning of this bizarre incident was, Claire never knew, but like the mistresses before her, she suspected the worst. To her, the letters were proof of Byron's incest, and perhaps indicated that Augusta's daughter, Medora, was in fact also her brother's. But Claire's suspicions were not Shelley's. Honourable to the last, he defended his fellow poet and declared that the ciphers were most likely used to convey news of his illegitimate children, and nothing more. It was a poor argument, since Byron was never shy in announcing his bastards, as Claire was to find out for herself. However, the subject was dropped and Byron never mentioned it again. When Claire returned to resume her copying, he behaved as though nothing had happened and as if he hadn't seen her for days.

If Augusta, however, was not discussed publicly, she, nonetheless, preoccupied his thoughts night and day. To her, he wrote two poems within a week of each other:

* Claire Clairmont, letter to E. J. Trelawny, *c.* 1870.

> My sister! my sweet sister! if a name
> Dearer and purer were, it should be thine;
> Mountains and seas divide us, but I claim
> No tears, but tenderness to answer mine:
> Go where I will, to me thou art the same—
> A loved regret which I would not resign,
> There yet are two things in my destiny,—
> A world to roam through, and a home with thee

Hardly perhaps, the sentiments of a disinterested younger brother. And again:

> From the wreck of the past, which hath perish'd
> Thus much I at least may recall,
> It hath taught me that what I most cherish'd
> Deserved to be dearest of all:
> In the desert a fountain is springing,
> In the wide waste there still is a tree,
> And a bird in the solitude singing,
> Which speaks to my spirit of thee...

Whatever the truth of the accusations of incest, if it is ever to be found (burnt letters, vague innuendoes, mendacious mistresses), there is no doubt that Byron was prepared to confess all, and would have done if his Memoirs had not been burnt by fearful adversaries. Instead one is left with the high-pitched clamours of Caroline Lamb,* the incensed suspicions of an abandoned wife, and

---

* *She then confessed as follows, with an unfeigned degree of agitation; That from the time Mrs L. (Augusta Leigh) came to Bennet St. in the year 1813 — Lord Byron had given her various intimations of a criminal intercourse between them — but that for some time he spoke it in a manner which did not enable her to fix it on Mrs L — thus — 'Oh, I never knew what it was to love before — there is a woman I love so passionately — she is with child by me, and if a daughter it shall be called Medora' — that his avowals of this incestuous intercourse became bolder — till at last she said to him one day 'I could believe it of you — but not of her' — on this his vanity appeared piqued to rage and he said 'Would she not?' — assured Lady C. L(amb) — that the seduction had not given him much trouble — that it was soon accomplished — and she was very willing.*

the intriguing speculations of Byron's own actions. That he loved Augusta is undeniable; that he slept with her can only be speculation, though Byron undoubtedly was haunted by the *idea* of a brother/sister affair. It appears in *Manfred* (written in Geneva), and in *The Bride of Abydos*, written after living with Augusta for the first time as an adult, and after the birth of Medora, whom Byron darkly hinted was his own. *Oh! but it (the baby) is worth while, I can't tell you why, and it is not an* Ape — an allusion to the medieval superstition that children of an incestuous union are born monsters. Ape or not, Medora Leigh seemed aware of her dubious parentage and grew up to be a haunted child, who at the age of seventeen was seduced by her brother-in-law, and conceived two children by him before being cast out to die, like Byron, in exile, and like Byron also, in her thirty-sixth year.

I have never ceased (wrote Byron to Augusta) *nor can cease to feel for a moment that perfect and boundless attachment which bound and binds me to you — which renders me utterly incapable of real love for any other human being — for what could they be to me after you? My own **** we may have been very wrong — but I repent of nothing except that cursed marriage — and your refusing to continue to love me as you have loved me — I can neither forget nor quite forgive you for that precious piece of reformation — but I can never be other than I have been — and whenever I love anything it is because it reminds me in some way or other of yourself.*

It is doubtful, however, if Claire ever reminded Byron of his sister,* even in appearance. She was taken as a

---

(Minutes of a Conversation between Lady Byron and Lady C. Lamb. March 27th, 1816.)

* To be accurate, Augusta was Byron's *half*-sister, being the daughter of John Byron and Amelia, Baroness Conyers, by his first marriage. Byron himself was the son of the second marriage, when John Byron married Catherine Gordon of Gight in 1785. Augusta was four years older than her half-brother, and in 1807 married her first cousin, Colonel George Leigh.

mere distraction when her lover was at the depths of despair because of the scandal, found to be nothing more than a reminder of his past melancholy, and so discarded when that melancholy returned. To her credit, Claire never charged Byron, while he was alive, of using her as a substitute for one he could never possess. To her eternal discredit, however, she never forgave him when he was dead, nor ceased waging a war of hatred on his name. But at the moment, in this July of 1816, she, like Polidori, still tried the patience of their employer, though their welcome at the Villa Diodati was no longer enthusiastic, and their presence appeared increasingly precarious. Little wonder then that Claire began to copy the required poems as slowly as she dared, and that Polidori remained conspicuously out of the way for a week or more. To add to the gloom, news reached the villa that one of Byron's closest friends had suddenly died in London on July 7th. He was someone whom Byron adored and admired without question. *I liked his voice, his manner and his wit: he is the only one of them all I ever wished to hear at greater length. In society I have met him frequently. He was superb! He had a sort of liking for me, and never attacked me—at least to my face, and he did everybody else—high names, and wits, and orators —some of them* poets *also.*

The man, who was not only a wit, but a statesman, a playwright and a drunk, was Richard Brinsley Sheridan.

* * *

'Sherry's dead,' Byron said. 'That's the sum of it. There'll soon be none left. Brummell's fled, Sherry's gone ... mourned by the bailiffs, both of them. But Sherry never had a shilling to his name and I have heard him announce that more than once. And if he did have a shilling, it was drunk away. He told me that on the first night of *School for Scandal* he was so drunk he was knocked down and put into the watch house for making a row in the street. When asked his name by the watchmen, he replied "Wilberforce". Fortunate Wilberforce to have his name taken so wisely. I wish it had been mine ... '

They were in the garden, not walking but sitting on a wall gazing out at the lake. There was some breeze from the north but the sky was cloudless and blue and ideal for flying kites or releasing a balloon. Realizing this, a group of children on the shore below the two men had cast a giant scarlet kite into the sky and were watching it and calling out to each other and running up and down as the kite flew higher and higher, straining the cord. It attracted Polidori's attention too as he sat, arms folded, nodding sympathetically to his companion's lament. Behind both of them, a gardener was cutting the grass.

'I remember one day he was offered a bet by Monk Lewis. They never liked each other, but that is by the way. "I will bet you, Mr Sheridan," said Lewis, "a very large sum. I will bet you what you owe me as Manager for my *Castle Spectre*." "I never make large bets," replied Sheridan, "but I will lay you a very *small* one. I will bet you what it is *worth*." '

Byron then talked for another hour, hardly caring if Polidori was listening. He had been asked to write a piece on the death of Sheridan to be spoken at Drury Lane; a Monody out of respect for Sheridan's Monody on Garrick. It was a task he welcomed out of admiration for the dead playwright, but found himself incapable of producing satisfactorily. *I did as well as I could: but where I have not my choice, I pretend to answer for nothing.* The poem preoccupied his mind, adding more fuel to the nostalgic depression, and did little to raise anyone's spirits. Even

Polidori, conscious of his own digressions, was finding his employer hard to bear. 'We sat for hours, I saying not a word, he soliloquizing like an Attic hero. I prayed for a *deus ex machina* to descend from the sky, but I was given only a child's kite, a blessed distraction, that fluttered about our heads like a spectre. By late afternoon, my back ached and I yearned for peace. Then suddenly, extraordinary thing. L.B. leaps up, Albanian yell, gardener drops scythe, and he is pacing up and down slapping his hands together. *"Tonight we will go to a ball, Polly,"* he told me, as if it were to be his debut into society. *"You and I will go to a ball."* '

It was to be given by a certain Lady Dalrymple Hamilton, an English hostess and beauty of some repute in high circles, who, besides being an expert on childhood lore, was the daughter of Viscount Duncan and the wife of Sir Hew Dalrymple Hamilton. Her dinner parties and soirées were as well known as her personal attributes, and she had been anxious for weeks to be the first to enliven her salon with the notorious Lord Byron himself. Tonight, it seemed, her prayers would be answered. At ten o'clock, Byron appeared in the main drawing-room at Diodati, dressed impeccably in a dark suit, buff waistcoat and pristine white cravat. Proud of his dress, he was not quite a dandy in the best tradition of Brummell and Alvanley, though he admired their attitude to life and their arrogant disdain for society. *I like the Dandies*, he once wrote, *they were always very civil to me, though in general they distrusted literary people. The truth is, that though I gave up the business early, I had a tinge of Dandyism in my minority, and probably retained enough of it, to conciliate the great ones, at four and twenty. I had gamed and drank and taken my degrees in most dissipations, and having no pedantry, and not being overbearing, we ran quietly together. I knew them all more or less, and they made me a member of Watier's (a superb club at that time) being I take it, the only literary man in it.**

On this particular evening, he was, however, at his best. He was also, so Polidori noted, unexpectedly nervous, and as if to give himself courage to enter the affray drank half a bottle of wine before leaving the house. In the carriage, he chatted excitedly about a million things, none either important or even worth discussing, and constantly took sips at a flask of brandy he kept in a locker beneath the seat.

He even asked Polidori about Mademoiselle d'Alvers, though warily and without malice, regretting that he had not met her or that they had not invited her to the ball. Then, as the carriage approached the Dalrymple Hamilton house and lights were seen, Byron suddenly became silent and began to toy with the knot of his cravat. 'Stay with me, Polly,' he said, almost in a whisper. 'We'll battle this out together.'

It was obviously a popular evening, for news having spread around the salons that Lord Byron himself would be present had brought out the gawpers and socialites in droves. Carriages and horses blocked the drive up to the house, and guests made excuses to remain on the steps, craning their necks for the appearance of the familiar Napoleonic coach bringing their devil incarnate into their midst. It arrived at eleven o'clock, stopping on the gravel before the pillared portico; immediately, dozens of faces appeared at the windows, noses pressed to the glass, and others, more bold in their curiosity, jostled each other to swarm on to the steps and nudge each other and stare, like members of a celebrated school posing before Alma Mater for a group portrait.

---

* Byron, in fact, belonged to many clubs, including the following: The Alfred, the Cocoa Tree, Watier's, the Union, Racket's (at Brighton), the Pugilistic, Owls, the Cambridge Whig Club, the Harrow Club, and the Hampden Political Club. He did not, surprisingly, claim to belong to the more notorious and exclusive clubs of the time — White's, Brook's and Almack's.

It was the utter silence that first disturbed Byron. It was as if he were under glass, or a specimen on a slide, scrutinized by mute beings looming over him. He could see them, as he glanced apprehensively around the curtains of the coach, watching him silently from the house and disturbed only by a nervous giggle from an unseen girl. Polidori descended from the carriage first, aware of the concentrated attention (trapeze artist about to attempt the impossible) and stood self-consciously on the gravel avoiding the stares, and waited for his employer to follow him. He could see him, white-faced, sitting well back in the darkness of the interior, his eyes flitting nervously to the scene outside. Then, his mind resolved, Byron turned quickly to the postilion, his voice low, and said, 'Tell the driver to take me back. I have changed my mind.' At first, the remark was not understood and Byron had to repeat it, painfully and much louder. 'I said, tell the driver to take me back. I am returning to Diodati.' And then, to the amazement and fury of the spectators, the carriage suddenly leapt forward, a whip to the horses, and was driven fast back down the drive and was gone. The last they saw of the occupant was a brief glimpse of his face as he leant forward and closed the curtains around him. Before anyone could react, the carriage was out of sight, leaving only Polidori standing self-consciously and very much alone in the centre of the carriage park.

When he himself returned to Diodati three hours later, Byron was in his room. A light could be seen but the door was closed. In a letter to Florence, Polidori talks agonizingly of the embarrassment of the evening (he was apparently cut dead by the guests at the ball, who considered that second-best was worse than none at all) and of his return to the villa. However, whether out of tact or merely propriety, he refrained from noting his discovery, on entering the salon, of a woman's blue cloak and bonnet lying on a chair. *Miss Clairmont has returned*, was all he would say without elaboration, but perhaps, with regret.

Byron, however, breakfasted alone the next day. Realizing almost immediately the error of his actions (despair perhaps was a poor excuse), he had sent Claire away before it was light, terminating the affair for a third time after a mere couple of hours. He had wanted a whore, and had made the mistake of choosing a mistress, whether out of spite or laziness, and therefore could not be surprised when the notes reappeared once more. *If you want me or anything of, or belonging to me, I am sure Shelley would come and fetch me if you ask him — pray do.*

It was a familiar letter, filled with the usual coy demands and fluttering eyelashes. Byron had only himself to blame, as he well knew, and could be consoled only by the fact that Claire would soon be leaving Cologny for a few days in the company of Shelley and Mary on a tour to Chamonix and Mont Blanc. It could not be said, however, that their absence would be regretted, as they all knew too well.*
'Seven days?' wrote Polidori. 'Why not seven weeks? Or seven *months*? I would not wish Mister S. to miss a thing, overlook a flower, ignore a stream. I cannot wait till they are gone — though we have seen little of them of late — since L.B. and I have many plans. He has offered to introduce me into *real* society — not the tracasseries of the English *belles dames* and their kind.† No more Ly. D.H. for me.'

* *We go I believe — in two days — are you satisfied! — It would make me happy to finish Chillon for you. It is said that you expressed yourself so decisively last Evening that it is impossible to see you at Diodati; If you will trust it down here I will take the greatest possible care of it; & finish it in an hour or two ... When you had such bad news to announce, was it not a little cruel to behave so harshly all the day.* (Claire Clairmont, letter to Byron, July 16th, 1816.)

† Confirmed by Byron: *I went into Society solely to present* him (*as I told him*), *that he might return into good company if he chose; it was the best thing for his youth and circumstances.* (Letter to Murray, May 15th, 1819.)

One *belle dame*, however — though *jeune fille* is perhaps more appropriate — was far from tiring Polidori's patience. He had met Mademoiselle d'Alvers again, a week after Brerier's soirée, and had not been disappointed. 'Her kiss transports my soul and ricochets through my very existence. I can write nothing of her that is not a mere cameo to the colossus of her beauty. We sailed alone on the "crystal face" of the Leman, as Byron writes it, when the sun was low and the mountains were gold. We were alone, she and I, drifting on the water, saying little to each other, but in our paradise. We landed on a deserted shore, like mariners in the Isles of Odysseus, and walked slowly side by side along the grassy bank. The sound of cicadas, the smell of newmown hay, of wild thyme, a panoply of stars.'

The letter is long and yet strangely euphemistic, as if the writer is honourable enough not to record a seduction that evidently took place on the grass beside the lake, and yet unable to contain his pride in the achievement. There is, however, a curious footnote. 'I do not think,' Polidori writes on the final page, 'I will call on Mademoiselle d'Alvers again. She is after all, only an actress, and if I am to appear in society with Lord Byron, I have to sacrifice my own preference in favour of decorum.' On the other hand, Polidori was only a physician, and an attractive, accommodating girl needs also to sacrifice her own preference in favour of higher goals and more eligible companions. Doctors, like hussars, should be discarded in one's minority. It is perhaps superfluous then to state that Madame Janine d'Alvers was never seen again.

As if in compensation for the tears, however, Polidori, in the second week of July, was introduced as promised into the *real* society of Geneva. There were no half measures about his debut this time, for on the 12th he was presented to the leading hostess not only in the canton, but perhaps in the whole of Europe. He was taken by Byron to Coppet across the water to meet the celebrated, and legendary, Madame de Staël.

[11]

OLD MOTHER STALE

THE coach had now left the outskirts of Geneva and was making its way along the north shore of the lake, keeping close to the water and moving at an easy pace. Inside, Polidori sat silently, knees together, arms folded, listening patiently to the voice of his employer, like a child *en route* to his first day at school. A nervousness, tinged with excitement, eager to present the best impression.

'Above all,' Byron was saying, 'speak as little as possible, and only when she addresses you. That way you will be assured of being invited a second time, or at least will be acknowledged in the street. Do not try to impress her — you cannot. She has met everybody, and after Goethe and Napoleon, we are all inferior. Bow, eat silently and praise her hands. If she provokes an argument with you — and she most certainly will — I beg you neither to raise your voice nor strike her with a poker. Instead, present your case if you have one, and refuse to budge from it. On second thoughts, agree with her. That way she will consider you more intelligent than you are and consequently will tolerate your abuse in future. But do not fawn, Polly. That is anathema to her. Nor address her husband as her husband. *I* know Rocca is, *you* know he is, the world knows he is, but to her it is a secret. So therefore you must respect that. Besides, Rocca is a bore — though *she* is not — and consequently should be ignored. In short, I recommend you say nothing whatsoever. Not a word. If they ask, I will say you are a mute. You will therefore be ignored and be allowed to listen *and* eat without fear of having to sing for your supper. You are young, handsome and Italian, and consequently, as far as she is concerned, have an advantage over all of us. Read *Corinne* and discover that. On the other hand, don't read *Corinne*. A meal of *that* and you are sure to make a fool of yourself. Mark my words.'

Polidori certainly marked them well, eager as he was to enter high society with impunity. Consequently, as the coach moved closer to Coppet, he listened attentively to Byron's monologue, nodding only occasionally and hardly moving for fear of creasing his clothes. His employer had met Germaine de Staël before, three years earlier in London, and had been suitably impressed, despite his natural aversion to the dominant and garrulous female. She was, however, a tragic figure, as all knew, and this perhaps endeared her to him. He told Polidori of her life, of her banishment from France at Napoleon's request, and of her unhappy love affairs. 'On this very road we are now travelling, she first met Benjamin Constant, who was never constant, especially to her. A pale young man with red hair, galloping on his horse after her, broke her heart and it has been broken by men half her age ever since. Rocca is twenty years younger than she in age, and a hundred in intelligence. I think the only man who ever returned her love was Necker, her father, and when he died, she became the ghost she now is.* She seeks a father in other men's sons, and has succeeded in being only a mother to everybody. Old Mother Stale, Polly. Old Mother Stale.'

Byron told his listener how Madame de Staël had been hounded by Napoleon's spies, forced to remain in exile

* One of the greatest regrets in Madame de Staël's life was that she was not present when her father died. In a poignant letter to Benjamin Constant in 1804, she contemplates suicide in her despair, writing: *Farewell, my dear Benjamin, I hope that you at least will be near me when I die. Oh, I did not close my father's eyes: will you close mine?*

from her native country. He told him how she had contemplated suicide on discovering that Constant had secretly married another, and how she had been abandoned by almost all her friends except 'her younger sister' Juliette Récamier. *My life is like a ball when the music has stopped*, she wrote in 1810, aged forty-four, when she found herself alone, imprisoned in Coppet, wandering the empty drawing-rooms where years before she had held court to hundreds. Now, in 1816, some had returned to listen to her again, but it was too late. 'Madame de Staël, Byron told me,' wrote Polidori, 'has returned to Coppet to die.'

The château, surprisingly, was originally medieval, belonging to generations of peers from across the lake, who planted flower-beds along the western wing, then allowed the building to burn down before they eventually returned to Savoy. In the eighteenth century, however, it was rebuilt and sold to Jacques Necker, a minister to Louis XVI, whose taste reflected perhaps the austerity of his profession, for the design of the château was almost pedantically formal and unrelieved by any curve, carving or pediment, resembling more a school for the poor or an English seminary than a country estate. It sprawled arrogantly above the sepia tiles of the village; a grey-stone, two-storey edifice with an iron balcony running along the lakeside wall, over which roses entwined to create, in early summer, the only pattern of colour.

If one approaches Coppet by the south-western route, with Geneva behind the carriage, as Byron did, one travels first along an avenue of elms and plane trees, planted in regular lines for about a mile, and guiding the visitor directly through the gates of the château into a cobbled courtyard the size of a croquet lawn. Other carriages are there, assembled against the stables on the left, or waiting by the Gothic doorway of the wine-press separating yard from lake, and covered in autumn by virginia creeper. Two stone water troughs (dated 1766 and 1768 respectively) have been set out for the horses, fed by a continuous running stream of mountain water that appears through the mouth of a triton. Opposite the gates is the south wing, and beyond that corridors of stone, two turrets, another wing, a small portico. The whole château is surrounded by a high metal railing, entered by two main gates, in which one at least betrays the pride of the owner. The initial letters N(Necker) and C(Curchod) are entwined together and set in the heart of the entrance, surmounted by a crown. It is a rare moment of sentiment on the part of Jacques Necker, for nowhere else on the exterior of the house is there any other personal design whatsoever, as if one is conscious that the occupants moved to Coppet not out of choice but because of exile. A coat of arms discovered on a wall belongs to the architect, and the monogrammed gate opens out, not to the road and the town, but to a lawn and a small pond.

Visitors to the château, however, in the days of its greatness, fortunately did not travel to admire the architecture, but to admire Necker's daughter. The memory of Germaine de Staël is everywhere, and it is she, not the father, who was responsible for the interior. Touring the rooms quickly, one has an impression of pink and green in the décor, echoing the roses outside, and above all of an influence that is not only feminine but exquisite. A bed, where Germaine herself slept, resembles an enormous cradle, over which coy cupids support a canopy of fuschia damask, resting in the centre of a magnificent Savonnerie carpet. Near by is another bedroom, *une chambre des oiseaux*, where the walls are covered in Chinese wallpaper representing birds of paradise, each painted by hand. The two rooms have an adjoining door. 'It is here,' wrote Polidori, 'in this room of birds, that Madame Récamier stayed; that friend of de Staël, who is an enigma to us all. She is acclaimed the beauty of the age and has conquered every man from Emperors to Princes, yet I know nothing of her except gossip, and gossip of the most bizarre kind.'

If the gossip about Juliette Récamier was bizarre, the facts themselves, if facts they were, were no less intriguing. Married at fifteen to a millionaire three times her age, she remained a virgin throughout her married life, and, some say, died a virgin. And yet she was without doubt the most beautiful woman of her time, painted by adoring artists who invariably portrayed her reclining on a chaise-longue, arms hanging loosely by her side, palms up, eyes staring wistfully out to the viewer. Her clothes are draped over-casually around her as if the painter would have preferred to depict her naked and is irritated by the barrier of white mousseline imposed upon him by a coquettish yet coy sitter. The gowns fall eagerly away from her shoulder, exposing curves of breast and, at times, thigh, and her feet (blessed triumph) are bare. Gérard portrayed her resting on a padded chair, her clothes in disarray, as if she had just woken up and was surprised to find an artist standing before her. In another, more famous study, she reclines for Jacques David in white once more, but more formally, like a member of a Grecian chorus, feet bare, palms up, eyes attentive. *Do you know why she always wore gloves, even at meals?* commented Madame Hamelin, a rival cynosure. *It is because she has practically no nails, just little claws. That is why David painted her hands with the palms upwards.* It was praise indeed, but her critic was not alone. Men also, tantalized by a woman who flirted but never submitted, accused her of every inhibition in order to justify their own failure to seduce her. In part, they may well have been right. She was on the surface a professional virgin, considering that as long as she didn't, no one would ever suspect that she couldn't, though the true cause may be more sinister. Madame Salvage, a notorious Lesbian of the period, wrote of her: *Madame Récamier became my great friend, because I paid her debts and the rent of her second suite of rooms at the Abbaye-aux-Bois. In Rome, she used to meet me behind Saint John Lateran. I rented a summer residence for her, but found to my dismay that I was not invited there. Once, to soothe me down, she gave me a bracelet with a secret spring; when I opened it, I found a miniature of her, naked to the waist, with two serpents twined round her.* 'Gossip,' scoffed Polidori, 'clings to the celebrated like birds on the back of an alligator, who pick the teeth of one who could eat them.'

But such alleged unorthodoxy in Juliette's sexual life was not total, even if true. There is no doubt that she was passionately, if passively, in love with two men at least, one of whom she met and lost at Coppet itself,* gazing out through the windows of her room for the arrival of her lover's carriage. There was even a desire in 1807 to leave her aged husband and elope with Prince Auguste, but this was denied by the man who, it is claimed, was not her husband at all, but was, in fact, her own father. Bizarre gossip indeed.

In the summer of 1816, the *chambre des oiseaux* was empty. Madame Récamier had not returned to visit 'her elder sister', and Madame de Staël was alone, surrounded mostly by strangers. She waited now in the gallery with her handsome second husband, John Rocca, her daughter and son-in-law by her side, and a crowd of visiting English

---

* *The memory of those fifteen days (at Coppet) and that of the first two years at the Abbaye-aux-Bois, at the time of M. de Chateaubriand's love, are the most beautiful, the only beautiful ones of my life* ... (Madame Récamier to Louis de Lomerie.)

aristocrats, the enemies of her country, as company. Now fifty, she looked older, though the brilliance of her eyes was undimmed, and so too, as Byron was to discover, her conversation. When Polidori first saw her, she was standing by one of the french windows that overlooked the roses, the village roofs and the lake, and for a moment he thought she was someone else, a colonel's Staffordshire wife or the widow of a London banker. She appeared shorter than he had expected, shorter and much older, and her black hair was now greying and hidden under a form of turban. Her head was turned away from him and she seemed lost and very alone. One hand was nervously clutching a long-stemmed rose, and, unaware of being observed, she could be seen glancing furtively into a circular mirror like an ageing mannequin. It was difficult to believe that this was the woman who had captivated the salons of Europe, and of whom one admirer had written: *If I were a queen, I would order Mme. de Staël to talk to me always.* 'An old woman in a shawl,' wrote Polidori, 'vain and tired and absurdly conscious of her hands.'

This glib aside was perhaps unfair. Madame de Staël had never claimed to be a beauty, unlike Juliette, nor was she celebrated as such. Vain she may well have been — her portraits are vaguely unreal as if the sitter had presented a mask to the artist, an impression of herself rather than her reality. In a celebrated portrait by Gérard, she resembles an Eastern gypsy (jewelled turban, ebony eyes, the shoulders of a fishwife) and in another, a different woman peers out from the canvas, posing it seems behind a gauze. And yet young men half her age had been captivated by her, if only for a brief moment, fascinated by her charm. *Detestable beauty which causes everyone to lose his head,* wrote one admirer, overwhelmed by the mere presence of the woman. She possessed a magical gift of seduction that few could resist and all envied, even, let it be said, Byron himself. *Ugly,* commented Polidori in his Diary, two months later. 'Beautiful? Ugly?' remarked Madame de Tesse, 'I do not know. I was listening to her and I believe I never saw anything else but her eyes and her mouth.' Nor, on reflection, did John Polidori, when he was finally face to face with his subject.

However, an incident took place before the introduction, before the doctor had even entered the room, that was to astound everyone, and add even more fuel to Byron's reputation as a devil incarnate. When the visitors from Diodati arrived at Coppet (courtyard, arch, courtyard, door), most of the guests were already assembled in the gallery on the ground floor. Calling cards were presented to a manservant and both men were guided towards the closed doors across the hall. The doors were opened and Byron *found the room full of strangers who had come to stare at me as if some outlandish beast in a rareeshow. They looked as if his Satanic Majesty had been among them.* Satanic Majesty or not, the impact of his arrival caused more than impertinent stares, for as the name 'Lord Byron' was announced to the room, one woman at least, a Mrs Hervey, unable to control her excitement, promptly fainted and had to be carried out in a coma. The fact that she was far from being a young girl only served to heighten the astonishment. *'This is too much,'* exclaimed the Duchesse de Broglie as the unfortunate woman was picked off the floor, *'at sixty-five years of age!'**

'It was as if she had been struck down by his fist not by his name. A woman of her age collapses before our eyes just on hearing L.B.'s name, and is carried out like a tavern drunk before the very man who had transfixed her so. For God's sake, L.B. had not even opened his mouth or entered fully into the room and half the women in Coppet

---

* *The sight of him quite disordered me, and he affected tender melancholy and much agitation* ... (Elizabeth Hervey, letter of August 1st, 1816).

are fainting dead away. What better introduction into a room can a man demand?' What indeed.

* * *

It was later that same evening that Madame de Staël, now the centre of attention—and attraction—first informed Byron of the book *Glenarvon*. Dinner had been served,* Germaine had talked, Byron had listened and Polidori had eaten. The atmosphere was more relaxed as guests grew accustomed to the outlandish monster in their midst (Mrs Hervey creeping back, face flushed) and Byron himself, relieved of the burden of being the figurehead, was happy to be merely an attentive audience to the hostess. He had always liked Germaine de Staël, with reservations, even though he had to admit that she thought like a man, but *felt* like a woman, and there was none to whom he would rather pay silent attention. Besides, the fellow guests interested him in no way whatsoever, not even Schlegel, the celebrated writer whom he considered, like Polidori, to be nothing more than a *presumptious literato, contradicting à outrance*. 'He translates Shakespeare for the Germans, Polly,' Byron had said as they sat down to eat, 'which I think is remarkably tolerant of the Germans.' Others: white-faced Scottish peers, cantering daughters, a Swiss botanist on one's right. Relatives too. De Staël's daughter, Madame Albertine de Broglie, *a beautiful, dirty-skinned woman* in Polidori's words, and her liberally pompous husband who sat on his mother-in-law's right and said not a word very noisily.

After eating, the stage-set was struck and all assembled in the grand salon on the first floor. It was perhaps the

---

* Eaten, no doubt, on the celebrated de Staël crockery; white, translucent *porcelaine de Paris*, very simple with cylindrical cups, decorated solely with gold rings and a single Gothic initial S capped by a crown.

finest room in the château, hung with eighteenth-century Aubusson tapestries (hunters, shepherdesses, lambs in the ruins) and tinted in pink. Oval-backed chairs in salmon Lyon silk embroidered with silver roses, brown velvet walls, and portraits of Auguste and Albertine, the only surviving children — another son, Albert, had been foolishly shot in a duel — and miniatures of Madame Necker and of Bernadotte. It was a warm, comfortable room, where guests could sit where they wished and not be out of earshot of any worm of scandal, or be too far from the decanter. It had space but not size, and the furniture was carefully placed so as not to discourage amourettes if that was desired. It was here that the great celebrities of the past had discussed the politics of the Empire and where Madame Récamier herself, for a brief moment in the life of Coppet, had played the harp, eyes and bosom lowered, to entertain the men. Here, now, only Lord Byron remained worthy of Germaine's personal attention, though she talked, surprisingly, of his ex-mistress Caroline Lamb.

To the poet's surprise, the mad Lady Caroline, as if she had not wreaked enough havoc in his life, had written a novel, based very obviously on himself, called *Glenarvon*, which had just been published in England. Byron himself had seen only the motto, taken from his *Corsair* —

> He left a name to all succeeding times,
> Link'd with one virtue and a thousand crimes.

— and consequently expected the worst. He was not to be disappointed. The hostess, without too much detail, described the book in which the monstrous cold-hearted seducer of a thousand crimes, Glenarvon, is described with the venom of a cast-off lover, as well as other equally recognizable models, including the Duchess of Devonshire, Lady Oxford and Lady Jersey, together with a certain pathetic heroine, Calantha, who was none other than the authoress herself. *Glenarvon,* wrote Hobhouse, *the hero is a monster and meant for B ... I called on the bitch and was asked whether any harm had been done by her book ... she showed me half bawdy pictures of hers of B.**

The book naturally was the rage of the year, especially as its hero was unable to defend himself, even if he cared to. To Byron, Madame de Staël's report of the *grievous things,* well-intentioned as they might be, filled him only with rage, and it is not surprising that his phraseology in a letter to Murray is more than usually blunt, as well as being perceptively apt. The last phrase alone is eternal in its sentiments: 'The generous moment selected for the publication [of *Glenarvon*] is probably its kindest accompaniment, and — truth to say — the time was well chosen. I have not even a guess at the contents, except from the very vague accounts I have heard, and I know but one thing which a woman can say to the purpose on such occasions, and that she might as well for her own sake keep to herself, which by the way they rarely can — the old reproach against their admirers of *"Kiss and tell",* bad as it is, is surely somewhat less than *"F**k and publish".'*†

* * *

Despite Lady Caroline's uninvited appearance on the stage, that first evening at Coppet was a success for all. Even Polidori, manners impeccable, impressed the hostess, so that she took him for a poet like his companion, or at worst, an exiled prince. 'I told her I was a physician and she considered it a pleasantry, believing all doctors to be old, grey and half-witted. L.B. reassured her that I was as I professed, and still I saw an air of disbelief in the lady's eye. "I will bring you my thesis to prove it," I declared,

* Hobhouse, Diary, May 10th, 1816.
† Byron, letter to Murray, July 22nd, 1816.

remembering that it still lay, unopened in the depths of my locker. "And what is your thesis about?" she inquired. "Sleepwalking," I replied. "Sleepwalking? Then I must read it immediately since I am so often confused with Lady Macbeth, and yet I have not a drop of Scottish blood in my veins." At this, I smiled politely. I was accepted.'

Polidori indeed was accepted, and yet he could not ignore the fact that it was Byron, not he, who took the limelight. Grateful that his employer had introduced him into *real* society, he nevertheless was well aware that he was below the salt in the favours of Madame de Staël, thesis or no. 'I am not unreasonable nor, let it be said, ungrateful, but I found myself so often behind L.B. in protocol and attention that I felt like that Roman plebeian whose task was to whisper constantly in the ear of the Emperor: "Remember thou art only mortal. Remember thou art only mortal." But even if I had said that to L.B., history no doubt would prove me wrong. Madame de S. has an odd conception of physicians, wishing me to be a poet. Perhaps there *is* more weight in it, for after all, what profession other than medicine strives so hard to make its practitioners redundant?'

Sensitive as he now was to his status in society, Polidori nonetheless returned to Coppet twice more (thesis under arm) before politely declining on the grounds of other distractions.

'Why will you not accompany me?' Byron had asked him a week later as his employee sat whey-faced in the salon.

'I would rather not, my lord. Your offer is very kind, but no.'

'Do you not like Madame de Staël then, Polly? Is that your dilemma?'

'No, my lord. I like her well enough. I would just rather not go to Coppet.'

'Ever?'

'Ever, my lord.'

And so it was. What the reasons were were never fully divulged openly, but it appeared that paranoia had once more set in. *Today I stayed in my room and said not a word.* And yet, curiously, there was no element of malice towards Byron himself, as if the doctor had mellowed, become less impulsive, preferring to remain alone rather than thrust himself into the centre of the crowd. It was a moment of withdrawal that did not last longer than a fortnight but was significant enough. Left in the Villa Diodati while Byron travelled to Coppet,* Polidori would sit alone, either reading or merely daydreaming, often writing not a word for days on end.

'A strange sensation follows me wherever I am, as if I were wedded to Lethe. I feel alienated from myself, suspended from my being by a silver thread, viewing myself in the darkness of my room, mirrored in my unreality. I eat little, speak to no one, not even Fletcher, and yet I feel no unhappiness. I am embalmed in my own disaffection. Yesterday, for example (I say yesterday, but time is now meaningless), I took myself on a walk along the shore and discovered I had journeyed for perhaps a mile when I encountered a figure of a familiar person before me. Approaching I saw that it was Mademoiselle Odier (forgotten creature) and she was sitting in the tide, dressed in blue and was playing a piano. A man was standing near her slowly taking off a glove and replacing it. Taking it off and putting it on. The man, of course, was myself. And yet, it was not a dream for I was awake, and so I believe it was a mere hallucination. Mister S. himself could do no

---

* Where Byron was constantly made at home, as he often professed later: *Madame de Staël I saw frequently at Coppet, which she renders remarkably pleasant. She has been remarkably kind to me.* (Letter to Moore, November 6th, 1816.)

better. I am not however disturbed by this occurrence, and perhaps one day I will include its image in a sketch. The colours were to me quite pleasant.'*

Mister S. on his part, however, was remarkably free from hallucinations. He had set off on July 21st with Mary and Claire (leaving William behind with Elise) to visit Mont Blanc and tour Chamonix. It was a memorable excursion, where they marvelled at the glaciers, bought a squirrel in a cage for William and where Shelley, declaring his atheism to all, wrote Εἰμι φιλάνθρωπος δημωγράτικος ν'ἄθεοςτε† in all the hotel registers. The daily walks or mule rides, the sensations at climbing the Alps, were detailed at length by both Mary and Shelley, and yet nowhere is there a mention of Claire, though she was with them constantly. Without doubt, Mary by now must have noticed a change in her half-sister's behaviour, even if she did not as yet recognize the cause. Nevertheless, Claire was now almost four months pregnant, and such a condition could not easily be disguised for long, especially under the watchful eye of one such as Mary on an arduous journey such as this. But it was not her companions she feared, but her lover; and she knew that before very long, on returning to Cologny, the secret would be exposed. It was a moment she dreaded, not because she resented bearing a child, but because she knew she would lose Byron for ever. The moment, inevitably, was near at hand. On July 27th the party returned to Diodati, and within a week the truth was known.

---

* Polidori in fact had a somewhat modest reputation as a sketch-artist, especially of the human form, and contributed some drawings of Lerici women for the book *Sketches, Illustrative of the Manners and Costumes of France, Switzerland and Italy.*

† Democrat, lover of mankind, and atheist.

[12]

REVELATIONS AND ANNIVERSARIES

ON FRIDAY, August 2nd, Mary Godwin writes a pertinent entry in her Diary: *In the evening Lord Byron and he [Shelley] go out in the boat and after their return, Shelley and Clare go up to Diodati; I do not for Lord Byron did not seem to wish it.* The implications, under the surface, are obvious, though why it is Mary and not Shelley who is barred from the dramatic meeting is puzzling. Perhaps it is Claire who requested the presence of Shelley, believing him to be an intelligent mediator between her and the wrath she expected, but if it was, Shelley made no mention of it. Indeed, he made no mention of the occasion in any way even long after the event was over. Claire too, in her way, is equally silent about the occurrences leading up to the disclosure of her pregnancy, for in her own Journal, all references to the lover who cast her aside are brutally destroyed by her, erasing his image from her memory. The circumstances therefore can only be speculation.

One member of the Diodati clique, however, was well aware of Claire's secret long before his employer was informed of the fact. 'The Shelleys returned today. Ah well. I saw their carriage arrive at nine and they burst into the villa like the avalanche they've just visited. Miss C. looks pale.' Byron at first was pleased to see them and invited them to stay and tell him all, though Mary first ran down the slope to see her son before returning to talk till midnight. In the excitement of narrating the events of the journey, Claire was ignored and remained seated in the far corner of the room, looking at no one. At ten o'clock, she muttered an excuse and left the room, reluctantly resigned to returning to Maison Chappuis and sleep. However, as she made her way along the hall towards the main door, she became aware that she was being observed. Stopping, she looked up and saw in the half light the figure of Polidori leaning against a panelled wall, watching her. In his hand was a book he had obviously taken from a shelf, and yet his pose indicated that he had been standing there for some time, near the door of the salon, and may well have been eavesdropping. Claire's discovery of him, however, afforded no surprise on the doctor's part.

'Good evening, Miss Clairmont,' Polidori said quietly. 'Are you leaving us so soon?'

The implication in the voice was obvious and Claire, without replying, turned and hurried out of the house. On reaching the garden of the villa, after walking down the steps past the fountain, she found herself face to face once more with Polidori, who had obviously hurried down the kitchen stairs to intercept her.

'One moment, Miss Clairmont, if I may speak with you.'

'Why?' inquired Claire coldly, making no effort to push past him. 'Did you not find that lady-love you sought?'

For a moment, Polidori hesitated as if unsure of his ground, then the smile returned and he replied, his voice steady, 'Miss Clairmont, I just think you ought to know that Lord Byron and I have been visiting Coppet while you have been absent. We have been visiting Madame de Staël.'

'That is not news, Doctor. Besides, what you do is of no concern to me.'

'But what *is* news to you is that Madame de Staël has been persuading Lord Byron to return to his wife. And may I add, Miss Clairmont, Lord Byron is not averse to the idea.'

The reaction was immediate, though Claire tried hard to disguise it. A gasp, a sudden reddening of the cheeks, a turning away, to recover quickly and reply, 'I do not believe you, Polidori. I know Lord Byron loathes his wife. He has told me so often.'

'Ask him, Miss Clairmont. I heard it with my own ears. At Coppet. Just across there.'*

Polidori pointed across the lake into the darkness as if emphasizing the truth of his statement. But Claire needed no such graphic proof, for she had hurried away, down through the vineyard towards Chappuis. For a long while, Polidori watched her till she was out of sight, and there was silence; then, casually, he returned up the steps to Diodati and to his room to read, after first asking Fletcher to send up some tea.

* * *

In the next few days the routine returned to the villa, with the exception of Claire's presence at night. It was also a week of anniversaries, four in all, though only two were occasions for festivity. On July 28th, Mary and Shelley celebrated the second year of 'their union', as Mary put it, though they had known each other for longer. They had first met at the Godwin house (Shelley already married to Harriet) and had fallen in love almost immediately after

---

* Polidori, in fact, is telling the truth. Madame de Staël did attempt a reconciliation between Byron and his wife as Byron himself told Medwin: *I believe Mme de Staël did her utmost to bring about a reconciliation between us. She was the best creature in the world.* But such maternal considerations achieved little. On August 24th, Byron wrote with impassioned tolerance: *The separation may have been my fault, but it was her own choice. I tried all means to prevent and would do as much and more to end it — a word would do so, but it does not rest with me to pronounce it. You asked me if I thought that Lady B. was attached to me? To this I can only answer that I love her.*

visits to St Pancras cemetery. Conscious however that their affair could not be happy unless they were together night and day — threats of suicide, passionate declarations — they had eloped in the night for France and it was this day they honoured modestly at Diodati, by spending the evening reminiscing over green tea with Byron. The second anniversary was Shelley's twenty-fourth birthday (on August 4th), on which day he received a telescope from Mary as a present, as well as a balloon which they floated above the lake as they read Virgil and Curtius to each other. It was a quiet and instructive celebration, but the sentiment was there.

The other two anniversaries, however, did not honour births but deaths, and for Byron they both brought back more sad memories of his past, though it was the past of his adolescence. On the first day of August five years before, his own mother died, drunk and raging, after receiving a bill from an upholsterer. He had never loved the gross, bad-tempered woman who had borne him, and who had dismissed him from her sight as nothing more than a 'lame brat'. *Am I to call this woman mother?* he once wrote. *Am I to be goaded with insult, loaded with obloquy, and suffer my feelings to be outraged on the most trivial occasions? I owe her respect as a Son, but I renounce her as a Friend.* And yet on her death, he could not deny his filial affections, despite it all, and declared that she was the only friend he had in the world. She had now been dead five years and his memory of her was still more tender than he had felt in her lifetime.

The fourth anniversary of that first week in August was perhaps the most tragic. In the same month as his mother's death, a boyhood friend, Charles Skinner Matthews, was drowned near Cambridge and was found entangled in weeds, like a trapped fish, at the bottom of a stream. It was a death Byron was never to forget; even in his last years he claimed the drowned youth as one of his few true friends. On first hearing of his death he wrote to Scrope Davies, *Some curse hangs over me and mine. My mother lies a corpse in this house; one of my best friends is drowned in a ditch. What can I say, or think, or do? I received a letter from him the day before yesterday. My dear Scrope, if you can spare a moment, do come down to me—I want a friend ... Come to me, Scrope, I am almost desolate—left almost alone in the world—I had but you, and Hobhouse and Matthews, and let me enjoy the survivors whilst I can ...* *

Byron, in 1816, still had the survivors, and no doubt on recollecting the death of Matthews he was reminded that Davies and Hobhouse would both be arriving at Diodati before the end of the month. Three months earlier, anticipating their visit, he had told Hobhouse that *they would buy females and found a colony* at Geneva, but such initial frivolity had long since died. No females had been bought, not of any kind, and he no longer desired to found a colony as Claire was to discover all too harshly on August 1st. 'Gloom, gloom, gloom,' wrote Polidori, eavesdropping once more. 'Gloom and shouts. All afternoon, I have heard their voices in the room below. Miss C., I fear, has finally revealed her condition.'

At six o'clock that evening, Polidori was sent for.

The expressions on the faces betrayed all. Byron, white-faced, head lowered, standing in the centre of the salon; coatless, a kerchief knotted around his neck, pale waistcoat unbuttoned. Across the room, Claire, eyes red, staring with hatred at Polidori as he cautiously entered the room. At first glance, it was Byron who seemed more at ease, but Polidori knew that controlled anger well. He trod warily.

* Byron, letter to Scrope Davies, Newstead, August 7th, 1811.

'Polidori,' said Byron, looking up without raising his head, 'how long have you known about that woman?'

Conscious of Claire's eyes cutting into his head, Polidori resisted an urge to glance at her, but by her silence he knew that it was his employer who was now solely in command.

'How do you mean, my lord?'

'That woman is pregnant, Polidori. She *claims* by me. I ask you once again — how long have you known?'

'I have not known —'

'Don't lie to me, Polidori. You are a doctor and I know that bitch would confide in you.'

'I did not confide —' interrupted Claire but was silenced before she could continue.

'Polidori?'

'I never *knew*, my lord. I suspected.'

'Then why did you not tell me before?'

Behind him, Polidori heard Claire gasp with alarm as if suddenly realizing that the doctor had indeed not informed on her.

'I believed it was of no business of mine, my lord. I felt ... that it was between you and Miss Clairmont.'

'No more, Polly. No more.'

On the next day, Mary was told to remain at Chappuis as Claire, Shelley and Byron (Polidori not being present) discussed, like solicitors around a defaulting client, the mode of procedure regarding Claire's unborn child. There was no question now, as Claire had feared, of her remaining with Byron — he did not love her, he did not want her, nor did he care to have her in his sight. She should return to England as soon as possible and give birth to the baby there. It was conceived there and would be born there.

'I do not believe,' Byron told her, 'that you were unaware when you followed me here, despite my wishes, that you were in this condition. I cannot believe that. You deceived me for four months, and why? I cannot see what you hoped to gain ... I have given you more than I have given anyone else, at least on the terms we had. The child when born will be placed in my sister's care and not yours. That is all I care to say.' *To this I objected,* wrote Claire long after, *on the ground that a Child always wanted a parent's care at least till seven years old ...He yielded and said it was best it should live with him—he promised faithfully never to give it until seven years of age into a stranger's care. I was to be called the Child's Aunt and in that character I could see it and watch over it without injury to anyone's reputation.**

The terms so stated were accepted by all though as yet they did not hint at the tragedy and hatred they would incur in the years to come. However, Byron, whatever his feelings towards the mother, now recognized the child as his own, even though there was little initial affection.† In a letter to Augusta there is revealed only veiled paternal pride, almost as an afterthought, but for Claire's sake, at least, there is a positive claim: *I forgot to tell you that the demoiselle who returned to England from Geneva went there to produce a new baby B. ...*

The demoiselle, however, on August 2nd, was to remain in Geneva for three more weeks, her role now being reduced solely to expectant mother and reluctant amanuensis.

* * *

* Claire Clairmont, letter to Trelawny (*c.* 1870).

† Though later, regarding the child's paternity, a curious statement is made and quoted by Claire: *I got a letter from her* (*the child's nurse, the daughter Allegra now being two years old*) *in which she told me that the day before Lord Byron had been in the nursery and sat some time observing Allegrina at play. Of a sudden he said to the nurse,* 'She will grow up a very pretty woman and then I will take her for my mistress.' *Elise was shocked and said,* 'I suppose My Lord you are joking ... ' *He then said—* 'I can very well do it—she is no child of mine—She is Mr Shelley's child.'

If Byron, in those first days of August, believed that he had seen the last of his physician's *eternal nonsense and tracasseries*, he was much mistaken. The four-week amnesty from disaster since the bid for suicide was coming to a close, for on August 10th, Polidori, for the second time that summer, was arrested by the police.

The incident began, like all the others, in a relatively insignificant way, in which Polidori's own actions seemed, initially, to be well meant, and no doubt were. It began then with Byron's stomach, that perennial cause for concern, not only for the owner but also for the physician. On the morning of the eventful day, the stomach was more painful than ever and appeared to be afflicted by cramp, but this may well have been merely indigestion. Accordingly, a messenger was sent post-haste to Geneva to acquire some magnesia, which was dutifully bought from a myopic and hot-tempered apothecary called Castan. The medicine was brought back and swallowed by Byron who immediately collapsed in further agony, believing himself to be poisoned. To Polidori, there was only one conclusion: the magnesia must be bad. In order to prove this, he mixed the remainder with sulphuric acid, whereupon it turned a red rose-colour, justifying Polidori's suspicions. The messenger was now sent to collect the apothecary himself, in order to confront him with the evidence and demand damages. Castan, however, fearing the worst, refused to leave Geneva, declaring that he never sold bad magnesia, not even to the sixth Lord Byron himself.

'There was only one thing I could do,' declared an angered Polidori, 'and that was to confront this Borgia myself and drag him to Diodati to view his poison. My L.B. was lying on the floor as if dead and may well have been. The poisoner was called Castan, who called me a liar, a jew and a papist all in one, and then said "if Lord B. was dying, he was glad of it." I told him, quoting my employer, that people don't like to be told that those who give them pain are glad of it, and asked an apology. Thereupon, he refused to confab further and set about me, so I knocked his hat on the floor and broke his spectacles, treading on them—and his fingers—as he crawled like a roach. Even now, for God's sake, he would not see the experiment and climbed on top of a wall for three hours as if he were a manx, gibbering at me and throwing stones. Without doubt, the apothecary was insensible.'

Insensible perhaps, but also vengeful, as Polidori was to discover. *A writ of arrêt comes for Polidori*, wrote Mary in her Journal, summing up the events, *for having 'cassé ses lunettes et fait tomber son chapeau' of the apothecary who sells bad magnesia*. Apparently, the gibbering Castan was cleverer than his opponent had anticipated, realizing that as Polidori had physically struck him, he could be arrested for assault. *Brought me to trial before five judges; had an advocate to plead. Laughed at the advocate; I pleaded for myself.** Polidori no doubt pleaded favourably, as he won the case, while Castan lost his cause in the plea of calumny. The victor, however, was required to pay twelve florins for the broken spectacles and costs, but his honour was preserved, at least in the eyes of the law.

Regrettably, though Byron survived the poison and was fit in a day, and though his physician's intentions were unselfish, Polidori was not received honourably at Diodati.

'If you had not lost your temper, this would not have happened,' Byron had told him.

'But you would have still been ill, my lord.'

'And if you had lost the case, Polly, I would have been worse. Not only would I have been ill, but I would be prey to every predatory doctor from here to Pisa. I do not wish the devil I know to be in prison. It is too expensive.'

To Polidori, it was a barbed attack on his medical

* Polidori, Diary, September 5th, 1816.

talents, especially as they, of all things, had been up to now accepted without question. *He is not a bad fellow,* Byron told Moore in November, *but young and hot-headed and more likely to incur diseases than to cure them.* The doctor's pride was hurt, especially on a day when he had attempted to play the hero, not the quack. Accordingly, licking his wounds, he resolved once more to pursue another path of action, as he had so often done before on finding he was no longer appreciated, or wanted, in the salon of Diodati. Moreover, Percy Shelley was now back in favour (now that Claire was out) as Byron needed a conversational partner when not visiting Coppet. Polidori therefore abandoned them all each evening and sought a new society of his own where he was unknown and he could be accepted warmly, and where also, if fortune was on his side, he could fall once again in love. Reluctant to return to the middle-class follies of Geneva, and yet resisting the heights of Coppet, he remembered a conversation at Brerier's; and so, on Sunday the 11th, on the pretext of re-meeting Mademoiselle d'Alvers, Polidori set off to the canton of Genthoud and the amateur dramatics of the delectable Countess Breuss.

[13]

FLICFLAC

SOCIETY around Lake Leman, as in any socially conscious centre, protected its vain pursuits by being as insular as possible, adopting new members into its clique with caution, and preserving its *ton* by being totally ignorant of the existence of any other arena but its own. The faded aristocrats of Coppet not only knew nothing of the world of Geneva or Vaugeron, but they never cared to know, as if any hint of an entrée into another salon diminished their own. Their strength was their exclusivity, and gossip was only at its best if the subjects of that gossip were known to the listeners. To be told that X is on the verge of bankruptcy or that Y is drinking herself to distraction is to be told an enticing but dull anecdote of fiction, unless X and Y are politely sitting opposite one at dinner. Then scandal can become an appetizing truth to be embroidered upon and enlarged with all the resources of imagination endowed on one, and with the solitary requirement that the subjects remain there before all as visible proof of their clandestine vices. The fetishes of strangers carry little weight, and it is a poor story-teller who has to rely on alien follies to spice the brandy, unless, of course, they are the alien follies of princes.

Consequently, the social circle must remain intimate, with its boundaries inviolate, and its members, naturally, must be linked by the same class, profession or vice; for what peer wishes to hear of the indiscretions of a stable-boy, and what courtesan would pause to contemplate the lovers of a plebeian niece? There is, however, one other aspect of gossip, which all abided by, and that is when the topic concerns he or she who stands above them in rank, notoriety or intimacy; *then* and then alone is the carrier of such a germ of salacious information (night pranks, naturally, heading the list) recognized as a true brother whether he is a stranger or not. For scandal at root is fed by envy, and one's own private foibles assume a cosy glow if one is informed that one's overlord is buggering the sweep, or that a well-known marchioness wakes up each morning with a jockey. Then, with triumph, all barriers are thrown aside to the spy who peddles the scandal of the socially superior, especially if the socially superior is an incestuous English lord and the spy is known to be intimate with the bed manners of that same English lord, even though he himself is only a humble physician. For such an informer, in the summer of 1816, there was no shortage of buyers and so it is not surprising therefore that the garrulous, open-faced visitor from Diodati was welcomed by the clique of Genthoud with open ears.

Within an hour, Polidori, introduced into the house at Vaugeron by Saladin, was the centre of attention, surrounded by man and daughter alike as he chattered about the 'extraordinary passions' of his notorious employer. 'Did you know,' he asked them, 'that when Lord Byron arrived at Ostend, that he fell upon the chambermaid like a thunderbolt?' 'No,' cried the chorus and moved closer. 'And that two frauleins emerged from his room at Ghent, one naked save for a shoe?' It was an indiscreet revenge on Polidori's part for the recent snub and he was well aware of it. *I found them eager to listen and I eager to tell; but Judas is not my role & I resented the playing.* Nevertheless, he remained on stage all evening and if he did not receive any silver in recompense, he did at least receive an invitation to the homes of all who listened, and the dubious pleasure, sad as it perhaps was, of being the subject of squabbles to obtain his favours. These, however, he endowed first on the hostess of the salon—the Countess Breuss herself.

Being as prominent in Genthoud society as she was, the countess had no shortage of detractors. Consequently, it did not take long for Polidori to learn that not only did she have a husband in Russia, but she also had another lodged in Venice. Neither of the men, however, were on speaking terms with her, for she had turned her back on both of them in order to create a menage of her own at Vaugeron. Her villa was a landmark in itself, surrounded as it was by a gallimaufry of summer-houses and baths, islands and follies, where guests would float on streams around a bizarre landscape that rivalled in imagination, though not in indelicacy, the Dashwood estate at West Wycombe. Instead of carefully planted bushes and triangular shrubs representing female forms, Countess Breuss had chosen Babylon as a theme and had erected, as Polidori noted, a Tower of Babel above it all built around the trunk of a chestnut. On summer evenings, plays would be performed on the lawns (farces, charades) in which bewigged young girls in scooped dresses would cavort with elegant bucks, always within the boundaries of propriety, reciting lines written by the countess herself. The dramas bore little weight outside their surroundings, for the players mocked each other and characters were based unashamedly on the spectators. Recognition and satire were the thing, and the audience waited expectantly to see themselves portrayed before them, each member leaving disappointed if he or she had not been viciously lampooned at least once. 'I sat next to one aged madame,' wrote Polidori, 'who almost burst a blood vessel laughing at a grotesque caricature of herself that spared no sympathy and was as subtle as a painting by Bosch.' Even the doctor himself was not spared, though it was he who was the last to laugh as a black-haired dwarf wearing a butcher's apron appeared clutching the coat-tails of a limping dandy escorted by two identical girls. 'The women exchanged wigs with the man, who I took to be L.B., until all three wore clothing of each other and spouted verses to the world. The dwarf I took to be myself and responded accordingly though I found much malice in the portrayal. However, I congratulated C.B. and professed the desire to perform myself. C.B. agreed.'

It was the beginning of a new chapter in Polidori's artistic career (dramatist, artist, actor) that was to be as short-lived as the others and as painfully unfruitful. Anxious to play, if not Hamlet, then at least Rosencrantz, he was somewhat piqued to discover that he was cast in his first appearance on the stage as a long-haired, bosom-padded chambermaid, and that his moment of glory (red-faced, the grin of a portcullis) consisted of the single line *Votre lit est prêt, Monsier l'Abbé* repeated in a high falsetto inaudible to all. It was a beginning that could well have elevated him to the status of Mrs Siddons, but his heart was not in it. 'I am aware, Florence, that Ophelia at the Globe was a boy in rosemary and thyme, and Cordelia the son, no doubt, of a blacksmith, but this is 1816 and a woman is a woman. My only consolation was that Charles Saladin, whose birthday it was, portrayed the Countess B. herself (and very badly may I add) and Madame Gatelier, in habit and cross, tottered on as the Abbé. The absurdity of myself, in cotton cap, telling *her* in tonsured perruque that her bed was ready *ad infinitum* amused me in no way, but apparently appealed to the audience for they applauded rapturously as if I were Edmund Kean before them.'*

---

* Polidori, however, took prominence after the performance, by reciting a verse of his own to Charles Saladin—it being his birthday—who had been a soldier with Napoleon:

Such dedication to the craft was soon rewarded, and a week later at a grand ball Polidori appeared as his own sex, portraying Flicflac in a play especially written for the occasion by Countess Breuss and called *Le Pacha de Suresne*. In this, Polidori not only showed his worth by upstaging all, including the writer herself, but even sang a song and had a conversation with a dog—an additional piece of *mise en scène* which Flicflac claimed brought character to the part. He also, need it be said, fell in love with the leading lady, a winsome brunette called Madame Clemann, who was not only twice his age but also possessed a daughter of seventeen (Harriet) who appeared at rehearsals and fell violently in love with the doctor himself. Such a situation was clearly bound to end in disaster, and was averted only by the presence of yet another beauty, renowned throughout the canton, called Madame Brelaz, a Portuguese lady, who played Guinevere to Polidori's troubador. 'I am surrounded by such delicacies, that I feel like Paris on Mount Ida presented with a golden apple. If wisdom were to be my guide, I would leave Vaugeron before I am shot by a husband, but the play must go on, though my head is turned to the wings.'

It is obvious, from Polidori's succinct and yet chaotic notes in his Diary, that the role of the actor has many advantages outside the text for a passionate male, even though one is billed as a Flicflac or a chambermaid. Green thought in a green room was for the aged and the impotent, as Polidori soon discovered. Within a week, his

---

> Jeune guerrier dans l'armée du premier des héros,
> Dans la cause de la France dédaignant le repos
> Que la chute de vos ans soit tranquille et heureuse
> Comme fut l'aube de vos jours éclatante et glorieuse.

It will be noted that the verse, remembering pronunciation of the final mute 'e', scans very badly.

desk drawer was filled with billets-doux and locks of hair, and his pannier overflowing with lockets and borrowed fans. His popularity was endless, especially as his rivals were few; and in time he courted, rendezvoused and made love to at least half a dozen breathless mothers and daughters, who believed, perhaps, that within this handsome physician there lay also a trace of Byronic magic. 'Odd role: elude mother to meet daughter. Abandon daughter to seek mother. All harmless.' Surprisingly, it appears to be beauty alone, though all were eligibly desirable, that prompted Polidori's pursuits, despite one brief change of face: *Jacquet Madlle., got half in love with her — no, her 8000 a year; her face and bad-singing exposures cured me.*

After all this picaresque and reckless flirtation, there had to be, as the protagonist knew, a retribution. Polidori, the intruder, had trodden on too many male toes and broken too many female hearts to be allowed to continue with impunity. And so, in the best Romantic tradition, vengeance came one afternoon on a lonely stretch of road back to Diodati, when the Lothario was alone save for the companionship of a Welshman, Ap Lloyd, whom he had met at Vaugeron. They were both sitting in a gig that was making its way leisurely along the coastal road, as both occupants daydreamed in the heat of the sun. Suddenly, two carts appeared from nowhere, approaching the gig at a gallop, until Lloyd realized that he would either have to stop or be involved in an accident. Reining the horse, both he and Polidori waited for the carts to pass, and were puzzled when, in fact, the wagons stopped on both sides and half a dozen men appeared from each vehicle, all of whom seemed intent to do them harm. *The carter struck me,* wrote Polidori in his Diary, *upon my back with a whip: I jumped down, and six jumped at me. I fortunately was between a wheel and a hedge, so that they all could not reach.*

Lloyd, seeing this, jumped down also; then three left me and went to him, and another untied a piece of his wagon with which, while I defended myself from the two (one with a whip), he struck me while fortunately my arm was striking a blow, so that it did just but touch my face. He lifted again; I sprang back and with all the force of my leap struck him with my fist in his face. His blow fell to the ground, and with his hand to his nose he retreated. They then seized stones to throw, but we closed with them.

The victims, valiant as they were, were still obviously outnumbered and outmatched, and the fracas might well have ended grimly if it had not been for the arrival of an English carriage, which Polidori recognized as belonging to Doctor Gardner. He called out to him and Gardner stopped, and by using his whip drove the assailants away, undefeated but exhausted. When asked the cause of the attack, Polidori shrugged and suggested that they may well have been robbers or thugs who had mistaken him for someone else, and refused to say any more. However, he refrained from adding that he had in fact recognized two of the men, and that a third had threatened him before.

Two days later, Countess Breuss received a letter stating that John Polidori was unfortunately unable to attend any further rehearsals for *Les Ricochets*, since circumstances demanded that he remain at Cologny for the present time. His absence, by some, was not regretted.

* * *

On August 14th, many miles away from the intrigues of Vaugeron, women working in the vineyards beside Cologny were suddenly disturbed by the sound of singing. The voices were obviously male but the tune was unfamiliar and seemed to be some kind of ballad or worksong, sung with great enthusiasm and joy. Raising their heads to see the source of the music they saw amid the dust from the road a large carriage making its way up the slope, pulled by four horses and attended on top by three Negroes, dressed not in traditional livery, but as dandies — lemon-slice hats, starched cravats, highly-polished boots. It was these Negroes who were singing, though the tune was unrecognizable, as were the words, which seemed to be a mixture of English and some obscure patois. Startled by this extraordinary sight, the women hurried to the road in time to catch a glimpse of the passenger in the carriage, who, thrusting his head out of the window and waving, appeared even more remarkable, being white, with the bulging eyes of an insect, and wearing a large panama hat.

As the women approached closer, one of the Negroes asked in fractured English the way to the Villa Diodati, and was confronted by a puzzled concentration of thought and nothing more. Realizing that the women did not understand, the passenger himself repeated the question in perfect French and was relieved to hear a chattering of voices and much pointing towards a house below. With a nod of thanks, the passenger retreated from the window, the carriage moved on and the black postilions resumed their singing until they were all out of sight, disappearing over the rim of the hill down towards the villa indicated. Within an hour, the news had spread along the lake-shore that a trio of Africans had arrived to visit Lord Byron, and by evening, there was talk of nothing else.

The women, however, were inaccurate in their assumption, for the Negroes were not Africans (though they may well have been born there) but Jamaicans, who only a few months before had been slaves on the passenger's plantation, and who had left their native island to visit Europe for the first time, proud to accompany a man who, as their employer, had made them free men, as he had made all the five hundred slaves on the plantation free men in so far as they were no longer in bondage and treated like animals. The employer and passenger was in fact the remarkable writer and poet, Matthew Gregory Lewis, known as 'Monk', after writing his successful horror story in 1795 at the age of twenty. Elevated to fame in the palaces of England at this early age, he had become the courtier of the elite, lover of Lady Charlotte Campbell the daughter of the fifth Duke of Argyll, and the friend of Brummell, Sheridan and Byron. Then, suddenly, in 1815, on the death of his father, he had inherited the Lewis plantations in Jamaica and had visited them the following year to be welcomed as a god. *Nothing could equal the rapture of the poor people on my arrival,* he wrote to his mother,* *and the noise which they made was something wonderful; they all said, that 'Till now they were afraid that they had no massa' and all the old people were in one story—'now they had once seen massa, they did not care if they should die tomorrow!'* Moved by the reception, and yet horrified by the conditions of the slaves, he realized that at last he had found his true vocation, and resolved to spend the rest of his life, he being now forty years of age, improving the welfare of those who worked for him. Though the slave-trade as such had been abolished, in so far as no more Negroes could be forcibly carried away from Africa, Lewis nevertheless recoiled against the idea of compulsory servitude, and even objected to the word 'slave' itself. *It seemed to imply that although he did feel pleasure in serving me, if he had detested me he must serve me still. I really felt quite humiliated at the moment, and was tempted to tell him, 'Do not say that again—say that you are my Negro, but do not call yourself a slave.'*

Inevitably, this ugly, bulbous-eyed man, who had quit his chambers in the Albany to live among the Jamaicans, was worshipped like a king. Each night celebrations took

* M. G. Lewis, letter to his mother, Jamaica, January 10th, 1816.

place in his honour (played on *gambys, eboe-drums, shaky-shekies and kitty-katties*) and Negroes from other plantations begged to call him master. Within a month, he had abolished the lash, visited the home of every man on the plantation, built a hospital, increased all holidays and pay, and had given all Negroes, without discrimination, fair and equal rights with the whites in every respect — this in 1816, without pressure and guided only by his love of his fellow man, since to Lewis that was all that mattered.*

He also attempted, without being dogmatic, to break down the superstitions of his employees, as the following anecdote illustrates. Monk Lewis is writing of a Negress whose four children had died after being entrusted to the voodoo Obeah: 'I told her that God was a great personage, who lived up yonder, above the blue, in a place full of pleasures, and free from pains where Adam (a witch doctor) and wicked people could not come; that her pickaninnies were not dead for ever, but were only gone up to live with God, who was good, and would take care of them for her; and that if she were good, when she died she too would go up to God above the blue, and see all her four pickaninnies again. The idea seemed so new and so agreeable to the poor creature, that she clapped her hands together, and began laughing for joy; so I said to her every thing that I could imagine, likely to remove her

* A code of laws was also drawn up, regarding punishments, as follows: *That a book register of punishments be kept in which the name, offence and nature and quantity of punishment inflicted, must be carefully put down, and also a note of the same kind given to the negro, in order that if he should think himself unjustly or too severely punished, he may show his note to my other attorney on his next visit, or to myself on my return to Jamaica, and thus get redress if he has been wronged. No negro is to be struck, or punished in any way without the trustee's express orders: the black driver so offending to be immediately degraded, and sent to work in the field; and the white person, for such a breach of my orders, to be discharged on the spot. No negro is to be punished till twenty-four hours shall have elapsed between his committing the fault and suffering of it, in order that nothing should be done in the heat of passion, but that the trustee should have time to consider the matter coolly.*

prejudice; told her that I would make it a crime, even so much as to mention the word Obeah on the estate, and that if any negro, from that time forward, should be proved to have accused another of obeahing him, or of telling another that he had been obeahed, he should forfeit his share in the next present of salt fish ... '

After four months in Jamaica, Lewis had been obliged to return to Europe to settle his affairs there, and on journeying across Switzerland with his servants, decided to visit Byron in Geneva to renew a friendship. They had last met when both men were in England before their respective departures, and where Lewis, then a discontented man, had found himself drifting idly through the salons of the rich, courting the favours of the titled, who invariably turned their back on such an unattractive creature who had never married and who spent each day writing epistles to his beloved mother. *Lewis at Oatlands*, wrote Byron, capsuling the Monk's image in society, *was observed one morning to have his eyes red and his air sentimental: being asked why? he replied, 'that when people said any thing kind to him, it affected him deeply; and just now the Duchess (of York) has said something so kind to me that ... here 'tears began to flow' again. 'Never mind, Lewis,' said Col. Armstrong to him, 'never mind, don't cry. She could not mean it.'*

More often than not, Lewis was also a bore to Byron as well, and yet he considered him a good and clever man who, *if he would but talk half, and reduce his visits to an hour, he would add to his popularity*. Nevertheless, Byron welcomed Monk's arrival, at least for a while, on the evening of the 14th, when Lewis's carriage finally arrived at the gates of the villa, and Lewis himself emerged, suntanned and grinning, to be the first guest that summer at Diodati.

It was a brief stay, a mere seven days, but in many

respects, though Byron was reconfirmed in his view that Lewis was *a damned bore*, it was an important visit for Byron the poet, if not for Byron the man. In his youth, Lewis had met Goethe, had been captivated by the man and now, in the salon at Diodati, introduced his companion to the German writer's greatest work, translating endless passages of *Faust* to his enthralled listener. *I would give the world to read Faust in the original*, he later told Medwin, and betrayed as early as this summer of 1816, his admiration for 'the greatest genius of the age' by writing *Manfred* unashamedly in genuflection to Goethe. Though he later denied the influence, claiming that *it was the Staubach and the Jungfrau and something else, much more than Faustus that made me write Manfred*, the critics were unconvinced; they could see Goethe within the poetry, for the signs for them were unmistakeable. They also saw, digging like moles between the lines, the *something else* that Byron had alluded to, hardly literary but infinitely more fascinating. Remembering — and indeed not wishing to forget — the character behind the writer, they reconfirmed their suspicions as overt hints of incest were unearthed in the drama, and gossip once more made Augusta's life unbearable. 'No avowal can be more complete,' wrote the Honourable Mrs Villiers gleefully to Lady Byron. 'It is too barefaced for her friends to attempt to deny the allusion. All that appeared to me practicable I have done with her own family, who have all spoke to me about it. I have said that I had long been aware that his whole object was to ruin others, and particularly those to whom he owed the most, and that I had long been convinced of his wish to confirm the reports of last year to Augusta's prejudice. Did you see the newspaper called 'The Day and New Times' of the 23rd June (1817)? There is a long critique on "Manfred" ably done, I think, but the allusions to Augusta dreadfully clear. Lady Chichester brought it to me!'

Lady Chichester, no doubt, travelled post-haste, book and paper in hand, to rekindle the scandal, though Byron himself, safely in Italy by now and unaware of the havoc he was creating so abstractedly, wrote to Augusta to ask if *Manfred* had caused, of all things, a 'pucker'. Not for the first time, he was understandably rebuked by elder sister: 'A propos of "puckers" I thought there was unkindness which I did not expect in doing what was but too sure to cause one — & so — I said nothing — & perhaps should not but for y^r questions.'

This rebuff, however, was not to occur for another year, for Byron at Diodati was surprisingly unaware of the trials of Augusta Leigh in England (harangued unmercifully by a smiling sister-in-law), being only concerned with his own. Claire, need it be added, was no longer present after dark, and the evenings retained a singularly masculine air — long conversations around the hearth between Byron, Shelley and Lewis. A visit was made to Ferney to pay homage to Voltaire, but otherwise, Diodati was never abandoned. Lewis talked, naturally, of slavery, one of the few subjects he cared passionately about, and to such an extent that he feared, on his death, that his measures of reform in Jamaica might be curtailed. Worrying about this incessantly, he returned one evening to the villa and declared that he had written a codicil to his will which all must witness.

'I cannot bear to contemplate the disaster that might happen,' he told his companions, 'when I die, if my estates are handed over to anyone who does not *care* about my Negroes. I do not want my heir to govern from Cornwall, but from Jamaica. These people can be exploited too easily and are too innocent to protect themselves.'

Accordingly, the codicil stipulated that all heirs to the Lewis estate must spend at least three months in Jamaica or forfeit all rights; that no Negroes must be sold on any grounds, and that these same Negroes had a right to be set free. *My whole object in writing this paper is to secure my Negroes a visit from some person of my family who is interested in their welfare, and to prevent their being abandoned to the unlimited superintendance of an attorney or overseer, and I most earnestly and solemnly entreat the assistance of the Law to carry an object of such importance to the happiness of so many human beings into effect.* The paper was then signed by Lewis and witnessed by Byron, Shelley and Polidori. Relieved now that he had secured the future of all his dependants, Lewis relaxed, and to the delight of the others, who were finding such revolutionary passions, though noble, yet a little tedious, the Monk turned the conversation to his first love and the source of his fame. On this occasion, Mary Godwin—now deeply involved in writing *Frankenstein*—was lured from her desk to join the men at the villa for a now familiar evening.

'We talk of Ghosts; neither Lord Byron nor Monk G. Lewis seem to believe in them; and they both agree in the very face of reason, that none could believe in ghosts without also believing in God. I do not think that all the persons who profess to discredit these visitations really discredit them, or, if they do in the daylight, are not admonished by the approach of loneliness and midnight to think more respectably of the world of shadows.'* Whether Byron believed in ghosts or not, however, he was nonetheless frightened of them as well as being fascinated by Lewis's stories.

Here are two.

A man, visiting a friend who lived on the outskirts of a vast forest in eastern Germany, lost his way. After wandering for some hours among the trees in the darkness, he suddenly saw a light in the distance, and so made his way towards it, hoping that he would find a path out of the

* Mary Godwin, Journal, August 18th, 1816.

forest. However, on approaching the light, he was surprised to discover that it came from a monastery, now in ruins, and overgrown with weeds. Puzzled by this, the man thought it wise to peer through a window before making his presence known, and so made his way towards the nearest wall. It was then that he saw the extraordinary sight: a dozen cats were assembled around a small grave, four of whom were at that moment letting down a coffin upon which rested a crown. The man, startled by this sight, and imagining that he had stumbled upon a coven of witches, turned and hurried away as fast as he could without looking back. At dawn, he was fortunate to arrive at his friend's house, who had been waiting anxiously for his arrival. 'I will tell you why,' replied the man, 'though I know you will not believe me', and so began to recount everything he had seen at the monastery. No sooner, however, had he mentioned the coffin with the crown upon it, than his friend's cat, who seemed to have been asleep by the fire, leapt up, saying, 'Then I am now the King of the Cats', and scrambled up the chimney, and was seen no more.

A young man who had taken Holy Orders arrived at his church for the first time on a Saturday night in summer. Being tired after the journey, he went to bed immediately and fell asleep; waking however at three o'clock in the morning, he saw an old man sitting at a desk in the window reading and weeping, while two beautiful boys stood near him, gazing at the man with the most profoundest sorrow. After a while, the old man rose from his seat and left the room, followed by the two boys and they were not seen for the rest of the night.

The next morning, the young priest, puzzled by the hallucination, decided to take a walk around his new parish in order to dismiss the image from his mind. He therefore walked first through the church, which the sexton was preparing for the first mass. Suddenly the priest was struck by a portrait on one wall which bore the exact resemblance to the man who had been sitting in his room. Pointing to it, he was told that it was the custom in the district to place a portrait of each priest after his death in the church, and that the young man's predecessor (whose portrait it was) had been universally beloved as a man of unexampled integrity and benevolence, but that he was the prey to a secret and perpetual sorrow. His grief was supposed to have risen from an attachment to a beautiful young girl, whom, as a priest, he could not naturally marry. However, many witnesses testified that they were indeed lovers, and that they had seen the girl bring to the priest's house two beautiful boys, the children of their affair. Winter arrives, the portrait is forgotten, and the young priest decides to light a fire in his room. But as soon as the wood is alight, a nauseous stench rises from the hearth from beneath the logs. Pulling these away, the young priest discovers the bones of two male children lying side by side.

Such were the stories told—hardly blood-curdling but curious enough to be remembered. Mary herself even took the trouble to write four of them in her Journal, and in fact copied the first, more comic than horrific one would think, in her essay 'On Ghosts' for the *London Magazine*. Byron and Shelley shrugged the tales aside and they were never mentioned again. Cats and priests were hardly their ingredients for horror. 'Well, if nothing else,' Byron told the storyteller, 'you have spared me a sleepless night, I will not be stark-eyed at the moon over those. Not only are the tales insignificant, you also tell them so badly.'

The next day, a Wednesday, Monk Lewis, his Negroes, his carriage and his will, departed from Diodati without being persuaded to stay longer, and set off for Italy. On the Thursday, Shelley and Mary paid a visit to the local cemetery to pass the time, found it lacking the baroque extravagance of its English counterpart, and left disappointed. It was on this day, also, just before dinner, that the thieves arrived.

* * *

It was the sail of the boat that was taken first. 'Taken before our eyes while I am at Chappuis attending the Shelleys' sick child. Taken in broad daylight with Maurice (the boatman) not twenty yards away. But it is I, Florence, who is held to blame. L.B. in a rage once more, discovers the loss when he and Mister S. are planning to sail on the lake. But no sail; I, scapegoat *évidemment*. The last three days have been my pillory.' To a degree, Polidori was right, in so far as he was not responsible for the protection of the sail, but it was only one more episode in a series of minor quarrels that had taken place almost religiously over the last week. The reasons, perhaps, are obvious. Byron was not in the best of tempers, partly owing to Claire's continued inconvenient presence, and partly because he was now restless to leave Switzerland. He had tired of Diodati and only the forthcoming arrival of Davies and Hobhouse obliged him to remain in Cologny for at least another fortnight. Moreover, he had been hearing distressing news from England, including reports that his wife was ill. This, in itself, did not unduly depress him — she was not his most affectionate friend, after all, and the illness was far from serious. *To say that I am merely sorry to hear of Lady B's ... illness is to say nothing, but she has herself deprived me of the right to express more.* Nevertheless, Byron did express more in a few lines of verse:

> I am too well avenged! — but 'twas my right;
> Whate'er my sins might be, *thou* wert not sent
> To be the Nemesis who should requite —
> Nor did Heaven choose so near an instrument.

> Mercy is for the merciful!—if thou
> Hast been of such, 'twill be accorded now.
> Thy nights are banish'd from the realms of sleep—
> Yes! they may flatter thee, but thou shalt feel
> A hollow agony which will not heal,
> For thou art pillow'd on a curse too deep; ... *

Other irritations followed, trivialities if set against the anguishes of the past, but thorns nevertheless. Polidori is discovered borrowing the carriage without permission; is caught neglecting a sweating horse and is accused of laming another. The reluctant copyist is reduced to tears by a vindictive physician, and Percy Shelley is sent on a fictitious errand under the impression that the request had originated from Byron. A yellow parasol is found hanging from a tree and Claire's hat is fished out of the Leman. One morning the words IVORY TOWER are found pinned to Polidori's door as its occupant recites nursery rhymes within, changing the words in a veiled attack on his employer. *War* writes Mary in her Journal, but it is a cold war as yet, in which the opponents use cardboard swords as if to emphasize the kindergarten tactics. Item: Shelley arrives at Diodati to encounter his fellow poet emerging from his bedroom. *Good morning, Shelley,* murmurs Byron wearily. *Good afternoon, Byron,* replies the other. *Good-bye, Shelley,* echoes a third, sniggering above them on the stairs. 'I do believe,' mused Byron an hour later as he sat on the balcony with his visitor, 'that Polidori is going out of his mind at last. He devotes his day to plaguing me, insists on addressing Claire as Medusa, and sends notes to the cook complaining of toads in his soup, signed "Flicflac". Flicflac? Who, God help us, is he? I would give him his *congé* this minute if I did not fear I would have a suicide on my hands.'

Byron's anxiety was understandable but his diagnosis

---

* Byron, 'Lines on Hearing that Lady Byron was ill', 1816.

inaccurate. Polidori was not as yet insane, nor even slightly so; he merely wished once more to turn the eyes of the world upon him now that he was no longer actor and Romeo. The stage produces bizarre side-effects on its devotees when they move in private, reducing them either to acute introversion or to overbearing bombast and all the variations between. To Polidori, who bore all the more obvious traits of the actor (vanity, shyness, a need to be adored, an inability to be self-critical), his voluntary, though pressured resignation from the theatre on the lawns of Vaugeron had left him restless and frustrated, like a gourmet on a forced diet. His audience at Diodati neither applauded his entrance, nor threw flowers before his feet, nor made illicit, open-mouthed rendezvous with him behind the lime tree. When he spoke he was interrupted, and when he left the room he was requested merely to close the door. In short, Flicflac's dramatic repertoire was ignored. 'I receive less attention here than Mutz, as if I were a plague they preferred to avoid. If L.B. asked me to leave this minute, I would find it difficult to refrain from kissing his hand.' That pleasure was now, unknown to Polidori, only just around the corner.

'Polly—someone has stolen our sail!' The voice was accusing. 'Is this another of your demonstrations?'

It is late afternoon and the weather fine. Polidori emerges, sleeves rolled up, bare-headed, coatless, from Maison Chappuis, eyes narrowed against the sun. He stares down the slope past Byron, past Shelley, at the boat in the harbour, shrugs and returns into the house. Later, it is discovered that the anchors also have been stolen (empty boat disappearing out of sight) and Byron, now in a fury, rides off in pursuit in the direction of Savoy. In his absence, the thieves return and break into Diodati while the servants are below stairs, and steal some boots, two of Byron's walking canes, four decanters and a portrait of an old man with pipe and tankard. On the top floor, Polidori, calm and oblivious, writes a letter as the rooms below are carefully ransacked. At dusk, Byron returns, discovers the robbery, discovers Polidori, and wearily retires to his room, locking the door, pausing only to comment, 'I wish to God that Murray had given *me* five hundred guineas to write on *you*, for it affords me as much patience and effort to be the subject of your Diary. There is nothing more I can say to you that has not been said. There are no more words of correction or advice I can offer. Stay if you wish, Polly, leave if you wish. I no longer care to concern myself with your tantrums.'

It was the beginning of the end, and Polidori knew it. At first, he attempted to shrug the inevitable dismissal aside, convincing himself that he would be better off on his own, his small reputation intact. Besides, had not Madame de Staël given him three letters of recommendation? And yet, such superficial screens deceived no one, especially the fabricator. Without the cachet, irritating though it may be, of being personal physician to the sixth Lord Byron, Polidori was reduced once again to being a talented nonentity, ekeing out an underpaid living in an English country town, or, at best, as medical lackey to a rich and dictatorial family. A servant to the tantrums of others, perhaps, rather than master of his own.

'That is me at nine, fat and Tuscan; a noisy child, I am told by my mother, born to scream. Unhappy infancy, unhappy infant. I remember long walks with my sister C. through London, a visit to Scarborough to see the ocean, a falling where I scarred a knee — a permanent mark representing a lozenge. Now ... over here, a drawer of scraps: a lock of hair(?), letters, a Nelson, a sketch of Strachur House, a drawing of Emily, sweet Emily, dead at sixteen at Mark Cross. One glove. A scalpel. An anagram(poor):
O LIDO R.I.P.

Little else. Leaving Ampleforth for Edinburgh was a pleasant journey and bathing at Berwick. Medicine is a fine career and I like to think that there is nothing else in the world I would rather be other than a physician. But of course there is. There's a million things I would rather be. A local god, for one ... L.B.? Sometimes I feel we are very close and sometimes not. Mister S. I will not miss when he departs next week. Miss Godwin, however, has been somewhat kind and will meet her again. Window closed. I see Miss C. below looking alone; a Romney creation. She will go too. And I? What will happen to me? But I will not pack yet. I have not been told to go. Not yet.'

Five days after the arrival and departure of the thieves, John Cam Hobhouse and Scrope Davies reached the Villa Diodati from England and moved into the top floor next to Polidori. It was now August 26th, and for Polidori, as well as for Claire, the summer with Byron was almost over. They were both now an embarrassment to the occupant of the Villa Diodati, and for one at least, this embarrassment was demonstrated all too clearly, and, as events later proved, with tragic finality.

[14]

DISMISSALS AND ARRIVALS

When you receive this, I shall be many miles away; don't be impatient with me. I don't know why I write unless it is because it seems like speaking to you. Indeed I should have been happier if I could have seen and kissed you once before I went, but now I feel as if we had parted ill friends. You say you will write to me, dearest. Do, pray, and be kind in your letters ... My dreadful fear is lest you quite forget me — I shall pine through all the wretched winter months whilst you, I hope, may never have one uneasy thought. One thing I do entreat you to remember — beware of any excess in wine ...

Farewell then dearest, I shall love you to the end of my life and nobody else. Think of me as one whose affection you can count on and never, pray, never forget to mention your health in your letters. May every good and every happiness be yours.

Your own affectionate,
CLAIRE

It was on August 29th that Claire, her half-sister and Shelley left Cologny for the return to England. There were no tears, no emotional embraces at the gate; there was merely the carriage moving up the hill and along the lake carrying its silent passengers as quickly as possible away from Diodati, and away from its impassioned occupant who watched it leave from a first-floor window. For Percy Shelley and Mary the journey was not an unhappy one, for both looked forward to going back to their native country in order to set up a home together (despite the antagonism of relatives and Harriet Shelley) where

William could grow up. Even as early as July, Shelley had written to Peacock requesting him to prepare for their return: *I wish you to look out for a home for me and Mary and William, and the kitten, who is now en pension. I wish you to get an unfurnished house with as good a garden as may be, near Windsor Forest, and take a lease of it for fourteen or twenty one years.** They, in fact, returned to live at Marlow, as neighbours to Peacock, in a house surrounded by the garden they desired and where they could all take walks along the Thames or through Bisham Wood. For Shelley, the summer of 1816 had been nothing less than memorable; he had met and befriended one of the greatest poets of the age, and had left him in August with his admiration far from being dimmed: *You have already given evidence of very uncommon powers ... I do not know how great an intellectual compass you are destined to fill. I only know that your powers are astonishingly great, and that they ought to be exerted to their full extent.*

Moreover, Byron, in his turn, praised the talents of this as yet relatively unknown poet, and demonstrated his respect by entrusting Shelley with the manuscripts of the third canto of *Childe Harold*, *The Prisoner of Chillon* and other shorter poems, with the authority to oversee their publication. It was undoubtedly an honour since Byron was notoriously fussy about the presentation and editing of his works (as his endless letters of complaint to Murray emphasize) and was not eager to give *carte blanche* to anyone. That he gave it to Shelley may well have been as part reward for the second, and less happy, commission — that of playing guardian to Claire's unborn child and making all arrangements for its birth. Shelley accepted without complaint, though he had sufficient problems of his own, and agreed to look after the future baby B. until both men met again. It was a thankless task which he

* Shelley, letter to Thomas Love Peacock, July 17th, 1816.

performed admirably, but for which he was to receive little gratitude, either from Byron or from the expectant mother herself.

For Claire, inevitably, there was only unhappiness as the carriage moved further away from the Leman and headed back across the Alps on the road to France and Calais. The affair had ended for her in the worst possible way, despised as she was by the father of her child-to-be. At first, she wrote to him in order to show that she still loved him despite it all, and that she eagerly awaited a reunion which, unbeknown to her, was never to arrive. The letters begin casually, and cautiously, enough; merely garden gossip related in dangerously maternal terms. *England seems quiet enough; at least there is no mention in the newspapers of anything like disturbance. So, you little restless soul, you must in spite of all your hopes to the contrary* be content with a nice furnished house, petits pois for dinner and a smooth Lake to look upon. I am sure you will be very sorry to hear poor Shelley has dreadful health—violent spasms in the head; this is all that vile nauseous animal Doctor Polidori's doing. He will do you some mischief, so pray send him away, and hire a clever steady physician ... I wonder if you ever think of me. I daresay not.*

Her fears were right, for Byron never replied. The mother is now replaced by the bitch as a second line of attack emerges: *Don't look cross at this letter because, perhaps*

---

* Byron had expected, and indeed hoped for, a militant revolution on the part of the poor and unemployed against the landowners and capitalists who were exploiting them without mercy. By November 1816, however, riots did occur; the Nottingham weavers fortified a village in defiance and 20,000 people demonstrated in Spa Fields. Inevitably, Parliament was urged to intervene on the side of humanity, but the Prince Regent, a puppet to the Ministers whom Byron, as a former member of the House of Lords and defender of the under-privileged, despised, cowardly prorogued Parliament till the New Year. The final tragic act after the Derbyshire Rising of 1817 was the Massacre of Peterloo in Manchester when the 15th Hussars rode and cut down the people in the streets.

by the same post, you expected one from Mrs Leigh [*Augusta*], and have not got it; that is not my fault, dearest. One can hear the knife penetrate in that final *dearest*, but Byron, undeterred, ignores the challenge once again. Wide-eyed innocence now enters the stage. *I don't complain of you, dearest Albé, nor would not if you were thrice as unkind ... Indeed, my dearest dear, if you will write me a little letter to say how you are, how all you love are, and above all if you will say you sometimes think of me without anger, and that you will love and take care of the child, I shall be as happy as possible ...* And again: [*Mary*] *says 'my love' is too familiar, and so it is changed into 'remembrances', and she shall always be happy to see you, and if you will come you shall have petits pois for dinner. You see she don't promise you the other chose you are so fond of. I should be sorry if she did. She says that if she were ever so much determined not to like you, she could not help so doing, and so* I *like her... Kinnaird says you told him I was an atheist and a murderer. You see the stupidity of people, so be chary of my name. A fine character I shall have among you all, when I am nothing more than an innocent, quiet little woman, very fond of Albé ...* And yet, inevitably, again: *Write me a nice letter beginning, not those scanty words 'Dear Claire', but 'My dearest Claire', and tell me that you like me, and that you will be very pleased to have a little baby of which you will take great care.*

I do not like to be the object of pity, and nothing makes me so angry as when Mary and Shelley tell me not to expect to hear from you. They seem to know how little you care for me, and their hateful remarks are the most cruel of all. How proud I should be of a letter to disappoint their impertinent conjectures ... Shelley told me that you once said to him: 'You don't really think that Claire is in love with me?' and when Shelley said indeed he did, you replied, 'Oh, no, she is only amusing herself with me' ... if you write directly I should have the dear letter before I lie in, which would make me so happy — but if you don't, indeed I shall go quite out of my mind.

To all these, Byron never replied once, and even to Claire, out of her mind or not, it seemed obvious that he never would. What the distraught girl never knew was that she would never see Byron again. The moment she left Diodati on August 29th, he resolved to avoid her for ever, whatever happened. That final glimpse by Claire of Byron at the window of the villa was to be her last. Within three years, when love had turned to hate, she was glad of it. Within five years, when their daughter, Allegra, was dead, she wished she had never seen him at all. For her, the summer of 1816 ought never to have existed, and till the day she died, almost seventy years later, as an aged spinster, the love affair with Byron was never mentioned again.

* * *

Like many dedicated gamblers, Scrope Davies was an unswervingly honest man, prone to many acts of kindness that seemed at odds with his erratic life. Unlike Hobhouse, he did not jealously guard his friendship, but dealt it fairly to all without reservations. On one occasion, having bankrupted a young man over a game of faro, he had returned all the money to him plus some of his own, on hearing that the youth was on the point of marrying. *If he wishes to marry, he cannot be a true gambler. We at least demand more favourable odds.* Only once is it recorded that he failed a friend in need, though the failure this time was a savage one since the request came from none other than Brummell himself as he stood on the brink of penury. The incident happened while Scrope was dining with Byron, also on the point of departure, in Charles Street, Pall Mall, and has been held, perhaps justifiably, in evidence against them both. During the dinner, a note was handed to Davies by the waiter:

My Dear Scrope,
 Lend me two hundred pounds; the banks are shut, and all my money is in the three per cents. It shall be repaid tomorrow morning.
 Yours,
 GEORGE BRUMMELL

To this request for, to the diners at least, a meagre sum, Scrope replied:

My Dear George,
 'Tis very unfortunate; but all my *money is in the three per cents.*
 Yours,
 S. DAVIES

To Brummell, it was the last straw, and he fled England a month later. Perhaps because of this denial as well as the nudgings of his own conscience, Scrope Davies, together with Hobhouse, broke his journey from London to the Villa Diodati in order to visit the exiled dandy in Calais. It was a moment of homage appreciated by them all, but the damage, regrettably, had been done. Pleased as he may well have been to see them, George Bryan Brummell knew that this gesture of kindness was too late. 'Napoleon will die in exile, and so shall I; but we have both had our day, and mine was the brightest of the two, for it had no change till the evening. I am more happy than people would think for—*Je ne suis pas souvent où mon corps est*—I live in a world of recollections, I trample again upon coronets and ermine, the glories of the small great! I give once more laws which no libertine is so hardy as not to feel exalted in adopting; I hold my court and issue my fiats; I am like a madman, and out of the very straws of my cell, I make my subjects and my realm; and when I wake from these bright visions, and see myself an old, deserted man, forgotten, and decaying inch by inch in a foreign village, I can at least summon sufficient of my ancient regality of spirit not to sink beneath the reverse. If I am inclined to be melancholy, why, I extinguish a duchess. I steal up to my solitary chamber to renew again in my sleep, the phantoms of my youth; to carouse with princes; to legislate with nobles; and to wake in the morning and thank heaven that I have still a coat to my stomach as well as to my back, and that I am safely delivered of such villainous company; "to forswear sack and live cleanly" during the rest of my sublunary existence.'*

For Scrope Davies, it was a poignant encounter on a blustery August day in the attic above a bookshop. 'Arriving at Calais,' he told Byron, 'I inquired after his whereabouts and found no one who could tell me where he lived or even who he was. Brummell was a stranger to them. So Cam and I walked aimlessly through the streets asking at every shop, at every inn but Monsieur Brummell was not known. Finally, we arrived at the Rue Royale and were confronted by a sign over a bookshop. Three words: *Le Pauvre Diable*. There, I thought, must be Brummell, if anywhere. And, regrettably, I was right. The poor devil had rented three rooms on the first floor and had transformed them into a museum where he lived like a hermit. When we arrived, he was sitting at a circular card-table, piled high with gold snuff-boxes, pearl card-cases, ivory paperweights. An ormolu greyhound, God help us. A paper press of Sienna marble. A bronze eagle. And Brummell himself, hair thinning, face whiter than his cravat, hunched up in the half-light, dressed as if for the

* Lord Lytton, *Pelham*. A speech by Russelton, a character based intimately and accurately on Brummell.

London Opera. His sole companion was his dog, Vick; otherwise he is alone. "I am punctually off the pillow at half-past seven in the morning," he told us, "and my first object—melancholy indeed it may be in its nature—is to walk to the pier-head and take my distant look at England. I stand there for a long time merely gazing across the water recollecting the life I once knew, and then I return here to read and write my memoirs.* You may say I am sentimental, Scrope, and I say I am. I never could cloak my feelings. That perhaps is why I am here." '

'The subject depresses me,' Byron replied after a while. 'How can I forget the image of the poor wretch standing on the shore, gazing out across the Channel. If one turns one's back to England, it is the back England should always see. Otherwise, one might as well go mad.'

He is one of the three greatest men of the age, Byron had once remarked, *I place myself third, Napoleon second and Brummell first*. Now all three were in exile and seemed destined to remain so. At one time, at the height of his fame, Brummell was asked by Lady Hester Stanhope the reason for his success, since his family had no claim on society whatsoever—Brummell's grandfather being a valet. *Ah, my dear Lady Hester*, Brummell replied, *who indeed ever heard of my father, and who would have heard of me, if I had been anything but what I am? It is my folly that is the making of me. If I did not impertinently stare duchesses out of countenance and nod over my shoulder to a prince, I should be forgotten in a week; and if the world is so silly as to admire my absurdities, you and I may know better, but what does that signify?* What then indeed?

On August 29th, that same day that the Shelley party left for England, Byron, together with Scrope, Hobhouse

---

* Ironically, the Memoirs, like Byron's, were burnt and were never seen. The loss, once again, is immeasurable.

and Polidori, set out in two carriages for a tour of Chamonix, inspired perhaps by Percy Shelley's earlier visit in July. 'I am taken along,' wrote Polidori, 'as if I would do damage if left alone at Diodati. S.D. is a reckless, loud companion but likeable, though for Hobhouse I cannot claim an affection. He has changed since England and seems to be guarding a secret which he is reluctant to impart. L.B. asked him yesterday for the hundredth time how he had left Mrs Leigh. "Well enough," replied H., long face, nothing more. Pomp. Well enough? L.B. is quite out of his mind on such a phrase ... Florence, I fear I will be sent away before the week is out. L.B. under influence of H., who likes me not at all. I cannot fight him. Unlike Shelley, H. goes back too far.'

But for Polidori, such worries were put aside for the present as the party, in Shelley's footsteps, journeyed leisurely through the beautiful valley of the Arve, filled with wild flowers, arriving at Sallenches to stay the night. There, at the desk, Byron noticed the Greek inscription written by Shelley in July and turning to Hobhouse, asked anxiously, 'Do you not think I shall do Shelley a service by scratching this out?' Hobhouse, who would have been happy if *every* reference to Shelley could have been scratched out, nodded, and Byron *defaced the words with great care*. Unknown to both however, Percy Shelley, in bold defiance, had written the inscription in every hotel register in the area, as Southey discovered a year later.

Next day by Chede in two char-a-bancs, with each a guide; a fine pine-glen of the Arve, to Chamounix. Only one incident, an anecdote worth repeating, broke the travellers' unselfconscious admiration of the glaciers and mountains before them. At Chamonix itself, *in the very eyes of Mont Blanc,* Byron found himself standing beside an English tourist (female) who contemplated the breathtaking panorama of snow-capped mountains before her, then turned to her companions asking them if they had ever seen anything more rural? *Rural!* cried Byron in stunned amazement, *As if it was Highgate or Hampstead or Brompton or Hayes. Rural! Rocks, pines, torrents, Glaciers, Clouds and Summits of eternal snow far above them — and Rural!*

On the next day, the weather suddenly changed for the worse; mists blocked out the mountains and rain began to fall. With reluctance, the party returned to Sallenches, and then back to Diodati. On the journey back, Polidori sat alone with the servants in the second carriage, frozen out of the company ahead by Hobhouse's animosity. Surprisingly, Polidori made no complaint, but stoically sat stony-faced, uttering not a word, in the corner of the coach, and stared out at the passing landscape. At varying stops, only Scrope Davies walked back along the road to talk to him, commenting on the weather and standing silently beside him before returning to the others. It was a small gesture, much appreciated by the young physician, who now felt an anachronism on the scene, as if he belonged to another play and had, by some oversight, been forgotten. Davies and Hobhouse had been the friends of Byron for ten years at least, and their intimacy was undeniable. It was the intimacy of the London clubs, of Cambridge and Newstead, and of the salons of Byron's fame. Polidori was only a part of that summer in Geneva, as Shelley and Claire had been a part; he was now superfluous, ignored, and the tragedy was, as he had told Florence, that he could no longer fight that indifference. Hobhouse's and Davies's friendship was too deep. Instead, Polidori submitted — with cold reluctance but submitted nevertheless — waiting for the inevitable moment when his employer would pay him off. 'If it were not for Scrope Davies I would run away. We play tennis together. We talk. We reminisce. Without him, I sit in my room in silence. Below, visitors arrive, visitors depart, but I am no longer invited to the table. Only Scrope appears.' On September 5th, together with Robert Rushton, a servant, Scrope Davies left Diodati to return to England. When Polidori rose that day, he discovered all too soon that his sole companion had gone. Only Byron and Hobhouse remained. That day, abandoned in his room, Polidori recommenced his Diary, in order to relieve the solitude.

Two days later, almost driven to distraction by boredom (Byron and Hobhouse having gone to Coppet for the evening), Polidori rode to Geneva through the rain in the hope of meeting someone he knew. At Madame Odier's he was told by a bad-tempered servant that the Odiers had left for Germany on a visit to a first cousin, and would not be returning till November. The door was closed in his face as if he were a bailiff or a prospective burglar. 'I then visited La Poêle and found no one except Redford, who was drunk, and who invited me to dine with him. Reluctantly I agreed, for the man is a bore, but I was hungry and the room was full of strangers. All, it seems, have returned home now that autumn is here, and the rain is ceaseless. Not even a pretty face in the corner of the restaurant to decorate the atmosphere. Just I and Redford drinking together like stubborn guests who remain long after the party is over. I left him as soon as I could, a bottle of wine later, and thought to visit de Roche. He, hélas, also absent. If I suddenly encountered red crosses on the doors, I would not be astonished for Geneva is empty, and I feel as if I am almost the Angel of D.' An hour later, drunk and embittered, Polidori was involved in a brawl with the three French hussars who had been his rivals to the lamented mademoiselle, Janine d'Alvers. They had seen him wandering disconsolately along the Rue de la Cité, had attacked him and then had left him, face down in the gutter, bruised but conscious. It was an inevitable, but unjust ending to a day that had proved to be one of the unhappiest of the summer. It was also, as if to add salt to the wound, Polidori's twenty-first birthday.

A week later, on September 15th, Lord Byron walked slowly across the sloping lawns of Diodati towards a bench beneath a large chestnut tree. Sitting on the bench, shaded by the branches, was Polidori, his back to his employer, writing a letter, his head lowered almost myopically towards the page. As Byron approached, the younger man looked up and lowered his pen, conscious of the expression on the other's face, and placed the letter aside. When the dinner bell rang on the gable of the house, both men were discovered walking side by side along the shore, two yards apart and silent. At dusk, Byron returned alone, bad-tempered, brushing Fletcher aside and retired to his room, not reappearing till midnight, and then only to inquire after Hobhouse. He seemed to be disturbed, ill at ease, but when told that Hobhouse was in fact in the salon, Byron hesitated, turned his back and returned to his room. The door was locked but the candles remained burning till the early hours.

We have parted, wrote Polidori to his father,* *finding that our tempers did not agree. He proposed it and it was settled. There was no immediate cause, but a continued series of slight quarrels.* No final act of disobedience, no ultimate demonstration of defiance to provoke the dismissal; the curtain merely fell exhausted on a summer-length career of irritation and embarrassment. John Polidori had finally been dismissed. And yet, dismissed, in the final analysis, with reluctance, for both men seemed suddenly unwilling to leave each other, despite everything, as if aware that they had been much more than merely employer and employee. They parted friends, without resentment and

* Polidori, letter to Gaetano Polidori, September 20th, 1816.

without malice. *I believe the fault,* wrote Polidori, *if any, had been on my part; I am not accustomed to have a master, and therefore my conduct was not free and easy.* As equals, there may well have been no estrangement, but both men were ill-suited for the roles they had to play and so, inevitably, it ended; it is perhaps startling that the relationship lasted so long. Polidori was given seventy pounds (fifty pounds for three months' advance and twenty for the voyage) in generous gratitude, as well as his employer's best wishes. *His remaining with me was out of the question,* Byron told Murray, *I have enough to do to manage my own scrapes; and, as precepts without example are not the most gracious homilies, I thought it better to give him his congé: but I know no great harm of him, and some good. He is clever and accomplished; knows his profession, by all accounts, well; and is honourable in his dealings and not at all malevolent.* Years later, Byron appears not to have changed his affection, for he tells Medwin, *I was sorry when we parted, for I soon get attached to people.*

At six o'clock on the morning of the 16th, while all at Diodati were asleep, Polidori crept downstairs from his room, carrying all his possessions in the world, and left the villa without saying goodbye. 'If I had stayed to see L.B., I may well have been reduced to tears. I am not an unemotional man and it is difficult for me to turn my back on five months which were—in all reality—the saddest and happiest in my whole life.' When Byron awoke seven hours later, John Polidori was fifteen miles away on the road, walking to Italy.

[15]

EXEUNT OMNES

My friends, you are sorry for the Poet: still in the bloom of joyful hopes, not yet having realised them for the world, barely out of the clothes of infancy he faded away! ... And yet, perhaps ... he would have changed in many ways ... married, and in the country, happy though cuckolded would have worn a quilted dressing gown. He would have come to know life as it really is, would have got gout at forty, would have drunk, eaten, become bored, fat and ailing, and finally he would have died in his bed, surrounded by children, tearful women, and doctors.

Alexander Pushkin, *Eugene Onegin*

In 1824, on hearing that Byron had died suddenly of a fever at Missolonghi, Mary Godwin (now Shelley) collapsed and was in a coma for almost the whole day. *I knew him in the bright days of youth,* she wrote in her Journal, *when neither care nor fear had visited me ... Can I forget our evening visits to Diodati? our excursions on the lake when he sang the Tyrolese Hymn, and his voice was harmonised with winds and waves ... Albé—the dear, capricious, fascinating Albé—has left this desert world! God grant I may die young! A new race is springing about me. At the age of twenty-six I am in the condition of an aged person. All my old friends are gone ...* In the few short years since that single summer of 1816, Mary's life had been tragic indeed. Six weeks after returning to England, her half-sister, Fanny Imlay, was found dead in a hotel room in Swansea. Beside her body was a watch, a necklace, two coins, an empty laudanum bottle and an unfinished note: *I have long determined that the best thing I could do was to put an end to the existence of a being whose birth was unfortunate, and whose life has only been a series of pain to those persons who have hurt their health in endeavouring to promote her welfare. Perhaps to hear of my death may give you pain, but you will soon have the blessing of forgetting that such a creature ever existed as —*

Two months later, early on a morning in December, a small boy and an old man pulled the body of a dark-haired young woman from out of the Serpentine in Hyde Park, and informed the authorities. The dead woman, who was pregnant, had obviously committed suicide and seemed tragically to have had no friends, for she had been in the water for at least a week without being missed. A notice was subsequently printed in *The Times*: *On Tuesday, December 10, a respectable female far advanced in pregnancy was taken out of the Serpentine River and brought home to her residence in Queen Street, Brompton, having been missed for nearly six weeks. She had a valuable ring on her finger. A want of honour in her own conduct is supposed to have led to this fatal catastrophe, her husband being abroad.* The 'respectable female' was called Harriet and the husband, who it was believed was abroad, was Percy Bysshe Shelley. *My dear Bysshe* Harriet had written before drowning herself, *if you had never left me I might have lived, but as it is I freely forgive you & may you enjoy the happiness which you have deprived me of ... God bless you all is the last prayer of the unfortunate Harriet S.* The reasons surrounding her death and her pregnancy remain a mystery — some authorities claiming that the father of the child Harriet was carrying might have been her husband himself. Shelley, however, dismissed this idea in a letter to Mary: 'It seems that this poor woman—the most innocent of her abhorred and unnatural family—was driven from her father's house, and descended the steps of prostitution until she lived with a groom of the name of Smith, who deserting her, she killed herself.' Less than three weeks after Harriet's body was found, Percy Shelley and Mary Godwin were married at St Mildred's Church in the City of London.

The marriage lasted five years and was to end as tragically as Harriet's. In 1819, while in Rome, the Shelleys' son, William, developed a fever and became desperately ill. For five days he remained semi-conscious, then died during the night of June 7th. *It seems to me*, Shelley wrote to Peacock, *as if, haunted by calamity as I have been, that I should never recover any cheerfulness again.* Three years later, almost to the week, Percy Shelley, aged twenty-six, was drowned in the Tyrrhenian Sea; watched by Byron, his body was burnt on the beach, excepting the heart which was plucked from the flames and later given to Mary, his wife. She herself lived for another twenty-nine years, never re-marrying and wandering back and forth across Europe, a literary celebrity, recording her experiences in her Journal. Often she addressed her dead husband direct: 'Mine own Shelley, what a horror you had of returning to this miserable country. To be here without you is to be doubly exiled, to be away from Italy is to lose you twice. Dearest, why is my spirit thus losing all energy? Indeed, indeed, I must go back, or your poor utterly lost Mary will never dare think herself worthy to visit you beyond the grave. "Mine own Shelley". The sun knows of none to be likened to you—brave, wise, noble-hearted, full of learning, tolerance, love. Love! What a word for me to write ... for I am still his—still the chosen one of that beloved spirit—still vowed to him for ever and ever!'

Mary died, semi-paralysed, in her London house in

Chester Square, on February 21st, 1851. She was buried in a Bournemouth churchyard near Boscombe Manor, the home of her only surviving son, Sir Percy Shelley.

As for Claire, her life was to be the longest of all those who were at Lake Leman that summer. Her baby was born in January 1817, was christened Allegra, and died alone (of typhus) in an Italian convent. The child was five years old and her death, believed by Claire to have been caused by Byron's neglect, was to sever any remaining affection between her parents for ever. *For me*, wrote Claire later, *there could be no happiness, there could be nothing but misery in the presence of the person who so wantonly, wilfully destroyed my Allegra.* She was never to marry, nor indeed ever to love again. Only Shelley retained her affection and respect, and perhaps, her heart.* After working as a governess in Europe and Russia, she retired for the last thirty years of her life to Florence, living with her niece, Paula; two spinsters at 43 Via Romana. Byron was rarely mentioned, and then only with venom. *Never, never, neither here nor in Eternity can I, nor will I, forgive the injuries he inflicted upon my defenceless child.* When the writer William Graham visited Claire Clairmont in the Via Romana, he asked her if she had ever loved, and was told that she had. 'Shelley?' inquired Graham casually. 'With all my heart and soul,' Claire replied.† She died at the age of eighty-one, and was buried, as she had requested, clutching Shelley's shawl to her breast.

Of the others, Madame de Staël was to die first,

---

* A scandal of 1818 indicated that Shelley and Claire were lovers and that Claire had given birth to Shelley's child. *You must know then that at the time the Shelleys were here Clare was with child by Shelley* (Hoppner to Byron). Byron believed the story and was not alone. Claire certainly was curiously ill at the time, and it is known that Shelley had a baby baptized Elena in Naples, a girl who later died of fever.

† William Graham, *Last Links with Byron, Shelley and Keats*. The history of Claire, and especially her love affairs and her years in Florence, is the basis for Henry James, *The Aspern Papers*.

surviving only a few months after Byron's first visit to Coppet. Her coffin was placed in a vault within the garden of the château and the door was walled up for ever. In 1832, Madame Récamier and Chateaubriand returned to Coppet to find it overgrown with weeds and deserted. Slowly they both wandered the empty rooms and galleries and finally emerged sadly at the entrance to the monument. *Madame Récamier*, recalled Chateaubriand, *herself pale and weeping came out of the funeral grove like a shadow. If ever I have felt both the vanity and the value of fame and life, it was at the entrance of the silent wood, dark and unknown, where rests the one who had shone so brightly and who had enjoyed so much fame, and on seeing what it is like to be truly loved.*

Both Augusta and Lady Byron were to live into another age to become respectable upper-class Victorian ladies, the latter living politely in Brighton, yet still retaining her animosity towards her sister-in-law. After Augusta became a widow, Lady Byron arranged an historic meeting between them, to take place in a public house at Reigate. *My servant in Drab Livery*, dictated Lady Byron, *holding up my card will look into all the 1st. Class carriages and will have a Fly waiting to convey you to Reigate Town (a mile and a half from the station) where I shall be at the White Hart.* It was a bitter encounter between Augusta, now a shy, weak woman of sixty-seven, and her sister-in-law, who was accompanied by a handsome clergyman. There was no attempt at reconciliation, or of forgetting a scandal that ought to have been past history; Lady Byron merely opened old wounds, and Augusta left in despair. She died six months later, her hands clasped in those of her only surviving daughter, Emily. *Poor Mamma died this Morning, a little after three, having suffered most dreadfully since yesterday afternoon—it is indeed a most happy release, but her loss can never be made up to me.*

In May 1818, two years after leaving Byron at Diodati, Monk Lewis died on board a boat leaving the West Indies for Europe. 'All that night his groans were dreadful; I could only lie in my berth and listen to them, for illness rendered me powerless. By degrees, his moanings subsided into low convulsive sobs; they grew fainter and fainter, and became calmed into a gentle breathing, as though the sufferer slept. I was worn out, and lost all consciousness. From this state of stupor (for I can hardly call it sleep) I was roused by the steward, at a little past four on the morning of the 14th of May, calling me by my name. He came to inform me that "Mr Lewis was no more".' The next day, Monk Lewis was placed in a coffin, and after a brief ceremony the coffin was cast overboard into the Atlantic. By a strange chance it did not sink, but was seen by all on deck to be floating back towards Lewis's chosen country, Jamaica.

George Brummell, on his part, finally went mad. Abandoned and forgotten in Calais, he began to talk to himself, miming imaginary soirées in his attic in which he once again was host to the elite. As the years passed, his body also, ironically for the dandy, reacted against him and he began to lose control over his bowel movements, and would also dribble at meals. By 1830, with George IV dead, Brummell was a shabby, helpless wreck of a man, pitied by an age that was past and remembered only by two or three ageing friends. Finally, his mind snapped altogether and he was carried off screaming to an asylum where Beau Brummell, who, for a short time, was considered, incredible as it may seem today, the most important influence in English life, died. He was buried among weeds in the cemetery at Caen.

As for John Polidori himself, his career, after leaving Byron for Italy, was brief. After touring much of northern Italy, he returned to England in December and continued his medical career in Norwich, before finally abandoning it altogether. Some time after this, while staying in Great Pulteney Street, London, Polidori began to talk gibberish to a companion he had invited to dinner. The other, believing his host was merely drunk, ignored him and left early. At midnight, Polidori retired to his room, taking with him a large tumbler which he filled to the brim with prussic acid and then drank. He was dead within the hour. The incident was described as a 'Melancholy Event' by *The Traveller* and the verdict was given as suicide. John Polidori was just twenty-six years of age.